A MAD AND WONDERFUL THING

Mark Mulholland

SCRIBE
Melbourne • London

Without a sign, his sword the brave man draws,
and asks no omen, but his country's cause.
Homer, *The Iliad*

We used to wonder where war lived, what it was that made it so vile.
And now we realise that we know where it lives ... inside ourselves.
Albert Camus, *Notebooks*

Never think that war, no matter how necessary,
nor how justified, is not a crime.
Ernest Hemingway, introduction to
Treasury for the Free World

Principles

I WAS SIX YEARS OLD WHEN I WATCHED THE GUN GO INTO DAD'S MOUTH. Another would think that was the beginning of the whole thing — like it has to have one. Another would think that's what made me what I am. I'm not so sure. There were other incidents, too; another would call these pivotal events. Another would; I don't. I just think some of us are made this way. I had it all worked out. Okay, maybe not all of it, but I knew what my role was, what sacrifices needed to be made, what needed to be done, what I needed to do. Another would wonder about my role, and about the how and the why. That's fair enough — we are a curious animal. I don't know if I could give an answer, like wrap it up in a there-you-go-sir bundle. War isn't like that — not when you actually do it — but there is them and there is us and there is homeland, and that is the cause of the conflict. Anyhow, I had it all worked out. And then she came and everything is not where it was.

Eight days. That's how long I've known her. Mad, but that's what girls do, they wreck your head. She just came out of nowhere — I mean, not really nowhere, but she wasn't part of it, and now she is, like she was always there. Even when I'm thinking of something else, she is there, and that's not good when you do what I do, when nothing must be in my head but the gun and the bullet and the kill. But she is in my head, like now, and just then as I left my room, and all morning, and before that when I woke early and there was nothing for it but to lie there with her — well, not physically with her —

replaying those first conversations with her, extending the real here and there, redrafting, inventing. I am unable to think of anything else. Only the girl will do. And you know something? I'm happy with it.

I hear her voice — as if her face and body were not torture enough — and I am thinking of her as I step from the house into the bright morning. I tidy the fall of my overcoat and pull at my blue scarf. The dog slides in alongside, and I am ruffling my hand across his head as I reach the end of the drive where the gate is closed, tied with an old shoelace. The gate is low, and with one hand on the top bar I'm stepping over it when I hear the porch door slide behind me.

'Your mother asks if you will pick up the *Sunday World* on the way back?'

I turn. It's my dad. He is standing in the porch, with one hand holding the sliding door.

I lob a protest over the low gate: 'I'm not buying trashy newspapers.' I shake my head at the dog, and he barks once as if he agrees.

I look to the house where Dad, now retreated from the midday air, relays the refusal down the central hallway and then stands nodding with his big, dopey smile as he absorbs a long reply from the kitchen at the far end. I mean, the whole show is pure theatre.

'She says you won't be wanting dinner, then,' he summarises, his head re-emerging into the sunshine. This is Dad all over — he finds the middle ground and plays for loose change.

I look on a face that is held wide open to catch my answer. He knows he has me. 'Fair enough,' I say. 'The *Sunday World* it is.' Well, sometimes you just have to lose, and lose fast.

'That's great,' he replies. 'I love to see a man stick to his principles.' And he laughs.

'Will I get you anything?' I ask him.

'What are you getting, yourself?'

'The *Times* and the *Tribune*.'

'Pick us up the *Indo*, will you? And the *People*, if there's any left?'

'Sure, Dad. No bother.'

'Right you are, Son. Right you are,' he calls from the porch, as I set off on the short walk to the late-morning Mass. It is Sunday. It is April. It is 1990.

The Mass

I ENTER THE CHURCHYARD AS THE BELLS OF SAINT JOSEPH'S PITCH ON THE
first arc of the Angelus.

'Hi, Johnny.'

I look up. Some local girls are perched in a single row on the
church steps. Chatting and giggling, they are like unsettled starlings
stretched out on a power line. Girls, they wreck your head.

'Well, sisters. Are you all here for Jesus?'

'For Jesus, Johnny?' a girl I know answers. 'I don't think so. I'm
only here for the talent. What about you?'

'You're a shameless hussy, Siobhán McCourt,' I reply. 'But fear
not, you may be touched yet by the power of the Holy Spirit.'

'The Holy Spirit, Johnny,' she says, and laughs. 'We don't see
much of him in Dundalk.' She looks to me, a smirk on her pretty
face. 'And I won't be touched by anyone unless you're free yourself
for half an hour?'

'You are some lunatic,' I answer. 'And that's a fine offer. But I've an
appointment inside with the man himself.'

The girls laugh as I bounce up the granite to the church doors.
Girls do that to me — they make me feel as if I can run from here to
China.

'Another day, McCourt,' I call, thinking it best to play safe and pop
this one in the back of the wardrobe. You never know.

'Another day, Donnelly,' I hear as I push through.

I step into the left aisle and find a space in the rear corner, and there I stand silently, apathetic about the imminent hour of murmur, shuffle, procession, and sermon. I look across the heads of the seated faithful and watch the last-minute arrivals quietly, apologetically, nursing themselves in at the ends of pews. It is an odd event — the Irish Catholic Mass. It is adoration by stealth: an unenthusiastic ritual where joy is a stranger and where emotion is as welcome as a Protestant. I see Aunt Hannah among the gathering, and she sees me. She has a hand raised and her mouth is moving, and I am lip-reading as I signal: she's giving me jib for wearing 'that old coat' to the Mass. She would have been waiting just so she could give out — she constantly gives out about my old Dunn & Co coat — but that's spinster aunties for you. They're as bad as mothers. She'll be happy now she has the complaint registered. She turns to face the altar as the Mass eases through the early gears, and I am again with the girl as my mind slips from the church and drifts the short journey west to town, to where it all began, to where I first met Cora Flannery.

We were in a nightclub — we being the boys. We were camped at the bar when a group of girls approached and stopped nearby, their conversation busy as girls' talk always is, busy and speckled with bursts of rapid comment and laughter — you know the way they go on. She stood among the girls, but she looked to me. I can admit something: I was surprised by her attention. I glanced around, but there was nobody else in her view. I lowered my gaze to the ground to put some order to my thoughts while random matter flew around my head like kids let loose at McDonald's. I peeped, and could see that she was continuing to watch me. Girls bring out strange things in me, and suddenly the poet inside was busy working away and I was thinking that her eyes were the lightened green of an August meadow. Oh, sweet hallelujah. I mean, I just couldn't think straight — just mad poetry stuff. Slowly, I lifted my useless head. She wore

Dr Martens boots. They were red and they were tied in extravagant bows with green laces. (*Green for Ireland*, she says. *Green for Ireland* — like how good is that?) A long, beige skirt held to her slender frame and a white, knitted cardigan, unbuttoned, part covered a small white top. She had hair of gold, and long golden threads fell in soft waves over one side of her face, resting lightly on her pale skin. And I knew who she was. The town is too small for a girl as beautiful as Cora Flannery to go unaccounted.

I looked to her. Why not? Well, there was nothing to lose. Or was there? She passed close as the girls moved on.

'I like your boots,' I said, surprising myself, though nearly choking as I spoke. Where did those words come from? I hadn't meant to say anything.

She didn't respond, not really, but I saw her smile.

The Mass reaches a high point with the reading of the Gospel, and everyone stands. I feel a hand on my ribs.

'How's the boy?' my friend Éamon Gaughran whispers from behind.

'Never better.'

Éamon acknowledges with an upward flick of his head, and we both fall quiet.

It was Thursday when I saw Cora again. I was in town after work and on my way to the bank. Cora stepped out of the post office. I know now that she waited for me — how mad is that?

'Hi, Johnny.'

She surprised me. She knew my name. 'Ohh, well, eh, Cora. How'ye?'

'Sorry about the other night. I was just, ehm, too shy, you know, in front of all the gang. Anyway ...' and she just kept talking.

I stood silent. I had no idea what this girl was saying to me. Twice now in one week I had experienced shock, and both times were as I looked into the green eyes of Cora Flannery. My heart was racing, I could feel it, and — weirdly — I could hear it. I was conscious of blood rushing to my face. I was fighting for breath. The head was gone again, and now the ears and lungs, too. This girl was killing me.

'Are you going again this week?' she asked.

'Yes. Yes, I might.' I tried to remain calm.

'Right,' she said. 'That's a date, then.' And off she went.

I couldn't believe it. I just couldn't believe it, and I was halfway home when I realised that I'd forgotten to go to the bank.

Saturday night arrived, and we gathered in town for the eager consumption of alcohol, cigarettes, stories, and lies. The Dubchoire Bar is our regular meeting place. There is a dusting of magic or something about the place — I'm not sure what exactly, although to an outsider it would look pretty crappy. Townsfolk say that, between the thick walls and below the music, intrigue and conspiracy simmer in dark pockets. I don't know anything about that — I never hear any of it — but local heads have nicknamed it The Cooking Pot. Anyhow, back to Saturday. First in, as usual, was Big Robbie. Robbie is my friend from work and, to be honest, he's a bit of a header. Johnny — Johnny being me — and Éamon Gaughran were next. Conor Rafferty and Frank Boyle followed up. That is pretty much our regular form, though, on any night, any number of others might attach themselves to our posse. Other than the chatter on football or work or college, we usually talk about girls, and play our game of 'marks out of ten'. Eight-and-a-half is agreed to be the highest possible score to be found in the town; convinced as we are that faraway maidens just have to be fairer. I wasn't saying a word about Cora — I mean, let's be reasonable, I wasn't too sure what was happening. Was it a date? Or was it not? But she did say ... Well, I thought, if nothing happened and I fell on my arse, at least the boys didn't have to know.

'Big date tonight, Johnny, eh?'

I looked up to see Frank Boyle smiling at me over a glass of beer.

You see, these are the things that piss me off — and just when I had some sort of a plan together. 'What, wha', what makes you say that?' I asked him.

'Well, Johnny-boy, Cora Flannery seems to believe that she's meeting up with you later.'

'Cora Flannery!' was the cry around the table.

'Cora Flannery,' Conor Rafferty repeated softly, looking to me with his big brown eyes as he sat shaking his head.

Oh, sweet hallelujah, so it is a date.

'And how do you make that out?' I threw out the stall to get some thoughts together.

'That's the news according to Clodagh Breen.'

'Well, that's Clodagh Breen for you,' I said, looking to Frank and having no choice now but to reach down for the emergency supplies. 'She tells stories, that one. Wasn't it Clodagh who said that you popped Tootsie Roddy a fast one in the Friary Lane? That's just all-out madness. You can't believe a word she says.' It was a low attack. A liaison with Tootsie could only be absolute need confused with desperate want, and it could happen to any man. I take no pride now in the retelling. But I was rattled.

I saw Frank Boyle absorb the statement with panic, and his thoughts were all over his face. *Does Johnny know? How does Johnny know? Bastard!* For a moment, there was silence.

'Oh, I think he doth protest too much,' Big Robbie said, as he laughed. 'You know, I've said it before and I'll say it again: Johnny D could score at a funeral.'

I gave my best innocent grin. What else could I do?

Big Robbie lifted a pint of porter off the table and drank half the measure in one slow, easy gulp. 'Mother's milk,' he said, wiping his mouth with the back of his hand. 'You are some pup, Donnelly. That's all I'll say. You are some pup. I have you trained well.'

Big Robbie is an electrician who is one year ahead of me in our apprenticeships, and sometimes the seniority thing gets the better of him. I saluted him with my own glass and let his delusion stand.

'But Cora Flannery?' Conor continued, moving next to me and still shaking his head. 'Unbelievable. Jesus, Johnny, you have the luck of the Devil. How do you do it?'

'You smarmy git,' Éamon said from across the table. That would be Éamon: a bit off-time, a bit off-tone. It comes with trying too hard.

'Now, don't be jealous,' I defended.

'God-sakes, Johnny. Me, jealous? That'll be the day, Sunshine.' Poor Éamon. Nobody could believe that, not even himself.

The banter and drinking continued until a yet-to-be-vetted girl caused immediate debate, scoring highest with Big Robbie's declaration, 'That's class — definitely a seven-and-a-half.'

'And what more shall I say …' I am pulled back to the Mass, as the priest is lecturing us about heroes and conquered kingdoms and enforced justice and received promises and winning strength out of weakness and becoming mighty in war and putting foreign armies to flight. These guys know how to talk. But the thread has tangled and caught. Putting foreign armies to flight? Yes, that fighting talk is all very good in Saint Joseph's, but how about a cold, wet ditch on the border? There would be few then so loud and brave. It's all hell and thunder for Jesus. But for Ireland? Put foreign armies to flight? I don't think so. Only the few take on that foreign army. Our foreign army. And as I think on that, I see their faces, like I see their faces through the scope of the gun, those foreign faces, those foreign soldiers in Ireland. And that's not good, foreign soldiers. It never works out in the end. I know that not everyone thinks this way. Some don't mind them being here. Some welcome them. Some don't care. But that doesn't work either, the not-caring. If you don't care about who you are, then every day a little bit of you dies — a small bit, hardly noticeable, but day by day these bits add up, and before you know it you are completely dead. You are still living, of course, but you go through the rest of your life dead. That's the price you pay for not caring about who you are, and for not fighting. But not me: I know the danger. I know who I am: Johnny Donnelly, Irish. And I do care, and I do fight.

The priest continues his advice to the assembled heads, but my thoughts are gone again to Cora.

We had never been in the nightclub so early. Usually we would leave the pub late, and, via a side door and a damp alley, we would run the short distance across a back-street carpark into the side entrance of the main-street hotel. The empty interior was bizarre without the usual circus. For once we approached the bar in comfort, and had time to admire the decor and the light system.

'I hear it cost a fortune doing the place,' Big Robbie said, leading us to some high stools overlooking the dance floor.

'Bastard can well afford it,' Éamon replied, reaching into his shirt pocket and withdrawing a twenty-pack of Carroll's No. 1. He flipped the box open with one hand, withdrew two cigarettes, and tossed one onto my lap.

'Let's hope Cora don't mind you smoking, Johnny-boy,' he commented with an upward flick of his head.

As we settled into our seats, we watched a small man slip into the nightclub. He wore a tight cream suit, the suit's bright sheen radiant in the club's lighting. With an effeminate step he made a tour, stopping briefly to chat with each of the dark-suited bouncers.

It was Éamon's bastard — the hotel owner — and we watched as he inspected his troops. As he passed us he paused, and I could almost hear him chuckling.

'Hello, Mister Fitzgerald,' I called to him. 'That's a lovely suit.'

Slowly, the crowd began to trickle in. Time passed, the nightclub filled, and I was feeling the first pangs of disappointment when …

Suddenly, there is a lot of movement and everyone falls to the floor. We are at a moment in the Mass when we should all kneel down and check out the shoes of the person in front. I'm no spoil-sport; I get down on one knee. They are a pair of black loafers, low cut, and they expose bright white socks that disappear up a pair of blue jeans. Well, that's a little sad. After sufficient time for reflection has elapsed, the priest gives a signal, and we all are allowed to resume our seat, or stand. In the resettlement, I have a quick look to those around me at the back of the church. It is the usual Sunday gathering of hung-over rogues. Survival can be that in an occupied state: an attendance granted, but collaboration withheld. To the left, annexed to the side wall of the church, there is a decorated shrine to the Sacred Heart of Jesus. The statue within it has always intrigued me; I don't know why. Above the electric ten-penny candles, a brightly robed man with a kind face looks down on the gathering. A small, vivid, pink heart glows from the centre of his chest, like some sort of suspended, chainless medallion. A tiny girl stands before the shrine. Under the watchful eye and arm's-length grasp of her father, she caresses the rows of switches she knows will trigger the candles. She turns and notices me. She turns again and watches her father, and waits. The tempo of the Mass shifts, and the pious in the dark wooden pews shuffle into a kneeling position for the next prayer. In the disruption the girl flicks two of the switches, and within the candelabra in the shrine two red bulbs come to life. The girl looks to me with her face held open as if she is willing some reaction from me. With a wink and a slight nod of my head, I acknowledge my approval. The girl is delighted.

She was standing with her friends on the other side of the nightclub. Unsure what to do, I held my ground. I can confess that I would have walked cold and naked over the Cooley Mountains to get to Cora Flannery. But to cross that dance floor and walk into an audience of curious girls was beyond me. My palms began to sweat and I stared at the floor. Should I go over? Could I go over? But when I looked up, she was there. She stood before me and, slowly, as she looked to me, she took my hand. And with that first touch my anxiety was dismissed with the force of the gods, and rushing into the void was joy.

'Come on,' she laughed, skipping towards the dance floor.

At the end of the night, Cora's friends came to take her, but she refused them.

'Johnny is walking me home,' she told them. 'Aren't you?' she added, squeezing my fingers. And indeed I was. It would have taken the ancient armies of Ulster to take Cora from me that night, and they would have had to fight.

'Okay, be good,' they replied, and made to go. Abruptly, one of them — a tall and good-looking girl — came over to us.

'So she finally got you, Johnny Donnelly,' she said. 'This one will never let you go now.' She kissed Cora on her forehead before turning to me.

'See you, handsome,' she said, and was off.

'Who is that?' I asked, bewildered.

'That's our Aisling, my big sister, and my best friend. My best female friend, of course. Isn't she beautiful?'

'Yes, Cora, she sure is.'

'She's studying medicine, in college, in Dublin.' She rushed the detail to me, the rush tripping her breath.

'Beautiful and clever,' I said. And then after a pause I added, 'So who's your best male friend then?'

Cora looked to me as though I had just asked her if she knew the capital of Ireland. 'You,' she answered. And she answered with such sincerity that there wasn't any doubt.

I felt as if I'd been substituted into another life and that I was being mistaken for someone else. We were queuing at the cloakroom to get our coats when I thought of the boys. I searched for them, and saw that they were still sitting where I had left them hours before. They caught my enquiry and all gave me an exaggerated wave, and Éamon shouted something that raised a laugh from no one but himself.

As we reached the exit I looked back into the club and caught a glimpse of Conor's shaking head.

We took our time on the walk home and stopped in the central Market Square for a snack from a late-night take-away stall.

'I'm always starving after a disco,' Cora said. 'Do you fancy a bag of chips, Johnny?'

'I'm that hungry, Cora, I could eat a small Protestant,' I quipped, and we both laughed as we fought our way to the counter.

'One bag of chips, *Mademoiselle*, and one large curry-chips and sausage, when you're ready?'

To eat the food, we sat on a bench opposite the stall, near the entrance to the county court-house — I insisted that it wouldn't do the supper justice to eat on the move. When we'd finished I crumpled the wrappings into a ball, tossed it into the air, and volleyed it into a litter bin. I moved beside her.

'So what's the story with that coat and scarf, Johnny? Are you ever seen without them?'

I take a lot of grief with the coat — people are unable not to comment. But that's fashion: yesterday's favourites are today's oddities. It is a dark-tweed woollen overcoat — a 1960s Dunn & Co of London that I bought used — and in different light the tweed is green or grey or brown, like Ravensdale Forest on a wet day. The scarf is blue. I like the coat and I like the scarf, and that's that. The world can think what it likes.

'No story at all.'

I removed the scarf. I put it around her and pulled her to me.

'Do you know something, Cora Flannery?'

'What, Johnny Donnelly?'

'It's time to go.'

When we arrived at Cora's house, we sat on a low wall that separates the small front and rear lawns. We watched a few other late-night travellers making their way home, some unsteady on their feet. We watched cars pass — some travelling too fast for the small road — as young men and women drove home from Dundalk to the outlying townlands in North Louth and South Armagh. I took the Dunn & Co off and put it over Cora's shoulders, closing the coat tight and lifting the collar up. She rested on me and I held her easy in my arm. It was joy itself to hold her. She moved closer. I could feel her breath on my throat. I raised my hand and touched the side of her face, and I could hear my own heart as I kissed her. And under the fall of the blue scarf, she rested her fingers on my chest.

'You are unbelievably wonderful, Cora,' I whispered to her. 'You are a mad and wonderful thing altogether.'

'A mad and wonderful thing,' she whispered back. 'Thank you. You are not too bad yourself, Mister Donnelly.'

We reach the serving of communion, the climax of the Catholic Mass. Those who stand around me at the back of the church are on the move — one or two toward the great altar to consume the body of Christ, and the rest out and away. I hold my place. To pass the time I lift a copy of *Parish Monthly* from the magazine rack on the rear wall of the church. I read about arrangements for daily Mass, weekly confessions, novenas, devotions, and a holy triduum; and news of baptisms, marriages, new choir members, a cake-and-bun sale in the parish hall, and a scheduled bus trip down the country to see a moving statue. 'I saw it sway a little,' Dad had said after the latest trip. 'It definitely moved all right. Didn't it, Kathleen?'

'Go in peace to love and serve the Lord.' The priest brings the Mass to an end, and I skip down the front steps to where Éamon is waiting. We buy newspapers from the Sunday stall at the church gate and we walk together the short distance to the junction with the Ramparts Road. We both scan the headlines.

'God-sakes,' Éamon comments. 'Listen to this, Johnny. IRA SNIPER WITH NEW DEADLY WEAPON AT WORK IN SOUTH ARMAGH.' Éamon has the same habit as Dad of reading aloud from a newspaper. 'Aren't you glad we don't live in the North, Johnny? Five miles away — it might as well be five hundred, it's such a different place. Thank God we live in the Republic.'

'Up the Republic,' I say, and we both laugh.

'So how's it going with Cora?'

'Great. She is a wonderful girl.' The thing is out and said before I have time to consider it.

Éamon flicks his head and gives me a look that carries both surprise and question. But he says nothing. Instead he produces a couple of cigarettes, and we stand and smoke and chat. We separate after the smoke and agree to meet up later, and as I walk away from my friend I consider the girl. That's what they do to you, girls — they're an unmanageable species. And once they make it into your thoughts, it can be impossible to think of anything else.

'John.'

[15]

I turn to the call. Behind me is a tall, elderly man buttoned up in a double-breasted charcoal-grey long coat. The man is Ignatius Delaney, and Delaney in the open is all John le Carré. Or so he thinks. The whole show is a bit Starsky & Hutch to me. Though the day is warm, he's wearing gloves, and as he approaches he's adjusting a gentleman's trilby. Two dark eyes peer out below the trilby, and a thin sneer is held beneath a greying, trimmed moustache. A Burberry scarf, neatly knotted, is offered through the lapels of the coat. Delaney, if needs be, is pure Hollywood.

'John, I thought that was you.'

'Hello, Mister Delaney,' I answer, playing along.

He extends one leathered hand. With the other, he gestures behind him. 'John, have you met my daughter Loreto? She's home from California.'

I am surprised — this is unusual. I look to the tall woman. She has a white powdered face and dark eyes. Her painted red lips roar against the pale background. She wears a long, black coat with a cranberry-red scarf draped across her shoulders like a shawl, and a cranberry-red velvet cloche hat. This woman, literally, is a doll.

'Forty years teaching, Loreto,' Ignatius Delaney says to her. 'Forty years. So many boys, so little talent. But there was one. One who could fly higher. One light in the dark.'

I ignore the story. I have heard it before.

'And do you know, Loreto? Do you know what he chose to do with this talent? Which higher school of learning does he attend? Which university, do you think?'

I look again to the dark eyes of the woman. She's watching me.

'What he chose, Loreto, was carpentry. Isn't that right, John?'

'Like I said before, Mister Delaney, I thought I might get a skill in when my hands are still young.'

'Yes, well, never mind, John. You were always the incorrigible.

[16]

Good to see you. God bless.'

We part at the fire station where the road forks. What was that about? Why was she there? This is not the Chief's form. But I've got the message — I will make a visit. I watch them as they walk away from me. I ponder on the woman below the velvet cloche hat. I know there is something there, but I let it fall from my thoughts as I walk home. Around me the air is bright and warm, the sunshine reflects off the ground, and I think again of Cora at the post office, at the nightclub, on the road home, and on the small wall in her garden. I skip along the footpath; secretly, I dance on the edge of joy. I bubble like milk on the stove just before the boil. I could break into a Michael Jackson routine at any second.

My old friend Bob appears beside me, keeping pace and in step. *We're in great form altogether,* he says. *There's no stopping us now.*

I pass an elderly neighbour I hardly know. She looks to me with a curious regard as I greet her.

'Hello, Missus Byrne,' and, unable to stop myself, add, 'How's the ould sex life this weather?'

'Not as busy as yours, by the look of things,' she shoots back.

Damn, that was quick. I can't think of a follow-up, so with a laugh and a wave I continue home. And I'm thinking things are looking up. Yes, indeed they are. Things are looking good for Johnny Donnelly.

The dinner

'WILL I POUR YOUR TEA?'

'Are you going to the match, Son?'

'Did you shift last night, Johnny?'

I have joined Mam, Dad, and Anna at the kitchen table for Sunday dinner.

'Please.'

'I might go up for the second half.'

'I sure didn't,' I answer, moving my cup across the table to within Mam's reach.

'Thanks. Where's the other fella?'

'Declan was away early,' Mam answers, pouring the tea. 'Peter collected him. Off to the Mourne Mountains, if you don't mind. Up at the crack of dawn, he was, making sandwiches. I had to hide the good ham.'

I don't say anything. My two brothers often take weekend mountain hikes. It's a harmless-enough activity, I guess. But they can get puritanical about it — you'd want to listen to them going on and on about it, as if not doing it were the vice of the Devil himself. It's the type of thing people do to help them feel better about themselves. I understand that.

'They'll be here later with yon one,' Mam continues — yon one being Aunt Hannah. 'I'm doing a pot of homemade soup.' An old pot rattles on the cooker behind her.

'Well, Johnny, spill the beans,' Anna persists. 'Did you?'

'And I've brown bread in the oven,' Mam says, continuing the account of her preparations for high tea.

'It should be good,' Dad insists. 'Derry will bring a great crowd.'

'I'd say you did. Who was she, Johnny-boy? Do I know her?' Anna probes again.

'Hey, nosey parker, eat up,' Mam admonishes. 'And eat them sprouts, they're good for you. I don't like them myself, but I eat them.'

I look across to my sister. 'Yes, Anna, come on, get them into you. There's a good girl.'

Anna Donnelly is twenty years old. She's a good-looking girl; well, she is my sister. She has long, dark hair the colour of old oak, and green eyes — forest green fading to an edge of azure blue. She has the same eyes as her brother, the brother who's sitting across the table from her. With the minimum of months between us, Anna and I had a shared childhood, and for all our young years we were often mistaken for twins. Through threads of her long hair, she gives me a warning.

'I might take a walk up for the second half myself,' Dad says with some finality, and rises. With his knife he pushes the scraps off his plate into a bowl set aside for the dog, and he carries the plate to the worktop.

'I'll wash them later for you, Kathleen,' he says. 'After a wee read of the papers.'

I also rise.

'I'll throw on some eggs,' Mam says to no one other than herself. 'I could do a bit of a salad.' She, too, rises and begins to clear the table.

I follow Dad to the living room and sit on the couch, with a newspaper in hand. I can hear the opening lines of a familiar tune as Mam sings as she works. She is singing 'Lizzie Lindsay'.

'If she had ever got her hands on Danny Doyle, I'd have been given the door,' Dad says from behind his newspaper.

'I think we'd all have got the door,' I say, laughing. I can't remember a day when I have not heard Mam singing a Danny Doyle song.

Kathleen Reynolds had already been working in the shoe factory for four years when she married Oliver Donnelly in the town's Saint Nicholas's Church in September 1959. She was just seventeen. Nine times she would feel the tightening of her belly and the nausea rush of early pregnancy. Those nine conceptions carried to just four births. I am the fourth-born of her four children. Mam was a bright student as a young girl: smart, capable, top of her class at reading and mathematics, and with the catechism. She had a sweet voice — the nuns had her to the front for visiting inspectors, priests, and bishops. In another time and in another place she could have been something. However, the end of primary school was the end of her education, and the end of her childhood.

Mam grew up in a house of twelve children, the youngest of eight girls. Granddad was a tradesman in the brewery — a good job at any time — but he suffered the schizophrenia of the Irish: generous and magnanimous in the pub, cruel and spiteful in the home. Mam says that her mother fought an endless war just to keep them all fed and clothed. And so, as her sisters had done before her, Mam took her small body from the schoolyard to the shoe-factory floor. Only five of the twelve children were to remain in Ireland, and two of them are dead and buried. The other seven left for work in England. Mam never saw the two eldest boys — they had been and gone by the time she was born. They never came back.

As I settle on the couch, a girl arrives at the back door, lets herself in, makes her way to the living room, and jumps up beside me.

'Caitríona Begley is calling me names again,' she sighs.

'Hello, Clara,' Dad says, without lowering his newspaper.

'Hello, Oliver.' She tugs at my arm.

I drop my reading and look to her. Clara Mulligan is seven years old and the youngest child of a neighbouring family. The Mulligans run a bar in the town centre, and Clara's parents are too busy with work to be busy at home. Mam has taken on the job of child-minding during after-school hours, school holidays, and weekends. Clara has known more child-minding than she has parenting, and she has adopted here as home, and me as big brother. And that's okay with me.

'Don't worry, baby. She's probably just mad jealous,' I say, putting my arm around her.

'Because she's fat?'

'No,' I laugh. 'Probably because you've such a handsome big brother and all she has is that Paddy Begley to look at. A brother with a face like that would upset anyone. He's not allowed pass the creamery, that fella, in case he'd turn all the milk sour.'

'That's true. That's it, isn't it?'

'Indeed it is. If I had to look at that ugly contortion every day, I wouldn't be too happy either.'

'Okey dokey,' Clara says, leaping off the couch. 'I'm going to tell her that.'

'There she goes,' Dad says.

I watch the girl skip out the door and I look over to my father. Dad can spend a large part of any day behind a newspaper, and I am never sure when he's beyond those pages whether he's reading at all or just taking cover to drift off to some other private world. I ponder on him for a while as he sits and reads. But sometimes it is impossible for me to think about Dad and not to remember the gun.

I don't have a good memory for most stuff, like what they try to teach you at school. I learn things, and they go in and linger a while, but they never stay any distance. It seems I can only hold on to the peculiar. I could never have been a great student, despite Delaney's hopes. And I don't remember much of my early childhood, the first five or six years or so. But I do remember the gun.

It must have been winter, because it was dark and wet and cold. We were on our way home from an afternoon's shopping in Newry. Mam has a thing about shopping in Newry — she says everything up there is great value. As it leaves the town, the road from Newry to Dundalk climbs a big hill. Near the beginning of this hill there is a junction where the main road continues south, and where a smaller road runs east along the coast of Carlingford Lough and then south around the peninsula into Dundalk Bay. The seashore route is a nice drive on a nice day. Dad had a habit of calling out to us kids in the back as we approached this junction, 'Turn or straight on?' We always shouted 'Turn', because the longer coastal road offered something of an adventure. Most times, Dad drove straight on anyway, whatever the vote, but once in a while — to keep the magic in the game — he turned.

There was just Anna and I with them in the car that day — I guess the two older boys were at home with Aunt Hannah — and we shouted, 'Turn, turn, turn.' I don't know why Dad turned. It was too dark to see anything of the drive, but maybe he fancied the spin or was in some sort of a comfortable daydream and needed the extra mileage. Whatever the reason, it was a bad choice.

The road we took runs next to the Newry Canal on a narrow strip between the broadening lough and the dark rise of Cooley Mountains. Four miles from Newry, the road crosses the border into the Republic of Ireland. There is a customs post on the southern side, and sometimes a police or army security-check on the north. Somewhere between Newry and the border, Dad suddenly slowed. I tried to look ahead between the two front seats, but it was difficult to see anything in the dark and the rain. Then I saw the slow arc of a lamp being waved. Mam and Dad's conversation died abruptly, and in the new silence I could hear Dad's breathing as he stopped the car and wound down his side window, his hand slipping once from the handle.

It wasn't the first time we'd been stopped on a trip to Newry, and I sat quietly in the back with Anna as Dad passed his licence out to the soldier and answered questions about who we were and what we were doing there. The soldier told Dad to get out and go to the rear of the car and open the boot. I heard the boot opening and the sound of muffled voices. Then there was silence, and waiting. Then another soldier stooped through Dad's door and pointed a gun at Mam and shouted for us all to get out of the car, and he stood us by the side of the road with his gun still pointing at Mam, and we watched in the cold rain as two other soldiers searched the inside of the car. The first soldier was still questioning Dad at the rear of the car as the search came to some kind of an end, and we cowered in the wet darkness as Dad lifted Mam's scattered shopping from the road and put it back into the car. Dad closed the boot, trying to lock it, but he couldn't get the key into the catch, and the first soldier pushed him towards the driver's door as the second soldier marched the rest of us to the car and shouted for us to 'Get in and get the fuck out.' Even as a six-year-old boy, I thought this to be an odd instruction.

Dad was fumbling and struggling to get the car going again, and after only a few yards the car stalled. Dad was breathing loudly, shaking the steering wheel with a tightened grip as if he were trying to force the engine by will and panic alone. It was then that the thing happened. Thinking on it later, I know that a soldier must have run from the ditch, but at the time it seemed as if the gun appeared from the dark air. Dad's window was still fully opened, and the first thing we all saw was the big black gun as it caught Dad on the side of his head. I heard Mam scream, and beside me in the back Anna gripped my left arm and froze. I saw Dad recover from the knock, but as he turned to the window I watched the gun go into his mouth. The only sound in the car was Dad's gulping for air. The next words were very clear, 'I'm going to kill you.' There was a long silence before the gun disappeared back out the window. Dad didn't move, Mam still stared straight ahead, and Anna was still frozen.

The silence went on forever. Then a head appeared at the window and leant in and retreated, and I heard voices and laughter. 'Pissed his fucking pants, mate,' I heard the soldier call. 'Pissed his fucking pants.' Dad just sat there, his head dropped and his body slumped and turned away from the window, as other heads gathered at the car and shouted at us, 'Get going', 'Drive away now', 'Move it, Paddy Piss-Pants.' The shouting and the laughing went on and on as Dad remained slumped in his seat. Mam was leaning over to him, her hand cradling his face as his shoulders shook. 'Oh Oliver, Oh Oliver,' she said, but he didn't respond and he didn't make any move to restart the car. Mam got out into the shouting and laughing, and took Dad out and walked him around the front of the car to her seat before going back to the driver's side and wiping the seat with the cloth that Dad used to clean the windows. Not once did Mam look at the soldiers. Then she sat in the car and drove away into the south.

'The children,' was all Dad said, and Mam shushed him with a touch, and we travelled home in silence. But I knew that one day I would take a big black gun to those soldiers.

Delaney's cabbages

I CALL TO SEE DELANEY IN THE MIDWEEK FOLLOWING THE SUNDAY MASS.
I rest my bicycle against the redbrick of the front wall and search for
him first in the back garden.

'Hey, Chief,' I hail him. He rises between rows of cabbages,
salutes, and moves towards me. The garden is a collection of square
enclosures, each enclosure partitioned by a clipped box hedge
enveloping straight rows of raised and planted earth. The whole
thing is as neat and tidy as a Jehovah's Witness.

'Is it about a bicycle?' he greets me.

'How's that garden treating you?' I ask him.

'Busy time of year. Can't turn your back for a minute.' He looks
to me as he removes his garden gloves and places one hand on my
shoulder. 'How's my boy?'

'Never better, Chief,' I answer. 'How's Miss California?'

He gives me that look of his, a look halfway between a smile and
a sneer. 'Out shopping with Delores, thank God. I have the place to
myself.' He nods towards the house. 'Let's have tea.'

We move inside to a back kitchen which could have come out of
a 1960s *Good Housekeeping* brochure, and probably did.

'We've had some leakage,' he says, as the kettle boils on the gas
stove and he stands at the window looking out over the garden.
'Nothing for you to worry about.' He turns to face me. 'I just wanted
you to know.'

'How? Who?'

'That doesn't matter, John.' He turns again to the window. 'It's dealt with. But it's nothing new. They tried before. They try now. They will try again. Now and again they get a talker. There are those who can be bought or flattered; it is a flaw in our human nature. But this one doesn't know anything about you — nobody knows about you — so let's just take it as a caution, a warning.'

I am cold as the threat registers. 'Informers,' I spit the word out.

He doesn't speak as he scalds a white-porcelain teapot with boiling water. He empties the teapot into the sink and spoons in loose tea before filling it from the whistling kettle. He stirs the tea, replaces the lid, and puts the teapot on the table. 'Now then,' he says. 'Let's continue to keep it tight, very tight. Just the two of us, and we'll have no loose ends and no loose talk or tout to worry about.'

I nod, and we drink the tea as he talks about cabbages, carrot fly, and fruit netting.

For seven years I have come to Delaney. He has never told me exactly how high he is in the IRA — it doesn't matter to what we do — but I guess he's somewhere near the top. I have helped with some other stuff, too, but he has kept me separate, secret. No one in the movement knows who I am; no one in the movement knows I exist.

It has taken time to get what I need and to know how to use it. I am still learning. 'I'll help you do what you do,' I had told him early. 'I'll help you do what you do, if you get me a big black gun.'

'Leave these matters with me,' he says now as we part, 'and don't annoy yourself about it.'

But I am annoyed, and as I cycle away I go over each step of our plan, checking every seal and strut. I get home and retie the gate with the old shoelace as Che, our German Shepherd, bounds to greet me, and I wrestle with him on the side path.

Bob stands by the garden shed where I store the bicycle. *Should we be worried?* he asks, as I park the bicycle and latch the shed door.

Have Delaney and Donnelly got a flaw in their great plan to free Ireland?

I ignore him. We should be good — we built the plan slow and well. It is leak-proof and it is failsafe.

That's what they said about the Titanic, Bob calls, as I play with Che on my way around the side of the house.

I see Clara out on the street. She is cycling on the pavement and concentrating hard. She knows I am there and she wants me to see her. I am afraid to call to her as I know she will lift an arm to wave. So I walk to the gate and lean over.

'You are going great,' I tell her. 'A pure natural. We'll have you in the Tour de France yet.'

She stops and looks to me, 'What's the Tour de France?'

'It's a race for lunatics,' I tell her. 'You're made for it.'

'Funny boy,' she says, and she cycles off, and I watch her go on the red bicycle that I bought her for her birthday.

The red bicycle

I WAS SEVEN YEARS OLD WHEN I GOT MY RED BICYCLE FOR CHRISTMAS. I had wanted it forever, and I couldn't believe it was actually there on Christmas morning. I couldn't believe it was for me.

I had learned to ride on Anna's small bicycle and then I moved up to Peter's, and when he was off playing football or away at the scouts or something I rode his Raleigh around the front garden. Peter's Raleigh was too big for me — I couldn't reach the pedals if I sat on the saddle — so I rode around the garden standing, with my little body going up and down with the effort, giving the whole adventure a fairground-ride feel to it. It was great stuff, and I always waited until the last minute before returning the bicycle to the shed and pretending all was as normal to Peter when he got home. 'He's going to catch you one of these days,' Mam would warn. 'And then you'll be looking for me to save you.' Declan never had a bicycle of his own; I don't think he liked cycling. Isn't that a peculiar thing?

But now I had one of my own — a beautiful red bicycle — and I rode around that garden every day. At the time we lived in a council estate of about a hundred houses. The estate had a rectangular block of houses at one end and an open U-shape of houses at the other, as if the planners couldn't agree on either and so included both. We lived on one of the entry corners of the rectangular block.

The street bully was Jimmy McCusker, and he was fourteen when I got the red bicycle. I think Jimmy was a bit slow or something because he never went to school. Instead he wandered around the street all day looking for trouble. But he never got it from me. I didn't go out there much, and I wouldn't have gone out at all, only I needed to walk to school. Out there were bigger boys and danger, and to me it all seemed rough and threatening. I stayed and played in our garden. Jimmy always had a couple of sidekicks with him — younger boys who would be replaced as they grew up and moved on from him. The McCuskers lived on the back row of houses in the rectangle block, and it was a blessing that I never had reason to be around there. All of my information was gathered second-hand. Sometimes I saw Jimmy about the street as I made my way to or from school, but somehow I managed to avoid him. Dad said that Jimmy was the image of his father and that there must be some class of a delinquent gene running through the McCusker family. Jimmy's father sat in his porch all day smoking cigarettes and abusing passers-by as his son made a nuisance of himself in the street. Dad said that the McCuskers had a fair share of insanity and a monopoly on inanity. It was years later before I knew what that meant.

When summer came, I started to cycle to the shop to get the *Dundalk Democrat* for Dad. The *Democrat* came out at the weekend, and so first thing on a Saturday morning I was up and away. The shop was just past the end of the street, and one morning in August I bought the newspaper, strapped it to the metal carrier, and headed for home. I don't know why I took the rear street through the rectangle block — I'd never done it before — but it was such a beautiful, warm morning and maybe I was daydreaming, or maybe I just wasn't thinking. Suddenly I had to brake hard not to crash into Jimmy McCusker, who was standing in the road. Jimmy put one hand on the bicycle and looked down at me. He didn't say a word. My back tightened, I felt my insides shrink, and I was gripped tight and sore around my middle. But Jimmy McCusker didn't touch me. He didn't beat me up. He didn't even push me off. He just took the bicycle from me and wheeled it through his own gate. He even took Dad's newspaper.

'Didn't you do anything?' Dad asked.

'No,' I said. 'I didn't know what to do.'

'Didn't know what to do?' Dad repeated my words to me, standing above me and shaking his head.

'I'm sorry,' I told him, but he said nothing.

I went to my bedroom and sat on my bed and cried, and Anna came in and held my hand. We heard Dad leave, and we ran to the window when he returned, but all he had with him was the *Democrat*. I figured it must be one that he had gone and bought himself.

When Christmas came around again I asked for a slingshot.

'Why do you want a slingshot?' Mam and Dad asked.

'To be like Cúchulainn,' I said. They thought this to be bit of a laugh, and they repeated it to all our relatives and callers.

'Going to be like Cúchulainn, this boy,' they told everyone.

'I need a good one,' I said to Mam when she was alone in the kitchen. 'A strong one, like a kind of sports-shooting one.' And I showed her models I'd found in books that I'd borrowed from the library.

Christmas brought the slingshot, and I had my plan made.

I spent the next six months with stones and marbles. I used footballs and tennis balls as targets, and I practised every day until the target was a golf ball and I could hit it from across the length of the garden. I was ready.

Between our housing estate and the next one were hilly fields. One hill had been part chiselled away at some time, leaving a face of rock exposed. It wasn't very high — perhaps some twenty feet — but to us children it was huge, and we called it the cliff. Anna and I climbed there when there was no one about.

The summer holidays came, and the children from both estates gathered in the common ground of the hilly fields. Jimmy McCusker and his gang held a raised patch near the height of the cliff like a pride of lions might hold some higher mound in the African savannah. The rest of us children, like a grazing herd, kept a distance. That year, McCusker's crew comprised the two Breen boys, and I waited for a day when the three boys were at the cliff height and no other children were near. I had my place in the long grass prepared, where I knew I couldn't be seen. On previous mornings, before anyone got there, I had checked the cover, I had measured the distance, and I had practised the range.

I first took one of the Breen boys. I hit him in the forehead and he fell. The other two had no idea what had just happened, and stood around him open-mouthed. I then took the second Breen boy, catching him in his open mouth, and he went down screaming. I could see McCusker was panicked as he searched out into the field for some solution or reason. He found neither, and I hit his right shoulder and then his right knee as I worked him backwards to the cliff. He was moaning and desperate for cover. But there was none — the long grass was all mine — and when he reached the cliff he looked over it as if unsure whether to jump or scramble down, and so he turned again to face me, and I hit him in his left eye, and he fell back and away.

What happened on the cliff that summer was a mystery that became a street legend. Nobody really believed the Breen boys' report of an attack from nowhere, and the cliff was full of stones anyway, so nothing could be found or proved. Most believed that there had probably been some row or incident among the gang and that the story was a cover-up, though some thought the Breen boys to be too young and their injuries too severe for it all to be a fiction. But nobody cared enough to give it a serious investigation.

Jimmy McCusker survived, though he'd broken his neck in the

fall, and when he got out of hospital he joined his father in the daily vigil on the front porch. I got a new bicycle the next Christmas — a blue Raleigh — and when dry weather came I took it for a ride around the block. When I passed the McCuskers I stopped and looked at the boy in the wheelchair as his father shouted abuse at me. But something had changed: the tightening in my back and the sore grip to my middle were gone, and I was no longer afraid of them. I waved to the McCuskers as I rode away.

We moved to a new house later that year, and I never saw Jimmy McCusker or my red bicycle again.

A black flag flying

It is the second week of May, and it is two weeks since that first evening with Cora Flannery. Two weeks. I am nervous. Today I'm to call at her house for the first time. Today I shall meet her mam and dad. I have held out for as long as I can, but Cora says that I am really pushing it, that at two weeks I am being just plain weird. What can I say? There is normal time and there is Cora's time, and well …

I tie the low gate closed behind me with the shoelace and salute Dad, who stands watching me from the front porch.

'All right, Son?' he calls.

'All right, Dad.'

Next door, in the front garden of an identical house, a small man is bent low at work among some roses and shrubs.

'She has you on your hands and knees again, Eddie,' I comment.

He barely looks up. 'Gobshite.' It is just a whisper, but I catch it, and too late he tries to run. Too late and too slow. Before he can get going, I have cleared the wall and have him in a firm grip.

Eddie Reynolds is my uncle. He is ex-army and he is a small man. But he is a proud man. He was, in his youth, the featherweight boxing champion of Leinster, and he held that title for five years. Eddie and Hannah are my mam's brother and sister, and live next door. The three of them do everything together — shopping, socialising, holidays, the whole fruit-basket — and the rest of time they give out about each other. Eddie and Hannah never married and neither one has children. When Eddie retired from the army he took me as his vocation, and many of his afternoons were spent teaching me boxing, arm-to-arm combat, and — removed from the eyes of others — how to handle a gun. Eddie delighted in the telling of tales of army life: the barracks, the rifle-range, the border, the Curragh, the Congo, and the Lebanon. I loved to hear the stories. Back then, Eddie could manage me, but that was ten years ago, when Eddie was fifty and I was nine. This is now. It is no longer a contest.

'Gobshite, is it?' In one movement I lift the small man up on my shoulders and spin him around.

'Johnny,' Eddie pleads as he tries to fight my hold. 'Let me down, you fecker.'

But I hold him easy enough.

'Hannah, Hannah,' Eddie calls out.

Aunt Hannah appears in the central doorway. She takes no notice of the scene at play on the front lawn. She turns to Dad, who still stands in the open front porch.

'A beautiful day, Oliver,' she calls.

'A beautiful day, Hannah. Thank God. A beautiful day.' He looks up to pencil-grey clouds that move below a blue-and-white sky. 'Though we could see a shower yet.'

'How's herself?' Aunt Hannah asks.

'Right as rain, Hannah,' Dad says, indicating over his shoulder. In the brief silence of his pausing, a few faint notes of song escape the hallway. 'She's right as rain.'

I let Eddie down, and have cleared the wall before he steadies and takes a swipe.

'Too slow, you old fox,' I call, pulling the Dunn & Co straight.

I take the bicycle from where it rests against the front wall, check the tyres for hardness, mount, and I am off. I look back as I go. The old soldier waves, acknowledges Dad with a salute, gives his sister a shake of his head, and returns to his gardening low among the roses.

I cycle out of the small estate and turn west onto the Ramparts Road. I pass the grounds of the lawn tennis club where on summer mornings Anna and I would climb the wall for a game before the caretaker arrived and threw us out. I turn north through Distillery Lane and then west again through Jocelyn Street, passing the office of a local newspaper below the first-floor snooker rooms of the Catholic Young Man's Society where Éamon and I played every week while the rest of the class took to the cold and windy sports-field. At the junction with Chapel Street I pass the Home Bakery where Mam queues on a Saturday morning for two French loaves and an almond ring, and every so often a chocolate or pineapple cake. I pass Saint Patrick's Cathedral and continue west through Crowe Street passing the town hall. I continue along the side wall of the county-court house and enter the Market Square. It was here I sat with Cora just two weeks ago. And it was here in this square where I first took notice of politics, first made conclusions on the story of Ireland, and first decided my role. That was 1981, and I was ten years old.

Bobby Sands, an IRA prisoner in a British jail in Northern Ireland, died after sixty-six days of a hunger strike. He was twenty-seven years old. Nine other men would follow him that summer on a demand for identity, a demand to be recognised as political prisoners. The streets and the television stations were full of it. The newspapers Dad brought home were full of it. Mam and Dad's talk at the kitchen table and neighbours' talk over fences was full of it. The walls, hoardings, and bridges around town were full of it. The list of the prisoners' five demands was everywhere, with SMASH H-BLOCK below them as a sign-off.

At the time I wondered why a people with so little, against an enemy with so much, would put all this effort into a battle for clothes and visits — a battle that could never affect the war. I asked Dad

what was going on. 'Politics,' he said. 'It is all a game of politics.'
A protest base was established in the Market Square throughout the
Bobby Sands hunger strike, and every day on the way from school I
walked through it just to try to catch some of the fever. I didn't. I just
couldn't figure the thing out. The black flags appeared on the day he
died; they hung from every lamppost. That day, a skinny teenage girl
in tight jeans and sporting a short haircut asked me to sign a petition.
'Why?' I asked, and the question seemed to throw her. It didn't make
sense. My ten-year-old head couldn't figure it out. Bobby Sands had
contested a Westminster seat during his hunger strike, and he had
won — graffiti on an old wall near the school read, THE RIGHT HON
BOBBY SANDS MP. I looked at the wall every day. *The Right Hon Bobby
Sands MP*. Why, I thought, are we celebrating participation in the
very thing that has persecuted us all this time? But celebration it was,
BOBBY SANDS MP was everywhere.

There were riots in the north when he died. We watched it all on
television: women blowing whistles and banging dustbin lids on the
pavements, youths attacking armoured cars, police lines behind riot
shields, and petrol bombs flying in the night. The funeral was like a
state affair — a long cortege of tens of thousands, a colour party, and
shots into the air. And everyone had something to say about it.

A week later, after fifty-nine days on hunger strike, Francis
Hughes died. He was twenty-five. So the whole thing was repeated.
And then another hunger striker died, and then another, and then
another. It seemed to go on forever. In the Republic, though everyone
was gripped by it, and concerned, we were yet distanced, kind of
detached, as though it were remote and happening in another country
altogether. We sat as spectators in our living rooms as bin lids rattled
in the mornings, stones were launched in the afternoons, and petrol
bombs flew at night. We watched the long funeral processions, the
stiff-stepped coffin-carrying, and the colour parties shooting bullets

up into a sky that never harmed Ireland. And here in Dundalk the black flags hung in the Market Square. Ten men were dead by the time it finished. I asked Dad why it had stopped. 'Politics,' he said. 'It is all a game of politics.' I didn't know it then — I know it now — but Dad was right. It was only ever politics, and we lost.

And we Irish are too used to losing. We are too fond of celebrating moral defeats; too fond of celebrating small victories that don't matter and are not victories at all; too fond of suffering; too fond of martyrs; too fond of the damned word *struggle*; and too fond of reverting to playing politics with the British, who have a long history of never doing us any good. The only thing that matters in this war is removing the enemy from Ireland. And to this end the hunger strikes changed nothing. They were an attempt at persuasion. But why bother? The only battle worth fighting is a battle that can help win the war. This was the lesson I learned in 1981.

A single black flag was erected in a lane near the school during the hunger strike, and was forgotten and left in place when all the others were taken down. For years, I watched that flag as it faded and tore, until one day the wood gave way to rot and it fell to the ground, where the cleaning truck brushed it up and dumped it along with the other unwanted things.

I cycle north from the Market Square through Clanbrassil Street, passing the narrow road where the school is. *Are you joining us today, Mister Donnelly? Would you care to share your thoughts with the class, Mister Donnelly? Is there something strange or startling out those windows, Mister Donnelly? Hello, hello, calling Mister Donnelly, come in please? Continue reading from there, Mister Donnelly. Well, Mister Donnelly, don't wait for the applause. Mister Donnelly …* I pass through Church Street to Bridge Street, a dull, narrow street that offers nothing but a last-chance saloon for desperate enterprise, where the few remaining shops sell everything nobody wants. Rough-looking men stand outside bars and watch me with suspicious faces as if the act of riding a bicycle is an indecent phenomenon and is likely to be of some threat. I pass two vagrants walking south with such slowness that it appears they would rather walk for eternity than reach the end of the street. This northern edge is where the town abandons pretence and ambition, settles for fate over fortune, and lies down with a bottle of cheap wine. I pull the zip on my high pullover and change gears. At the muddy river I turn and cycle west on Castletown Road. Some children are playing ball in the yard of the National Girls' School, and I have to stop to return a ball that has been kicked over the iron railings. I think of Mam. This was her school. Here in this same yard I know she must have sung, skipped, run, fallen, and cried. I try to picture her there, but can't. The children resume their game with gusto as I cycle west under the railway bridge. I slow as I approach the low-walled gardens of Níth River Terrace, and I stop halfway down the row of houses. The sky above has softened; the darker clouds have wandered off and the day has brightened again. I look to the chip shop where a girl polishes the front glass with a spray-gun and some loose newspaper.

'Hi,' I call to her.

'Hi,' she replies. She is a good-looking girl. Isn't the world full of them?

I push the low gate open with the front wheel, and rest my bicycle against the ashen-grey pebbledash of the side wall. I straighten the Dunn & Co, and run my finger and thumb down the length of my scarf, tidying it neatly parallel to the open coat. I walk to the front door, where two small brass numbers — a one and a six — are high over the central panel. I take a deep breath, and knock.

Bob

THE DOOR OPENS.

'Hello.' A boy stands in the doorway.

'Hello, is Cora in?'

There is a brief silence as the boy examines me. 'So you think you're Johnny Donnelly?'

'Eh, yeah. So they tell me.'

'So you do exist after all. She's been blabbering on about you for ages. We all thought she just made you up.'

'Right.'

Unwilling to let me stray from his gaze, the boy throws a shout over his shoulder, 'Cora, you're wanted.'

At the rear of the hallway a door opens and a woman hurries to the front, clipping the boy as she passes.

'Cormac, give over,' she says. She is an attractive woman. Her red hair is tied behind her, and her eyes are the lightened green of an August meadow. 'Come in, come in,' she says. 'I'm Fionnuala. I'm Cora's mammy.'

'Hello, Missus Flannery. It's very nice to meet you,' I say, stepping into the narrow hallway. I feel my breath quicken as I move inside the door. Suddenly I am unsure how to stand. I stand straight, I lean forward, I put my hands in my pockets, and I take them out. I settle on a partial forward leaning, and I clasp my hands low in front of me. The boy watches me.

There are footsteps on the staircase. It is Aisling.

'Hi, handsome.'

'Hello, Aisling.'

She approaches, kisses me on the cheek, and takes my hand. 'Listen, Johnny,' she says, 'there's still time to change your mind. Me and you, what do you think? We could be great lovers.'

I add a burning face to my struggling breath and my awkward stance.

'Mammy, quick, get her off him,' Cora calls, running down the stairs and pushing her sister away. The two girls laugh.

'Well, it was worth a try,' Aisling says. 'Right, I'm off. I'm meeting the girls. See you later, handsome,' she says, running her hand through my open coat as she leaves.

'Hey, you,' I say to Cora.

'Hey, you, yourself,' she answers, a blush ripening in her pale face. She leads me to the end of the hall and opens a door. 'Give me five minutes?' she asks, and disappears.

I push through the door. It opens to a kitchen. A large, ivory-coloured range stands against the opposite wall, and to the right of the range the back wall has been removed, and through a broad arch is an extended dining and living area. There is a long couch against the far wall of the extension, and sitting on it is Bob, a folded newspaper resting on the lap of his green overalls.

Isn't this just lovely? he says.

It was when I started my apprenticeship in the engineering works that I met Bob Hanratty. He was alive then. The old man was a caretaker in the machine workshop, and would spend one half of each day lubricating the various machines with his diverse collection of oilcans and grease guns. The other half-day he would empty the scrap bins and sweep the floors. At work breaks, Bob took his newspaper and ate alone at his workbench, preferring the peace and solitude of the oil store to the bustle and raucous banter of the works' canteen. He intrigued me, and I watched as he pushed his trolley to each machine, one after the other, lubricating the controls and levers, oiling the motors and greasing the machine beds, wiping each handle, point, and nipple, before and after, with a large, red rag that hung from the pocket of his green overalls. It was the old man's calm, methodical work and his quiet refrain from the coarse taunting of the factory floor that plucked my interest.

For weeks I observed him until, one Monday morning, I walked towards the centre of the workshop as Bob, pushing his trolley, approached the central intersection from the side. Grimes and McArdle were two buffoons who worked the inspection booth opposite the clerk's office. McArdle was unkempt — a slight frame in a dirty work coat, with a pitted weasel face under oily, brown hair. Grimes was clean, but he was a monster — a huge bulk of a body under a pink head.

'Did you ever get the ride, Bob?' Grimes shouted as the old man neared. 'There's still time. Is there life in the ould sausage yet? Are you still keeping palm busy?' he guffawed, leaning forward and signalling the motion with his hand. 'Hey, Bob, I gave it to her up the junction last night, like this,' he roared again, as he turned sideways and held his hands out and demonstrated. 'Then I went home to the wife,' he said, laughing loudly, slapping the table, punching McArdle, and turning to include all who could hear him. 'What about those lovely neighbours of yours, Bob? They'd love a fit man like me.'

I saw the flicker of rage that crossed the old man's face.

'Leave that man alone.' The words flew from my mouth before a consideration to speak was given thought. An abrupt silence tore across the workshop, and uncertainty hung in the hiatus of its tearing. Curiosity gripped the surrounding workers. Suddenly the thing was one big drama. And I was on stage, front and centre.

'What the fuck is this?' Grimes turned his pink face towards me. 'Who the fuck are you? You little cunt.'

Well, that just pissed me off. I knew Grimes could tear me to pieces in a struggle, but so what? To walk away would open the door for this arsehole to humiliate me every time I walked past his booth. I couldn't let that happen.

'A cunt,' I suggested, 'is the female genitalia. But you obviously don't know much about that. Are you sure it was a she last night? Did you look?'

There was a loud cheer and clatter, with the workers laughing and slapping hands and mallets on the side of their machines and benches. Men tend to do that — they love making noise and throwing verdicts down from the grandstand. Anyhow, Grimes's pink face reddened and his eyes filled with fury, and they bore into me with all the dangerous threat of an enraged and wounded bull. But he had no answer.

'Everything all right there, chaps?' A head popped out of the clerk's office window.

'C'mon, son, that's enough of that,' Bob said, leading me away. When we reached the end of the workshop, he turned to me. 'I don't approve of that abrasive language and bravado, young man.'

'I understand, Mister Hanratty,' I replied, surprising him.

Bob Hanratty paused and placed a hand on my arm. 'Those brutes have me tormented, son. But that's all they are — brutes, empty vessels. Grimes and McArdle haven't a brain between them. Give them no heed; it isn't worth it.'

I patted the old man on the shoulder and turned to go.

'And, son,' he added, 'thank you.'

The next day I approached him as he greased the tracks of a machine near the rear wall of the workshop.

'Excuse me, Mister Hanratty?'

'Yes, son,' he answered, turning and wiping his hands with the red rag.

'Why do you do this job here, amongst all this? You seem to be, you know, better than this?'

'Better than this does not exist, young man. I'm here because I'm here, and it's a fool's game for me now to think different.' He let his words stall for a moment and then continued. 'Maybe once, but that was long ago,' he said, as he slowly wiped each finger with the red rag. 'That's just the luck of the draw.'

'But you seem content here. What's the secret?'

'There's no secret, son. Look around. Most here spend all their time ducking and diving, and it only increases their misery. Whatever you do in life, even the simplest task, do it to the best of your ability. In that, there is a kind of happiness.'

I nodded to the old man.

'And, son, no more Mister Hanratty. It's Bob.'

The next day I took to the oil-store bench for my meal breaks, and Bob sacrificed his reading for our daily conversations — the two of us finding a common enjoyment in the transfer of what once was and what could yet be.

Cora returns and enters the kitchen, and is followed by a man I guess must be her father.

'Well, well. What have we here?' he asks. 'Cora Flannery, what have I told you about bringing home stray animals. Where on Earth did you find this thing?'

'Found him at the disco, Daddy. What do you think?'

'I think you must be mad.'

'I am mad.' Cora laughs. 'We're all mad in this house.'

I agree, but I say nothing.

'Gerry Flannery,' her father says to me, introducing himself and taking my hand. 'I hope we don't get the weather you're expecting.' I get this a lot from people — it comes with the coat. Usually I tell them to piss off, but not this time.

'You know something, Johnny,' he says, holding my arm as he points to a wall-mounted photograph of Cora, Aisling, and their mother. 'I have the three most beautiful girls on God's Earth. What do you make of that?'

'I'd say you're a lucky man, Mister Flannery.'

He nods his head solemnly, as if the comment was some sort of revelation to him. 'Some boy, isn't he?' he says to Cora after a time. 'He's some boy.'

Cúchulainn's castle

'OKAY, LET'S GO,' CORA SAYS, CLOSING THE DOOR AND SKIPPING TOWARDS the front gate. 'Come on, Donnelly.'

I run after her. I'm relieved to have the introductions over without mishap. 'Hey, hold them horses, Flannery,' I call, catching up and taking her hand. We stand on the pavement, momentarily lost for direction.

'I know where we'll go,' Cora says.

'Let me guess?'

'What?'

'Well, I think I know where you want to go.'

'You think you know where I want to go. What kind of a weirdo are you at all?' She gives me a questioning look. 'Well, then, lead the way, Johnny-boy,' she relents, teasing me as we take the footpath west to the edge of town.

'Cúchulainn's Castle.'

'Cúchulainn's Castle,' she replies, holding to the vertical struts of the wrought-iron gate and looking through to a shaded lane. 'How did you know?'

'Just a guess.'

'Just a guess, Johnny?'

'Yes, Cora. Just a guess.'

'My boyfriend is a genius. All right to call you my boyfriend, Mister Donnelly?'

I mean, sometimes life is just so good you have to let out a big laugh. I don't.

'All right?' I answer. 'Can I have that in writing?'

We are standing at the gateway to Castletown Mount, a hilltop ruin on the northwest edge of Dundalk. This mound is the location of the legendary fort of Dealga and the birthplace of Cúchulainn. Later the Normans settled here and built a motte-and-bailey stronghold, but local heads still call it Cúchulainn's Castle. Across the entrance, two high metal gates hang between round stone-pillars, and a padlocked chain secures them together. To one side of the gates, a stile is cut into the stone wall, and I hold Cora with both hands as she climbs it.

'That's a very fine arse you have there, Miss Flannery.'

She laughs as she turns, and offers her hand to steady me as I jump down from the wall. I take two thin broken branches from the ditch and I clean them of twig and growth. I give her one of the branches, and with my own I swipe in front of us as we walk, attacking the low weeds and grasses on the dark path.

'It's not the jungle,' she suggests.

I raise the thin branch forward, parallel to the ground, and hold it out chest high.

'En garde. A fair lady approaches.' I call. 'My lady.' I bow and swoop and beckon her forward.

'My knight,' she replies.

'On-ye on-ye,' I tease when I get her in front of me, tapping her very fine arse with the stick.

We climb the mound clockwise on the stone path. Below us, a wide fosse is dark under beech; sycamore, ash, and hawthorn are scattered in the outer ditch.

'You know, Cora, that ruin at the top?'

'Yes?'

'Well, Cúchulainn was a Gael, and Gaels didn't have castles. Castles came with the invaders.'

'I know that, Johnny-smarty-pants. But this hill was Cúchulainn's

[46]

home. This place is older than the English or the Normans, or the Vikings, or any of them. This is ancient Irish ground, a special place, a place before our history, a place before the Celts, a place before the modern Irish. This is a place of the Tuatha Dé Danann. And it's a place of magic.' She stops. 'If you listen very carefully you can hear their song. I believe that here, on this hill, is the gateway to Tír na nÓg.'

I, too, stop and listen, but I can't hear anything. There is only silence. 'You can't know those things,' I say.

'No, but I believe it. Can you imagine what's here, Johnny? Under our feet? This was the home of the king of Dundalk — a great chieftain, a chief among chieftains.'

'He wasn't called Bulla-Wolla, was he?'

'Shut up, Donnelly.'

We reach the top, and walk to the ruin of a square tower. There are remains of walls through the grass. A lone raven watches from high on the tower. As we near the tower, the dark bird shuffles on his stone perch. It lifts its head high to show a ruffled neck. Slowly, spreading its broad wings, it launches into the air. I salute the bird with a raised hand as we walk to the rim of the round plateau. We stand and look east over the town and the wide bay. To the north, the long, stretched arm of the Cooley Mountains cradles the bay until the eastern hills fall to the dark sea at Greenore. From the south, a beam of sunshine finds a gap in the scattered clouds and lights a patch of mountainside. The spotlight moves west to east, highlighting the dark greens of Ravensdale and onto the purples, blues, and browns of the middle mountains. Beyond the near mountains the higher Mourne peaks can be seen peeping through.

'Isn't it great, Johnny?'

'Yes, Cora.'

'This is where he was born, Setanta.'

'So they say.'

'In these fields here, he played. He was a born warrior. And when he was still only a child, he left and ran over those mountains to Emain Macha, all alone, all the way to his uncle, the King of Ulster, running all the way to join the great army of Ulster — the Red Branch Knights. And near there he killed and replaced the great dog, and so Setanta became Cúchulainn, the hound of Chulainn. And he was just a boy.'

'Yes, Cora.'

'And in that gap there,' she says, pointing north, 'he fought alone and defended Ulster against the attacking armies of Queen Medb. One boy against a whole invading army.'

I stand behind her, putting my two arms around her, holding her lightly. She rests on me, letting me support her.

'And over there,' she points to the south-west, 'that's where he held his ground and challenged the invaders, and one by one the greatest warriors of the attacking army took him on, and one by one he killed them. And then Medb sent Fer Diad — his foster-brother — down to fight him. Cúchulainn begged him not to fight, but Fer Diad had too much pride; he refused to retreat. Cúchulainn had to kill him, too.'

'Brother against brother. It's the curse of the Irish,' I interrupt, still holding her.

'And in this place here he loved Emer,' Cora continues. 'They say she was the most beautiful woman in all Ireland. I wonder was it here, on this hill? You know? I've imagined it so.'

I kiss her on the top of her head and she raises a hand to touch my face.

'All around here, he lived and fought. The greatest of them all, the greatest of all Irishmen.'

We look out from the mound, out across the land where young

Cúchulainn played. We see streams, rivers, marshes, fields, farms, hills, mountains, and bay.

'Wasn't it a fine place for a warrior to be born?' she says.

'A fine place indeed, Flannery. A natural academy. And you know something? The first-ever academy was associated with a great hero.'

She looks to me and it's a chance to impress, so I tell her about Plato and Athens and the hero Acadamus. I go on a bit.

'Aren't you a great fella, knowing all that,' she says when I finish, and we both laugh.

'So Johnny-know-it-all and still a little bit weird, what was that academy for?'

'It was to examine the world, Cora. And man's place in it.'

'Our place in the world,' she says into the May air, and she walks away to sit on a low wall on the northern edge of the plateau. A single oak grows from the north crest of the mound, and the green of its leaves frames her from above. Cora's fingers grip the sleeves of her white pullover, and her golden hair falls in waves over one shoulder. Above us, the gathered clouds break and drift apart, and behind Cora the stone tower cuts high into the brightening sky. I look to the girl on the low wall under the single oak. I was so sure of the war. Sure of what I needed to do. Sure of what I couldn't do — let anyone get too close. Now, looking at Cora, I'm not sure of anything.

I walk to her and take her hand, and we cross the rise to the ridge overlooking the town. I take the Dunn & Co and lay it wide on the grass. We sit down, and for a short time we are silent. I look to the sea. Below us the town of Dundalk stretches east to the grey waters of the wide bay.

'I was born down there,' I say, pointing to the dark roofs of a local-authority housing estate at the foot of the mount. 'It was our first house. We moved out when I was nine.'

'Did you like it?'

'No idea.'

'Don't you remember?'

'No. Not really.' I do remember the red bicycle, but I don't want to tell her about that. I don't want to tell her what I did to Jimmy McCusker. 'Except the songs — I remember the songs. Mam was fierce fond of the record player and the radio. She still is. I remember the record player sitting on the sideboard. It was a Reynolds. Mam told me they made it just for her, and I believed her. In a way, when I think of it, I still do. Isn't it odd the way the mind works? And I remember the records: Mario Lanza, The Clancy Brothers, The Dubliners, good old Danny Doyle, and the man himself, Jim Reeves. And then there was Leapy Lee, firing his little arrows out of the radio.' I face her and sing:

> Let us pause in life's pleasures and count its many tears,
> While we all sup sorrow with the poor;
> There's a song that will linger forever in our ears;
> Oh hard times come again no more.

'Do you know that song, Cora?'

'I do not.'

I go again:

> Now when we're out a-sailing and you are far behind;
> Fine letters I will write to you with the secrets of my mind.

'What about that one?'

'No. Are you making these up?'

I keep going, on a roll now:

> The secrets of my mind, my girl, you're the girl that I adore.
> And still I live in hope to see the Holy Ground once more.

[50]

'Have you gone mad, Johnny?'

'Here, you'll know this one. "O'Donnell Abú",' I call, and punch a fist into the air.

'No.'

'How about "Lizzy Lindsay"?'

'No.'

'Unbelievable. "Mary of Dungloe", surely?'

'Never heard of her.'

'How about "The Dutchman"?'

'I don't know any of them, Johnny. Are these songs or relations?'

'Songs. Do you know nothing? What about Liam Clancy? A singer, not a relation.'

'Nope.'

'Holy God, she doesn't know of Liam Clancy. If I could but speak a few words with the voice of Liam Clancy, Cora, I'd die happy. When Liam Clancy speaks, the world seems to find balance. And when he sings, Cora, I'm sure that from a distance you'd see the planet waltz.' I pause and blow a long, slow breath out into the air as if halted by the need to reflect on the weighty significance my own words. Cora gives me a look of disbelief and turns away and laughs. 'What about "The Rising of the Moon"?' I ask.

'Nope.'

'Ahh, you're only kidding. The whole country knows "The Rising of the Moon". Good old Danny Doyle does a great version. A top man.'

'I've never heard of good old Danny Doyle.'

'Mad,' I say, and we sit with two heads shaking in incredulity at each other. 'Will we sing a song together?

'Okay. What will we sing?'

'How about "Dear Dundalk"?'

'Never heard of it. Is it any good?'

'Nah. Load of old shite. You know, Cora, when I lived down there as a child I was afraid of everything.' I don't know why I tell her things like this — they just come out when I'm with her.

'Afraid of what, Johnny?'

'School, the street, strangers, God, the Devil, Jesus, everything.'

'Why?'

'Don't know why. No reason why.'

'Did it stop?'

'Yes.'

'When?'

'No idea. It left in little pieces.'

'Why Jesus?' she asks, surprised.

'It was one of those Sacred Heart pictures with the little red lamp and the big-heart thing. That worked every time.'

'How?'

'It scared the hell out of me.'

She laughs. 'Are you afraid of things now, Johnny?'

'No. I never think about being afraid. It seems ridiculous now.'

'Well, children see the world differently.'

'I think we all see the world differently.'

She takes the two broken branches we used as sticks, and places them side by side in the grass. We lie together on the overcoat. I am lying on my back, legs bent, knees raised. Cora is lying on her front, legs stretched, two red boots in the grass.

'I still can't believe I met you,' I say, looking up to the clouds. 'It's a small world.'

'Well, it's only Dundalk, Johnny. It's not that big.'

Fair enough. I pull a face, still looking to the sky.

'I remember the first time I saw you,' Cora says. She lies across me playing with the neck of my pullover. 'But you didn't notice me then.'

I wonder how it could be possible that I would not notice Cora Flannery, but our whole happening is still a mystery to me, so I let it pass.

'So why a carpenter, Johnny? Do you like it?' Cora asks.

'All my life, Cora, I was told to get a trade. My dad has a thing about trades. He has it up there with the rosary, the confession, and the annual weekend of starvation on Lough Derg. He sees it as a kind of salvation. *Get a trade under your belt, son*, he says. *Then the world is your oyster.* Whatever that means. *And you won't be counting piecework and be one week away from the poorhouse*, my mother chips in. They consider anything else to be "highfalutin talk". Just for a laugh, I suggested quitting the job and moving out to the Aran Islands to grow my own food and study philosophy. *A load of codswallop*, Mam called it. And she is probably right. Dad said it would be a waste of time — that you couldn't grow anything out there, that it was all rock.'

'What is philosophy anyway, Johnny?'

'It's the study of how we know what we know.'

'How we know what we know about what?'

'How we know what we know about who we are, about why we're here, about what *is* here, about what it means to be human. Like those early guns in Plato's Academy. *Philosophical perplexity is the first step to knowledge* ... That's what Plato said. Problem is he forgot to mention that it can also be the first step to a kind of folly, a world of baloney. Philosophers go on and on and on, adding ever-increasing layers of nonsense, thinking they're great thinkers; quoting on and on, in a way that would make a healthy man sick, the works of Descartes or Berkeley or Hume until it all becomes a thick soup of labels, mathematics, models, laws, rules, geometric extensions, astral planes, disembodied souls, and all the usual stuff men can't help adding. That's what academia can do. That's what men do. Like everything else, Cora, they tear the arse out of it. It's a search for enlightenment, but most wouldn't see light if you stuck a rocket up their arse and shot them off up into the Sun. They are blinded by the study of the very thing they are looking for.'

'Maybe you'll figure it out, Johnny. Maybe you'll discover who we are.'

'I have to tell you, Flannery, that's an unlikely occurrence.'

'Did you not want to go to college?'

'Not really. School just wasn't my thing. To be honest, I couldn't wait to get out. It's not universal, that learning-at-school thing — not by their rules, not at their schools, not for me. School, college, career: quick, quick, quick. Everyone seems to be in such a rush. Like a mad rush to nowhere. It seems to me they all end up against a wall and they don't know where they are.'

Cora watches me as I lie back on the Dunn & Co, stretch my legs, and place my hands behind my head.

'All too fast, I'm taking the slow road,' I say, looking up to her and adoring that arc of perfection that runs from jaw to neck to shoulder, before looking again to the sky. *All in its own good time*, my dad says. And you know something, Cora, he's right on that one.' I pause, and then continue. 'People are funny, aren't they? Most settle for mediocrity, and wrap it around them like a comfort blanket. And those who recognise this can be just as bad. Many are away with faeries altogether. And the path between the two is a narrow path.'

'What path, Johnny-boy?'

'The path between mediocrity and delusion. Enlightenment — the holy grail of the philosophers, although it doesn't burn too brightly around here. My old friend Bob called it a rope — a rope to pull you up the impossible mountain. Maybe he's right. Why not? Mind you, he wouldn't tell me where the ropes are, the old fox. He probably had a few stashed away in the back shed.'

'Do you miss him?'

'Yes,' I say. Well, I couldn't tell her everything — like that I still talk to him. She thinks I'm weird as it is.

'So how do you know stuff? You seem to know a lot for a carpenter.'

For a carpenter? I like that. 'I don't know anything, Cora, not really. I have a self-service approach to education — a pick-and-mix free from medals and ribbons.'

'How does that work?'

'Learning isn't exclusive to schools and colleges.'

'No, but they are good places to start.'

I consider her argument. 'A fair point, Flannery. I'll give you that.'

'You could go to college after your apprenticeship. You must go, if you want to or not.'

'That's what my mother says about eating vegetables. Anyhow, that's not my intention.'

'What is your plan, Johnny?'

'I don't have a plan, Cora.'

'You must go.'

'Yeah, well, let's see about that.'

'Will you go?' she presses.

'Do I have a choice?'

'No. You never know, Johnny, perhaps you'll find your own Plato's Academy.'

'This is Plato's Academy.' I wave an arm into the air. 'I'm not sure men cloistered behind walls ever get that.'

'And women?'

'That's different. Women get it. Malcolm X said that he'd put prison second to college as the best place for a man to go if he needs to do some thinking. He couldn't have been more wrong — with just one statement he was wrong twice. All a man needs to do to see the world or to do some thinking is to take a walk around the corner. If you took a slow walk around the town of Dundalk you'd meet all of existence. They think they can teach anything in colleges; they think they can bring a man to college and send him home a poet. How mad is that?'

We rest for a time and watch as slow clouds drift across the sky, and the light travels along the mountains.

'I don't think college is for me,' I continue. 'Many enter as lambs and leave as sheep. I couldn't do that.'

I see that Cora watches me, and I know thinking is going on in that pretty head of hers.

'So what will you do next year, after school?' I ask, rising again and sitting beside Cora on the coat.

'College. Belfast or Dublin. I'm not sure which yet.'

'Does it matter?'

'Not really. I think I'd prefer Dublin. And I could stay with Aisling; she's already in college there. I'd love to live a while with Aisling.'

'What will you study?'

'Irish.'

'Irish? Why Irish?'

'I love it. I want to teach. Don't you like Irish, Johnny?'

'Not really. I don't know. I never really bothered, I suppose. I had that madman Hogan for a teacher, and it all left a bad taste.'

'Well, we'll have to fix that.'

'Okay.'

'Let's start at the beginning.'

'*Bonjour*'.

'Shut up. Let's count.'

'Okay.' I grimace in concentration. '*Eins. Zwei. Drei.*'

'Shut up. Repeat after me, Donnelly.'

'*A haon.*'

'*A haon.*'

'*A dó.*'

'*A dó.*'

'*A trí.*'

'*A trí.*'

'*A ceathair.*'

I reach for her, pulling her to me and taking her down onto the open overcoat. I kiss her mouth, moving my hand to the small of her back, spreading my fingers on the soft wool of her pullover, pressing to her shape. I feel her take my head with both hands, allowing me to hold her tight. I kiss her hard, feeling her slide to me, her body fast to mine.

'Thanks,' I whisper. 'That was much tastier, I must admit.'

'I should hope so.'

'So you should, Cora. That fecker Hogan was a dreadful kisser.'

After a while Cora sits up and begins to recite a poem. In our two weeks together I have noticed that she does this kind of thing. And I like it.

I recognise the verse, and repeat a line when she is finished, '"The silver apples of the moon, the golden apples of the sun." That's a fine poem, Miss Flannery. A fine poem. I never could figure out what it meant, though.'

'Isn't it a beautiful thing, Johnny? And what's beautiful doesn't need figuring out. It just is.'

'You are right there, Flannery. Well said,' I respond. '"A thing of beauty is a joy forever."'

'Is that another Plato quote?'

'Not Plato, no, but another of the great masters: Mary Poppins. Now I have a poem for you. Have you ever heard of the child poet John Francis Donnelly?'

'Nope.'

'Well, hear him now, baby. It's called "The Blackbird". Are you ready?'

'Ready, steady,' she says. 'Off you go.'

Blackbird, Blackbird, cannot you see,
I left the breadcrumbs out for thee.
Blackbird, Blackbird, you are too slow,
Now they got eaten by the crow.

I deliver the lines confidently, and when I finish I turn to her. 'There you are, Flannery,' I say. 'That'll give your fella Yeats a run for his money.'

Cora shakes her head and laughs. 'What is that about?'

'That, Cora, is about the whole damn thing.'

We stretch out on the Dunn & Co together — quiet, comfortable, happy.

'You'll make a fine teacher, Cora Flannery.'

She lies across me, her head on my chest. 'Why?'

'You have kindness, and that's the magic key. In the long hours of teaching, it is an impatience or temper that will linger in the mind of the child. Remember that, Cora.'

'I will, Johnny. I'll do my best.'

'The wonder of the child, that's the golden ticket. And the heavy cross of the teacher.'

'You are a strange boy, Donnelly.'

'Just an observation.'

'Yes,' she agrees. 'It was.' And we both laugh.

We rise and prepare to go. Cora stands and looks out to the mountains. The border with Northern Ireland is just a few miles away, and a British Army observation post can be seen peeping over the ridge on the last western hill.

'Do you think we could build an army,' she asks, 'and run the invaders out of Ireland for once and for all?'

'If we could do one thing for Ireland, Cora, we should do that.'

She takes my arm. 'Come on, Mister Donnelly. Take me home.'

We walk down the mound. We walk through the fosse under the beech trees, and down the shaded path.

'C'mon, Flannery, we'll have a burst of a dance before we go.' I take hold of her two hands and swing her as we spiral down toward the gate, with leaves, pebbles, and two red boots flying through the dappled air.

We climb the stone stile at the round pillar and walk back into town. She slows at the corner of Castletown Cross where the country lane meets the main road. 'Thanks for telling me those things, Johnny.'

'What things?'

'You know, that stuff when you were a child.'

'Well, that was all long ago.'

'Telling truths is a brave thing.' She stops, turns, and looks to me. 'Shall I tell you one?'

'Sure, only if you want to.'

'I have dreamed about you since I first saw you. How mad is that?'

'I'd say that's pretty mad all right.' Like I said, sometimes life is so good you just have to let out a big laugh. And I do.

'You better come in for a cup of tea with Aisling before you go,' she suggests when we near the house. 'What about a bag of chips?'

'Better not. I'm dining with the Philistines.'

'A bag between us?'

'Okey dokey.'

We sit in the kitchen drinking tea, sharing the one bag of chips between the three of us. Aisling wants to know where we went, and she gets it on the first guess. Cora's mam joins us and asks how we got on.

'Johnny said I had a very fine arse.' My face immediately reddens. 'And he kept stroking it with his little stick.'

Hopscotch

WE MEET IN TOWN IN THE MIDDAY. SHE ARRIVES IN A GREY TOP AND a short tartan skirt over black tights, and she's wearing the red boots. She gives me that smile. There is an Irish adage I have learned from Delaney: *an rud is annamh is íontach* — what is seldom is wonderful. But I could look on Cora Flannery every minute of every hour of every day, and in all that time I could not but see and know that she is a wonderful girl.

We go to the Imperial Hotel, where Cora takes a table near the window, and I go to order coffees. An old woman stands before me at the counter. She buys a meal, and then with unsure steps tries to carry it to a table. I offer to help her, and I take her tray to a table next to ours. As she eats she coughs, and I go to the counter for water. When I return, Cora has moved beside her. I place the glass on the table, and she sips as she talks to Cora. I don't interrupt. They have settled into some sort of a comfortable exchange. I am introduced when the dinner is finished, and I return to the counter and order coffee for three. We sit and talk of family, of streets, and of Ireland. When the coffees are finished, she stands, and Cora helps her with her coat.

'Thank you,' she says to us both. 'That was a blessed relief from disappointment.'

'Disappointment?' I ask.

'With people,' she says, 'disappointment is the only consistent.'

We walk home and, passing the school on the Castletown Road,

Cora sees a hopscotch grid chalked onto the schoolyard ground.

'C'mon,' she says.

And we do, and I stand and watch the wonderful girl in the grey top and short tartan skirt above black tights and red boots as she calls and jumps and skips and laughs.

The meaning of life

It is a dry evening in the middle of May. I visit my friend Éamon, and enter by the back door.

'Hello, Missus Gaughran. Liam.'

'Well, Johnny,' Éamon's mother answers from the kitchen.

'How's the boy?' Éamon's father calls from the front room. 'Were you at the match?'

'No. No, I missed it, Liam. What was the score?'

'Two–two, last I heard.'

'Off gallivanting, were you?' Éamon's mother asks.

'Something like that, you know — places to go, people to see. There's just not enough time in this life, Missus Gaughran.'

'God almighty. Are you listening to this, Liam?'

Éamon arrives in the hall and signals with a flick of his head that we go outside.

'Another girl, is it?' Éamon's mother suggests as he passes. 'Here today, gone tomorrow, this Donnelly boy, I'm telling you. A fly-by-night.' She moves a teapot from the cooker to a tray. 'Come in and sit down with your father when you're ready,' she says to Éamon. 'The tea is made.' She carries the tray to the front-room table. 'Duffy's Circus, he is,' she calls to us. 'Duffy's Circus.'

Éamon Gaughran is an only child. His father, Liam, is a tall, quiet man who moves slowly, pulling reluctant feet behind him, as if head and feet are locked in some perpetual dispute. Liam is a retired garda. He was a desk-sergeant in the town's barracks, but he suffers from poor health; he seemed to spend more time out on the sick than he did in at the desk. Liam grew up on a small farm: a cottage and five fields forty miles away in east Cavan. Éamon and I often visited the farm to help out during weekends and school holidays. Well, we called it help. Éamon's grandfather, Ruán, was a kind and gentle man; life itself sat easy around him. Ruán, too, was tall and quiet, but — unlike Liam — he was blessed with natural strength and good health. But maybe that's just a head thing, and maybe that's where it's all gone wrong for Éamon: he takes after his dad. Liam is not Éamon's natural father, as it might be automatically assumed — I mean, not in the biological way — though they don't know that we know, but we do. I worked it out. Ruán Gaughran had something else, too: he had likeability. That's a slippery thing to measure, but once you see it in someone, you know. Many times I heard others speak well of him. And here's another odd thing: kindness is infectious. Whenever people spoke of him, I noticed a gentleness and a generosity about them. And people frequently spoke kindly of Éamon's grandfather.

Ruán had married Claire Clarke, the most beautiful girl in the parish — well, that's what Ruán told us — and I watched as their ageing was neither embraced nor rejected, but carried as easily and as unremarkably as a bucket carries water. Some people can do that, and it is a great thing. Ruán managed a big farm by day, and helped Claire tend their own few acres in whatever light could be squeezed from the evenings. They grew vegetables and they fattened a few pigs in the yard. Claire grew a herb garden next to the house and Ruán planted an orchard in the far field. Geese and chickens ran free around a tall ash tree in the front yard, and a single cow was kept in the near field for milk and butter. They had three children — three sons — and the boys grew tall, and they were well schooled by Claire, and one by one they followed each other into the Garda

Síochána na hÉireann — the Irish police force.

Liam graduated to a quiet rural posting and twenty years of bachelor life until a local priest intervened and arranged a marriage with the solidly built Annie Watson.

I assume Annie was uncomfortable with the notion of sex. I don't know this for sure; but then, somehow, I do. Éamon's mother has an aversion to affection — an embrace can put her off her whole day. Liam was forty-seven, and Annie forty-six, when the priest intervened again and suggested an adoption. This, I only know from observations, mathematics, investigation, and a little help from Delaney. I guess — with their ages — that rules were broken, but that might happen when it suits. Liam's poor health led to the offer of a transfer to desk-sergeant in the bigger town on the coast, and so it was man, woman, and boy that set up home in Dundalk. The matter of the adoption, once done, was never again discussed. The boy is Éamon, and he was never told. It was a matter left for another day, and that day never came.

Liam and Annie are too shy to be sociable. Having arrived as middle-aged strangers in a strange town, they exist on the edge of everything. For a peephole into the life that surrounds them, they cling to a daily ritual of Mass in Saint Joseph's — the Mass being part devotion, part habit, and part social outing.

But Éamon had a lonely childhood. With no brother or sister, and no relatives in town, I guess he was seen by other children as something of an oddity in the way that children mechanically see anything other than what is standard as an oddity, and ridicule it. I guess the faculty to be an occasional arsehole must be built into our DNA. Anyhow, Éamon retreated to places of his own construction, and without reference it passed Liam's and Annie's notice that some of these places were dark. How could they have known? And to Éamon it was normal; every childhood is normal to the child.

All this changed one day. It was a school day, and the morning lessons had just started when a knock at the door brought a new boy — me — to class. I was given the empty space next to Éamon on the double bench. I sat down, turned to Éamon, and smiled, and followed Éamon as we left the classroom for the morning break. Reaching the corridor, we walked side by side and, turning for the yard, I placed a hand on Éamon's shoulder and again smiled to him. 'Hello,' I said. 'I'm Johnny Donnelly.' Éamon smiled and, suddenly, life for us both sat lighter.

Although I was as shy then as Éamon was odd, our inhibitions were abandoned once we were free of the school. There was never enough time to do all we wanted to do. I insisted that we join the football team together. I planned the cycling adventures and fishing trips. I showed Éamon how to build forts and jumps, and how to play tennis and snooker. I brought Éamon to music and reading — passing records, comics, and books to my friend. And what did Éamon do? He stuck by my side, and I don't know how to explain it, but he gave me a kind of strength. And when I was figuring out what I was going to be and what I was going to do, I took a great comfort in Éamon being there. I decided early that I would never involve him; that Ireland's war was my war, and not Éamon's.

For the remainder of our primary schooling, we travelled together on the bus and remained side by side throughout the day. No longer did Éamon worry about the bullying of the schoolyard or the ridicule on the street. Although I was shy, I was never bullied. I'm not sure why, but maybe I carried some shadow of the incident with McCusker and the cliff, and bullies gave me distance. Or it may be like Éamon says: that I seem to be able to defuse a difficulty before the difficulty has time to form in others' minds. I don't know about that.

The primary-school bully was Tom Kinch, a big, unintelligent boy who only saw things in the immediate and the simple. Kinch's principal torture was to grab a boy's head under one of his big arms and knock the top of the trapped boy's head with his knuckles. I had just started at the school, and Kinch failed to notice the alliance of Éamon and the new boy. He failed to value the weight of our friendship; he did not know of the bravery of boys bonded. As we stood together in the morning line, Kinch — coming from behind — grabbed us both and held each of us by the head, crossing his forearms to rap each of us with his knuckles. The rest of the class laughed. The hurt was in the humiliation, and it was then that a silent oath was shared, a vow born of neither but of the union. We held back as the class removed their coats in the small cloakroom and filed into the classroom. Kinch was directing abuse from the rear of the line. Kinch was big, but Ruán had taught Éamon how to handle livestock, and he hit Kinch hard and drove the breath from his body. Kinch was smashed into the corner. He was trapped as I approached, and I saw he carried the same surprised look as McCusker had on the cliff height. And in his surprise I saw again the same confusion and fear. I was learning the power of those three weapons: surprise, confusion, and fear. I was learning that if a boy can bring those three into battle, he can beat anyone. I drove my arm through the face of Kinch. The class was seated and ready when the teacher noticed one missing. He found Kinch in the cloakroom with blood falling from his broken nose and running down over his mouth. I watched that bully glance back as the teacher led him past the open door. Kinch was afraid.

When we graduated to secondary school we formed new friendships with Conor Rafferty and Frank Boyle. And it was together as this group of four that we explored life further: the familiar worlds of school, sport, and adventure, and the fresh worlds of music, philosophy, poetry, and girls. I told them that, as fate would have it, we were meant for one apiece: Frank for the music, Conor for the big questions, Éamon for the poetry, and me for the girls. Those were just the hands we were dealt, I told them, and it was up to each of us to make the best job of it.

Éamon was fifteen when Ruán and Claire died. She died in September as the ash tree faded to a pale yellow, and Ruán followed in October as the leaves fell. It was typical of Ruán that he allowed Claire to pass first and then did not keep her waiting. At the funeral masses, all gave thanks for the long and happy existence they had both enjoyed and for the joy to have had them in our lives. Éamon didn't want to know any of it; he didn't want to give thanks. He had wanted them to live forever.

Éamon always knew that his future was certain and that it was in the police force. As he reached his mid-teens, however, he remained short, and everyone knew that he was never going to grow to the height required. And so the promises and expectations were dropped. Although the blow came slowly, it was crushing, and Éamon, his lifetime in preparation and certainty, was thrown on to unstable ground. Annie, seeing opportunity in a crisis, took the notion that Éamon's future could lie elsewhere in the law. In her dreams, she now saw him not in the dark uniform of a policeman but in the finely cut suit of a solicitor, with cuff-links and a pressed collar. She saw an office and a practice in town, a brass plaque at the door. She saw trips home to advise on serious matters. Perhaps he'd become a barrister? Perhaps a judge? And those dreams became plans. And those plans became expectations.

Éamon was a good student, but he was not brilliant, and he had to work hard on his schoolwork. I never had to do that. But we never cared about who got what in test results; there was never a competition between us. This wasn't so with Annie. She surveyed all of Éamon's results with the meticulous scrutiny of a beggar counting his coins, and after every careful reading she asked him the same question: 'And what did Donnelly get?' Such behaviour is an act of cruelty; parents can be bastards sometimes. But Éamon kept working. And as the exams got tougher, Éamon worked harder. He still does. His release is me. My job is to be dependable, solid, and happy. I tell Éamon not to worry about things that don't matter, and Éamon says that for me that must include nearly everything. I try to persuade Éamon to go easy. 'Does it really matter?' I ask him. If the answer is yes, I assure him that a solution will be found. If the answer is no, I take Éamon by the shoulder and say, 'Well, we won't give a flying flute about that then.' And that is that; we move on to the next thing, the matter resolved. But it never really is resolved, not really, and from me Éamon has never learned that which he wishes for most. And try as I do try to teach, there are things in life that cannot be taught, and for those without the preconstruction, cannot be learned. What Éamon wishes for most is my certainty about my place on the Earth.

We climb the garden wall, and from there we pull ourselves onto the flat felt-rolled roof of a single-storey extension. Éamon takes a pack of Carroll's No. 1 from his shirt pocket and we take one each, smoking in silence, sitting on the warm felt, leaning against the side wall of the house. We don't speak, and allow our silent gaze to follow pedestrians and traffic on the street below. I rest an arm on my friend's shoulder.

'Do you ever wonder what it's all about, Éamon? I mean, gravity, electro-magnetism, strong and weak forces, anti-matter, dark matter, dark energy, and all that mathematic conjecture are very reasonable, but, when you think about it, the whole construction is just things whizzing around other things. You see, these quarks and particles and protons and neutrons and electrons and neutrinos all whiz around each other to make atoms, and atoms get together to make molecules. And from that, well, it all gets big, and we get gas and solids and rock and planets and stars. And they are all surrounded by other whizzing things. And on it goes, with things whizzing around other things to make solar systems, star clusters, galaxies, galaxy clusters, super clusters, filaments, on and on with mad stuff altogether, on and on and on, well past the other side of the impossible. The stuff you see through one of those big telescopes is beauty mixed with a spoon of madness. You'd need a degree in complexity just to put a handle on it. And who's to say there aren't countless universes out there? But, I mean, once you get into the multiplicity of universes and dimensions, and how that all might look, well, it's very difficult to get some sort of a shape on; it's all very difficult to get it into some sort of a bundle so you can carry it in your head. And even if you could gather it all together, even if you could know it and understand it, it still wouldn't explain it all, it still wouldn't explain us.'

'God, would you look at that?' Éamon says, as a girl passes below.

'The belle Lucy Lennon,' I comment, blowing smoke high into the evening air. 'A very fine particle indeed.'

'I wouldn't mind whizzing around that thing.'

'Good man, Gaughran,' I tell him. 'Now you have it.'

'I'm telling you, Johnny, that arse has me tortured. I think about it morning, noon, and night.'

'You could ask her out.'

'What? God-sakes, Johnny. Would you feck off?'

After the smoke, we climb down from the roof. I fix the Dunn & Co, tidy the scarf, and mount the bicycle.

'Right, the snooker hall at half-eight,' I say, and Éamon sees me off with a flick of his head.

As I cycle, I am thinking again of things whizzing around other things, and I think that people, too, behave in that whizzing-around fashion: families, gangs, groups, organisations, societies, religions, nations, federations. It's all the same thing, isn't it? We love a bit of a get-together. We love belonging to an 'us'. It's only the peculiar who step out from the whole thing.

Bob cycles alongside, sitting straight and unhurried in the green overalls, with the red rag hanging loosely by his side. There's a touch of joy about the shape of him on the bicycle. *Isn't this what it's all about?* he says.

Reading for Rosie

I AM IN THE LIBRARY. IT'S NOT A GREAT LIBRARY, IT'S TOO SMALL, AND I cannot wait for the new one to open. But I love it anyway, and I am thinking and wondering why anyone with time on their hands wouldn't spend it in a library. I have never understood how anyone could ever be bored with all the books in the world that need reading.

I have always read. Well, not always — I wasn't born with a book or anything. But I learned young. Some people are born with a talent for things: some can pick out a tune and know it from hearing it once or twice; some have a voice for song; some can draw or paint or sculpt; some can write; and others can kick a football or swing a club or a bat with ease, grace, and accuracy. Me, I can read. It's nothing to shout about, really. It's not a spectator sport — it would be hard to sell tickets. And there are few prizes. But people do notice, and they use words like 'avid', 'keen', 'learned', and 'precocious'. Being well read is universally approved as a good thing. I don't remember how I got started; I guess I came to it myself. But I did have help and support, I do remember that, and that encouragement came from Granny Reynolds and Aunt Rosie.

Aunt Rosie, who's dead now, was my mam's sister, and she lived in Liverpool. She used to visit us for two weeks every summer, and every time she visited she brought a big bag of English sweets. English sweets are much the same as Irish sweets, and a child of any nation would find it difficult to see or taste a difference; but every year in advance of her arrival, Anna and I would think about those confections in blissful anticipation. For weeks we'd talk about what might be in Rosie's bag, what our favourites were, and what swaps we were prepared to offer and what we were not. And when the day came and Aunt Rosie arrived, and the contents of that glorious bag were allocated among us, we savoured those English sweets as though they were rarities from some far-flung jungle, or delicacies from another world.

As well as sweets, Aunt Rosie brought laughter. For the two weeks she was home, the house was full of joy. Some people are like that: they find life funny, and life — appreciating the applause — seems to reward them with a gentle passage. 'My Johnny', she called me. I think she took a shine to me early on; she was always poking and tugging me. Or maybe it was because Granny was fond of me, and she was so fond of Granny, and the affection was just relayed across. I don't know why these things happen — why some people take a shine to some people and not to others, and some get left out altogether. I wouldn't have noticed it then. Stuff like that only registers later on.

Granny Reynolds often took care of me when I was small. We went through all the old stories together long before I went to school, and Aunt Rosie took great store in this. On every visit I had to read for her, and every time it was the same tales she wanted to hear: 'Tír na nÓg', 'Cúchulainn and the Táin', 'The Children of Lir', and 'Fionn Mac Cumhaill'. I found 'The Children of Lir' sad, but Aunt Rosie loved it. She had one boy of her own, Donal, and two girls, and she was married to an Englishman — though she often said that she'd appreciate it if we kept that quiet, before she'd throw her head back and let out a big laugh. Donal is three years older than I am, and he got the *Beano* and the *Tiger and Scorcher* comics every week in Liverpool. The following week, when new issues were bought, Aunt Rosie would bundle those two comics and post them to me. From my sixth birthday, the bundle came every week; I thought it was sad that

[73]

Donal never got to keep his comics, but I didn't protest.

One day, when I was eleven, Aunt Rosie went into hospital and died, and the *Beano* and *Tiger and Scorcher* stopped coming. I thought it was an odd thing that she timed it like that — dying when I was just about to grow out of those comics. I never did get to thank her or Granny for giving me the gift of the habit of reading. With small kindnesses, people can make big differences for others without ever knowing it.

Anyway, I am dreaming of Aunt Rosie and English sweets and the *Beano* and *Tiger and Scorcher* when there is a touch to both arms. I step back from the shelves ready to apologise. It's a bad habit, the pulling of books and reading a little whilst taking a few steps and then squeezing the books back into wrong places. But it isn't library security; they haven't got any, of course, but you can get insecure when surprised. Who it is, is Cora and Aisling.

'Hi, handsome,' Aisling says. 'The how-to-handle-a-woman section is over there.'

'Thanks,' I say. 'But first I just need to catch up on the hydrodynamics of spherical imploding shock waves and a few other matters.' Sometimes that reading by browsing can be fierce useful.

'Right,' she says.

I turn to Cora, and she smiles that smile of hers — that smile that lifts the mood and air and light and weight of a whole day.

I smile, too, and reach for her and touch her. 'All these books,' I say, 'and the two most beautiful women in the world. All we're short of is a bag of toffee, and it's pure heaven.'

'A bag of toffee?' Aisling says.

'A bag of toffee,' I repeat, and I reach out to Aisling, too, and so make us into some class of a daisy chain. 'Did I tell you yet about Aunt Rosie?'

I get two shaking heads.

'Well then,' I say, 'how about we get some books and I take you both to the Imperial for coffee? And then I'll tell you about Aunt Rosie.'

Chips and eggs, and milk

IT IS A BRIGHT MAY EVENING, AND CORA AND I ARE TO MEET AT DUNNES Stores at seven. It is one month since we first met, and tonight we will go out early to celebrate. I watch for her as I pace around the wide pavement. She arrives smiling.

'The Imperial for coffee, the Cooking Pot for drink, or the Roma for chips?' I offer.

Cora chooses chips.

In the Roma, a middle-aged Italian woman is busy directing operations. She is short, and her dark head barely shows above a long serving-counter.

'Does your mammy know you're in there?' I say to her as we pass. She ignores me as she takes an order slip from the serving girl and shouts an instruction into the kitchen.

Cora and I take an empty booth at the far end of the restaurant. As we settle on the bench seats, the waitress arrives with the order pad held and the pencil already moving.

'What are we having?' she asks, and Cora orders for us both — chips and fried eggs, and two large glasses of milk.

'We should go down to Dublin for the day, sometime,' Cora says. 'We can meet up with Aisling.'

'Yes,' I answer. 'We'll go down on the train.'

Cora then goes into a long detail of what we will do in Dublin. Trinity College is first on her list, and then the National Gallery and some museums. I vote for cafés and bookshops, but she ignores me and continues her list-making. I don't mind; it's easy to listen to her speak.

The Dundalk accent is an odd thing on the ear. And like many Irish accents, it does have a peculiar attraction, though it would be hard to argue that there's any kind of beauty about it. It has a flat delivery; it's as if the language itself has been taken to a smith's forge and had any unevenness beaten from it, as though elevation or depth were impurities. But though the accent is flat, you can't really call it smooth. Each word is delivered separately — there's none of the stringing together of the north or the south of the island — so that, though they are spoken separately, the words have a levelled sameness about them.

The flat language of the town is an added pounding on the flat language of the county. But there is another voice here, too: the swinging northern accent of Armagh and Down. The county frontier is just a few miles from Dundalk, but the accent borders are much closer. The northern streets of the town are populated with northern voices, and conversations in town can carry one or both accents.

And there is another odd thing: not everyone in town has either accent. Some, by good fortune or accident, have avoided this fate. Most of these are women or girls; few men manage the escape. And like things disabused of some habit or torment, in the light of release they flower tall and bright. Those free from the local inheritance speak with some kind of purity, and every now and again I hear the notes of a harp plucked by the hand of child. This is the voice of Cora Flannery.

'To us,' I say, raising a toast with my high tumbler of milk.

'To us,' Cora toasts. 'Forever.'

I think it's mad the way Cora has slipped so quickly into 'us' as if we were some kind of preconstruction, prepared and awaiting assembly. I am convinced that Cora has already decided a future for us, that she fully expected our happening, and now that it has happened she has absorbed it as naturally as Ireland absorbs rain. I look to her pale face, and I know that in her beautiful head there are no doubts. But I know what I am. I know that what she sees is not true.

'What are you thinking about, Johnny-boy?' she asks, a chip held on her fork.

I look again on that face. 'I am thinking of you, Cora.'

El Cant dels Ocells

It is a wet day in June, and Cora and I sit in the Flannery kitchen and drink tea. Gerry Flannery enters and stands and looks at us in the way he does — half questioning and half laughing.

'So, has she told you yet how we all first heard of Johnny Donnelly?' he asks.

'Heard of me?'

'Yes,' Cora says. 'I heard of you, then I went to look. It was a story Daddy told us about a friend of his who is a musician, and this friend has a friend in the national orchestra in Dublin — a friend who plays the cello. That was a wonderful thing you did.'

'My friend still talks about it, Johnny,' Gerry says.

So now I know. 'Yeah, well ...' I say, remembering Bob's last day at the factory.

I'd been at the engineering works for two years when the day came for Bob Hanratty to retire. Bob never enjoyed factory life, and took comfort in the refuge of the oil store and the radio he kept there on a high shelf. One day, as I entered the oil store, Bob signalled for me to be quiet. I watched as he stood still, his head cocked to the radio on the high shelf. A piece of music played through the single round speaker, and when it ended Bob waved me in. 'Eh, what was that, old-timer?' I asked. 'That, my friend, was Pau Casals: "El Cant dels Ocells".' The old man looked at me. '"The Song of the Birds." Such a beautiful thing. And who is Pau Casals?' Bob tested me.

'Spanish,' I guessed.

'Catalan,' Bob corrected me. 'And a Catalan is Catalan first, and he is Catalan second.' I sat down at the workbench and asked no more about it, but I took note.

On his last day at work, Bob carried out his duties as normal. At the end of the day, he cleaned his workbench, tidied his trolley and oil-cans, removed and folded his green overalls, and took the radio down from the high shelf. He took a screwdriver and removed the brass plaque from the door. He put the overalls, the radio, and the plaque into a knapsack, and locked the oil store for the last time. He crossed the yard and entered the machine workshop to punch out. All the workers had already left, and the large workshop was silent but for the echo of his own footsteps.

He paused to look around. He had worked there for forty-nine years. I could see he was disappointed no one had waited. He was disappointed I had not waited. But, of course, I had — he just couldn't see me. Bob reached the time-clock, took his card from a rack, and punched out. The heavy clunk of the machine reverberated around the silence. Bob looked up to follow the sound, and only then did he notice the chair and the cello in the middle of the central intersection. Another set of footsteps echoed loudly in the workshop, and a man with long, wavy hair approached from the main external doors. The visitor wore a black formal suit and carried a dark-wooded bow in his right hand. He walked to Bob, and stopped and bowed before taking hold of the cello and sitting in the chair. He acknowledged Bob once more with a single nod. He rested the cello against his left shoulder and then, looking only at the floor some distance in front of him, he began to play. The bow, held in his right hand with four fingers showing, crossed the cello with slow, graceful movements. The fingers of his left hand punched and then nursed the four strings. Music floated through the building; vibrations carried around the machines and workstations, bouncing off the whitewashed walls and the high roof. Bob stood with his raised punch-card in shocked silence. He looked to nowhere as the workshop filled to 'El Cant dels Ocells'.

'He'd spent most of his life in that place,' I say to Cora and Gerry, 'so I called in a favour. He deserved one happy memory.'

'Well, you certainly achieved that,' Cora says. She leans into me, and I put my arm around her and hold her. '"El Cant dels Ocells"' she calls the title out into the room. 'We will have it played at our wedding, won't we, Johnny?'

Wedding? This girl is more crazy than me. I look to Gerry Flannery, but he just stands there, watching me with that look of his, as if Cora's mention of our wedding was normal and only to be expected. I look back to Cora.

'Yes, Cora,' I tell her. 'We sure will.'

A box of tricks

I WALK THROUGH EMPTY STREETS. THE TOWN IS DESERTED, AT REST, IN those few peaceful hours between late night and early morning. It is midsummer, and the advancing light of day begins to diffuse a night that never fully blackened. I take my time; I love the fade of the blue-black to a new day. I consider the girl. From the age of twelve I have decided my own fate. There was no question of what — just a finding of how. And I found it. Discipline, I learned from Delaney; conviction came with me. Each step along the way has been careful, meticulous, determined. This long war has fallen time and again on the rocks of indiscipline, recklessness, and treachery. On these, I will not be caught. And then, into all this, she comes.

The birds are busy at this hour: pigeons, crows, and gulls scavenge for scraps on the roads and pavements, and their hungry cries cut through the quiet. The air is mild. The sky above is showing grey, but it is high enough to offer hope.

I arrive at the engineering works, where all is quiet. The security guard in the small redbrick building by the entrance barely looks up from his novel as I pass through the pedestrian gate. I give a salute which the guard returns with a wave. At least once every month I make an exceptionally early arrival at the works, and at least once every month I stay exceptionally late. Familiarity as a disguise, the Chief has taught me, is as deadly as the greatest camouflage, and as I walk through the entrance and away from the guard I am already thinking of the gun.

I began with a .303. It was an old gun — an old Lee Enfield. It needed a lot of oiling and looking after, but it shot straight. Delaney kept me on that gun for three years. Then, one at a time, he brought me through the Armalite, the Kalashnikov, and the Heckler & Koch. I spent a year on each, and I have taken them all into action. I keep a Glock 17 as well, but it is a different gun for a different kind of action. It was only a year ago when, at last, I got what I was waiting for.

I move on between the tall buildings of the works, and I enter the machine workshop through double doors. The building is wide and long, and its high walls support a multi-pitched roof. Around me are relics of a former purpose: overhead are pulleys and apparatus for belt-driven machinery, and rail-tracks are buried in the floor. I cross the workshop, passing the time-clock near the clerk's office. I am careful not to punch in or out other than standard hours. I walk to the south-east corner, where a large, separate unit is contained behind high, block walls that offer no windows to the rest of the machine shop. This former store for components is now the carpentry workshop — 'Carpentry Corner', the men of the factory call it. I take a set of keys from the pocket of the Dunn & Co, and I open the lock of the steel door. I enter the workshop, trigger the switch for the low lights over the workbenches, and relock the door behind me. I settle at my workstation.

Only two workers are employed in the carpentry workshop — Jack Quigley and me. Jack is in his fifties, and has worked here for thirty years. He is a gentle soul. Jack isn't a carpenter at all; he trained as a fitter, and worked across the yard in the assembly plant. But fifteen years ago the carpenter died and the position needed filling. Jack enjoyed woodwork as a hobby, and built bird tables and dog kennels in his back shed at home. This was common knowledge — Jack supplied dog kennels to half of Dundalk. So when the vacancy arose, Jack was moved. Jack refers to it as the day of his great promotion, though technically that isn't so. Carpentry is incidental to the product of the engineering works — the demand for woodwork is restricted to odd jobs, and the making of frames and packing cases for shipping. Much of our labour in the workshop involves doing odd-jobs and making nixers for management and fellow workers. Mostly, we remain unbothered. It is perfect.

With just the two of us employed in the large workshop, each has an expansive space. I built my own in the first six months of my first year, and I took the whole south wall. I built a new dry-wall against the whitewashed brick, and on this I created shelves, racks, and tool-boards. Against this wall I built a large, square table, and two heavy benches. It took me six months. In the second six months I built my tool-chest. In fact, I built two, making one as a gift for Jack. The tool-chests are impressive pieces of work — over one metre in length, and half-a-metre high and wide. I modified an American design I'd found in a textbook, making the chests in oak and using complex and precise joints to ensure strength and durability. The chests have a deep space under a top-hinged lid, with various-sized drawers accessible behind a front panel. All the hinges, handles, and fittings are brass, and I fitted each chest with a secure lock. I lined all the internal spaces and drawers with a rich royal-blue felt cloth, and I finished the chests with a hand-rubbed Danish oil. So the chests could be pulled along like a trolley, I fitted each with a double-axle carriage and oversized wheels, and I attached a long foldaway handle at one end.

The tool-chests are a familiar sight around the plant as Jack and I pull them about on our various jobs. The men appreciate the craftsmanship — Jack says the chests are a work of art — and many ask me to help them build their own. I don't mind, and I am happy to help. In a way, it all adds to the deceit. All the tradesmen buy and maintain their own tools, so the bringing and the taking of tools to and from the premises is a common thing.

Once every two weeks I take the tool-chest home, taking a lift in Big Robbie's van. I make a point of stopping near the security office to open the chest and show off a new tool or some recent piece of work. Here, too, the tool-chest is a familiar sight: 'There he goes with his box of tricks', the men say as I pass. And they are right: built into the dry-wall of my station is a secret space, and in that space is a third chest.

I take a large, folded felt cloth down from a high shelf. Slowly, I spread it out smoothly on the table I've built for this purpose. I take the third chest from the wall. I gather the lubricants, polish, and cloths required from the shelving. I have hidden them here in full view amid the fundamental supplements of an engineering workshop. Maintenance and care, the American taught me, are as essential as both bullet and gun. Before I open the chest, I walk to the steel door and check that it is locked.

Is this what you choose for your life? To be a killer?

I turn. Bob sits on the end of my bench, a red rag hanging loosely from a pocket in his green overalls.

Johnny?

I ignore him. I return to the table, open the top lid, and set to work.

Soldiers' Point

In the early morning of a July day, I walk east along the embankment on the southern shore of the estuary. Che runs on ahead, stopping at intervals to check on me before running on again. The tide is ebbing, and the river is low as it empties into the wide bay. Below me the broad grey mudflats stretch and glimmer north to Bellurgan, Jenkinstown, Rockmarshall, and on east along the mountain peninsula. Herons hunt in the low tide and pools. The rivulets are populated with prowling oystercatchers, plovers, egrets, and grebes, and islands of green marsh are highlighted yellow before the rising sun.

I stop at the end of the embankment, at Soldiers' Point. I pull at the collar of the Dunn & Co and then push my hands into the deep side pockets. Inland, there is a terraced crescent of coastguard houses. There is no movement around the houses, and there is no one along the river — it is too early for early-morning walkers. I am alone.

Bob sits on a boulder that once belonged to a small jetty. *Hello, soldier*, he greets me.

I remember a day we sat at his oil-store workbench. It was summer, the door was open to allow a warm breeze in, and the bright light of the yard was framed in the doorway of the dark store.

Bob gestured to the doorway. 'Out there, life — it's just one impossible mountain.'

'A mountain, Bob?'

'Yes, son, a mountain. We all get born at the foot of the mountain, uncontaminated and ignorant. Our goal, young man, is to try and climb the mountain.'

'Why? What's on the top of the mountain?'

'Who knows? The meaning of life? Answers? Happiness? Maybe … maybe nothing,' he laughed. 'Who knows? Nobody knows anybody who has made it to the top and come back down. Anyway, it's the climb that counts.'

'Do many make it, Bob?'

'No, not many. It's a vicious mountain. Deadly. A person has to climb over all of existence just to keep moving up. The worst of humanity must be crossed: debauchery, savagery, greed. The relentless struggle slows you down, drags you back, stops you, swallows you up. Most settle for survival, and make camp wherever they can. The climb to the top gets lost.'

'Doesn't sound good.' I commented. 'Is there any hope at all?'

'Some have no chance. Some find a rope to help pull them up.'

'Hope on a rope, Bob. That's great.'

The old man took a drink from the teacup he held in one hand, and with his other hand he waved a slow finger to me.

'So where do we find these ropes?' I asked.

'Every man must find his own rope. They are found all around us, in the simple truths of life. But they are found, too, in our hopes and fears, and those need great care.'

'Why?'

'Without great care, a rope becomes a whip. The flesh of humanity is gouged deeply with the scars of those whips. Take care, my young friend, with what rope you take hold of in this life.'

I had no idea what the old man was talking about. 'So what's the secret, Bob? How do we get to the top of this impossible mountain?'

'You and your secrets, Johnny.' The old man looked to me. 'There are no secrets.'

'At a mad guess, then?' I pushed.

'Well, at a mad guess, I'd say it's a pure heart.'

After our lunch, I walked out into the sunlight of the afternoon. Across the yard the large steel doors of the workshop were open, and from the shadow Grimes and McArdle along with O'Connell and Cooney — two other buffoons — stepped boldly into the light, their work coats and shirts removed and tied around their waists. The four amigos approached the empty yard in broad steps, like out-of-town gunslingers looking for trouble. I laughed as I watched them.

'I know a problem we meet on that mountain climb of yours, Bob,' I said, popping back into the oil store.

'Yes, son, what is it?'

I pointed to the workshop. 'It's an avalanche of arseholes.'

On Bob's next birthday, I surprised him, replacing the 'Oil Store' sign with an engraved brass plaque I had made in the workshop. It read:

THE PHRONTISTERY
ROBERT J HANRATTY
PURVEYOR OF LUBRICANTS AND OTHER MATTERS

The old man polished it every day. He polished it every day until the day he retired. And Bob Hanratty was retired for only one week when he dropped down dead.

I stand looking out into the estuary. 'This is where they left from,' I tell him, 'the starving Irish. They went from here to Liverpool and then on to God-knows-where. That's what they did to us, the English: starved us or ran us out of our own land. They brought hell itself onto Ireland. And they had no right to be here in the first place.'

That's a long time ago now.

'Not really, Bob. And they are still here, still a pain in the arse. The partition they insist on is an open wound on this island. As long as it's there, it will fester and infect.'

But you'll make them pay, Johnny-boy. You'll see justice done. And who'll be next? The Vikings landed along this shore, and ransacked and plundered all before them. And the Normans sailed this very water, and what did they bring? Will you be off to Copenhagen and Oslo and Pembroke and London and Cherbourg next with that revengeful gun of yours? Don't you see, son? Once you start, where do you stop?

'It's not about revenge. Anyhow, they are gone; the English are still here.'

But that's just it, Johnny-boy, they are not gone. They, too, are still here. They are part of you; they were part of me. And the English? To many, England has been a refuge. To many, England has been a bright light on a dark shore. And to many, they are welcome here.

'They are not welcome,' I tell him, and the conversation ends as if it has dropped and fallen down the embankment and into the mud.

I find a stick on the shore and throw it far for Che to chase. I look out into the bay, where a boat sits at anchor and waits for the next tide.

You won't change anything, Bob says. *And you cannot win.*

'Maybe. But we didn't start this. A people who allow themselves to be occupied are taken as suckers. They will exist only in the shallows.'

Occupation is a slanted view.

'Slanted? We do not have an army over there, but they have one here. And by that, they force the Irish to be fighters or cowards. There is no other way; there is no middle way. Only the gutless apology of a politician.'

That doesn't mean anything. Do you think that you, Johnny Donnelly, can make a difference?

'So should I do nothing? Like a coward? If we do nothing, they win and we lose. If we don't fight, no other outcome is possible. But if we fight, we may win and they may lose; and the worst that can happen is that we both lose. It's the Irish dilemma. But fighting will produce the most favourable result: once we fight, they cannot win.'

That's the spirit, Johnny. There's nothing like a bit of warped positivity.

I look out to the mud, the water, and the mountains. 'By coming here, they started this whole thing. By bringing the gun into Ireland, they forced us, too, into lifting the gun. And by staying here, they take us all to hell.'

I summon Che and turn for home.

And what about herself? he calls after me. *Would you drag that beautiful girl into your war? Who gives you that right?*

Che runs on ahead as the sun climbs behind me, and I am walking into my own shadow. 'It's not my war,' I bark back to Bob. 'It is Ireland's war.'

I quicken my pace as if to get away from the annoyance of his questions, but it cannot be done. I try to push the difficulty of Cora away with every step, but, like my shadow below me, it remains connected and constant, and it too cannot be done.

Lifting mist in grey country

' "An accident happened", was all she said that evening. "An accident happened." And the next morning she didn't speak at all.' Gerry Flannery shakes his head as he drives the load of cattle-feed south and west on the N52. Ardee and Kells have slipped behind into the mist we lift from the wet road, and we are approaching Mullingar before he gets to the story he has brought me along to hear. The rain falls, and the wipers work to clear a view into the grey country. Gerry grips and turns and releases and grips the steering wheel again, pumping the pedals, pulling and pushing the gears, driving the truck forward, to brake and pull and grip again at the next bend.

I don't say anything. Whatever he needs to tell me, he'll tell me. I give him the space.

'She didn't speak for three months — we were worried, Johnny, really worried — and when she did speak again, it was all, well, you know, that poetry stuff and those old stories. I was right worried. I thought that the poor wee thing might, you know, be away with the faeries. I had an old aunt who suffered from the nerves, and I was afraid Cora could go that way. But then after her own short while she was back as she always was, that darling and innocent wee cailín. But she was different, too; I just can't explain it. It was Aisling who said to leave her and give her time, and Aisling then, too, was only a slip of a thing.'

'And Aisling?'

'Aisling was stronger … is stronger. Maybe stronger is the wrong word — I don't know how else to call it — she accepted it quicker and dealt with it, added it all up and settled on some answer she could handle. I suppose Cora did that, too, in her own peculiar way. But it was a different answer; she is a different girl. Aisling was that bit older, and maybe that helped — I don't know.'

He pushes through the gears, and brakes, and grips the steering wheel, pulling the truck left around a long, sweeping bend.

'Aisling was eleven when it happened; Cora was only nine. Nine is a young age for a bad thing to happen. God help us, but I still remember her wee white face, all her colour drained and gone, the sheer uncomprehending shock of it all in her eyes.'

I know the story. Every town has its tragedies, and everyone in a town knows the stories. But I ask anyhow. I ask because he wants me to ask. He wants the green light.

'So what happened?'

'It was a fine summer's day. I had to make a run to the west and Fionnuala had to visit her mother in hospital. There was no school, and it was too good a day for the girls to be in a lorry cab or in a hospital ward. The family next door used to look after them if ever we were stuck, and we did the same for them. Shane was the boy's name. He was fourteen. He was a lovely boy, Johnny, a shock of blond hair that had turned fair as he entered his teens, tall, and a good boy to his mammy and daddy. He was as nice and helpful and pleasant when he was fourteen as he was when he was five — he never changed in the way that boys do. Sue and Tom McEntee lived next door, and Shane was their only child. They were grand people altogether; it was a blessing to have people like that as neighbours.

'I was away early, and as I wouldn't be back before evening, Fionnuala left them all next door in the midday. Cormac was only a wee gassun, and Sue kept him with her in their back garden. Tom was at work. After lunch, Shane took the girls for a walk. In the summer, if it was a good day, they would go for a play in the fields or a run around Cúchulainn's Castle. That day, they walked to the bridge at Toberona, and to that blasted river.'

Gerry crashes through the gears and brakes only briefly before throwing the truck fast through a right-hander.

'The tide was on the full turn, and the river was high. They walked from the bridge along the bank — you know the way our two girls love all that green grass and wildflower stuff. They came across a small boat on the bank. It belonged to Cathal McGuiggan from Brid A Crinn. Do you know the McGuiggans, Johnny? Another grand family.'

I shake my head in the negative as Gerry continues without waiting for my answer.

'Cathal had been fishing that morning and intended to return later, and so left the boat on the bank. He didn't mean no harm, though afterwards he held himself to blame and never fished again.' Gerry chokes a little and gulps for air and stops talking as we approach Mullingar. He slows the truck into traffic.

'I suppose he was showing off a bit; it was nobody's fault. It was just a blasted accident. None of them could swim. Of Dundalk's four boundaries, north and south are rivers, and east is the sea. Surrounded by water, and yet few of us can swim — did you ever think of that, Johnny? How blasted stupid is that?'

I have thought of it, but again I shake my head in the negative, and again he continues without awaiting or checking my reply. We are now in the centre of Mullingar and turning west amongst town-centre traffic. The grey town merges with the dirt of the grey weather.

'Isn't this the most depressing place?' Gerry asks, looking about us.

I agree. Hell is to be condemned eternally to Mullingar.

[*93*]

Gerry pushes through the gears and presses the pedals as the truck rolls, and we break from the town and traffic on the western road.

'Free at last,' Gerry says, as he forces the truck forward. 'And a straight road. We have her by the hasp of the arse now.'

He goes quiet again until the town is lost in our rear mist. Then he resumes the story as if he hadn't paused at all.

'Shane pushed the boat into the water and got in. Only for Aisling's common sense, we might have lost them all, but she wouldn't get in and wouldn't allow Cora in, either. The current was in full flow, and the boat was quickly pulled to the middle of the river. Shane lifted one of Cathal's oars and stood up. He held the oar in one hand and saluted the girls. He was trying to look, you know, cool. Cora shouted at him to sit down; somehow she sensed the danger. But it was too late, and he fell as the boat rocked in the current. He was just doing what boys do — he was just showing off. The girls were too small and too young to help, and they cried in panic as the current pulled him away and under. They watched it all from the bank. They saw the terror in his desperate drowning. Half a mile they ran on the bank, until a fallen alder at a bend allowed the girls to grab him. Somehow, God love them, they managed to pull him out. And then the second terror of not knowing what to do. Aisling said that they tried to "wake him up"' Dear God. And then Aisling ran for help and Cora stayed with him. But the boy was dead. Sue and Tom moved away soon after.'

It is late when we get back to Dundalk. The wet day has dried to a mild evening, and I sit with Cora on the low wall that separates the front and rear lawns.

'Did he tell you about the accident?' she asks.

'Yes, Cora,' I tell her, and hold her close as we watch the traffic pass on the road.

The wedding

IT IS AUGUST. IT IS A BIG DAY FOR THE DONNELLYS. TODAY DECLAN marries Shauna Clifford. Following a midday Mass in the bright, oval Church of the Redeemer in Ard Easmuinn, we retreat to a hotel where the edge of the town meets the mountains. Shauna has gone mad altogether, and a lavish reception is provided for many guests — I don't know half the people here. The whole show is a bit stiff, but then people get like that about weddings: pedantic, formal, ridiculous. Shauna has manipulated us all into wedding suits, and the wedding troupe is large — there is a full orchestra of groomsmen and pageboys, she herself is gloriously resplendent in a white monstrosity, and a long line of bridesmaids and flower girls trail her every movement. It's all a big show. The whole thing would make you sick.

It is now four months since I met Cora Flannery. Four glorious months, where time together is never enough, and time apart is too long. It is an uncommon affair, I guess: the severity of our friendship. Every evening during the break of her summer holidays she waits for me at the factory gate. It is an uncommon occurrence: the waiting at the factory gate. The men of the factory pass as she waits; a few greetings have become many, with the men making an effort to soften and to greet the girl with the golden hair.

At the wedding, I introduce Cora to everyone I know and some that I don't. She gets many compliments, and as the day lengthens so, too, do the comments — well, that's what drink does. Near the end of the night, I surprise all and appear on the stage. Conor Rafferty stands beside me, carrying a guitar. We place two small wooden stools in the centre of the stage, sit, and pull the microphones low.

'For Kathleen Reynolds,' I say as Conor plucks the first chords and nods.

We sing 'Lizzy Lindsay', and long before we get to the last verse, the whole room is with us. Oliver Donnelly sways to the tune as if swaying for Ireland, with both arms raised, and I see Mam fight tears that escape and fall down her powdered cheeks. Frank Boyle and Éamon Gaughran join us, and we deliver our rendition of 'Sister Josephine'. We provoke laughter and abuse. We step from the stage as Cora steps on. She sings '*Táimse i m' chodhladh is ná dúisigh mé.*' — 'I am sleeping do not awaken me.' There is silence for the slow air. The song ends, and the room erupts with cheering and clapping. With the crowd still on their feet, we rush back onto the stage, and together we launch into 'The Rising of the Moon'. There is cheering, clapping, and the slapping of tables as song and dance engulfs the room. 'Have youse no homes to go to?' I call at the end of the set, throwing Liam Clancy's parting concert words across the room, and the party cheers.

'I thought I was Liam Clancy up there,' I say to Cora when it is over. 'It was powerful stuff.'

A mad and wonderful thing

THE DAYS HAVE SHORTENED, AND IN THE EVENING BEFORE THE LIGHT fails we walk to the river. We stand on the bridge at Toberona and look down on water that flows east. We watch brown trout, motionless, facing the current in the shade of the bridge. We don't say much, and I don't mention the accident. Some hurts don't need to be tackled. Some hurts cannot be healed. Coming here, we have acknowledged that there is a hurt, and we let it be.

'Setanta would have swam and washed here,' Cora says. 'He must have learned to swim here. Isn't that an extraordinary thing?'

'A mad thing altogether,' I agree. 'And the water that Setanta swam in would have flowed out to the bay and then have been pushed north into the Atlantic and have been lifted into the air as vapour and got blown across Norway or Sweden, where it fell as rain or snow and then gathered in another river, where it flowed cold to the ocean and fell low, where the great current took it and it was carried to the Americas, where the sun warmed the water and it rose again and was carried west, where it was lifted as vapour and fell again on Ireland, where it gathered in a river.'

'How long does that take, Johnny? Could this be the same water that Setanta swam and washed in, or the water into which Shane fell? Or both? Isn't that mad?'

'A mad and wonderful thing, Cora.'

'Just like me, you mean?'

'Yes, Cora, just like you.'

Slime

IT IS SEPTEMBER, AND IT IS ÉAMON'S BIRTHDAY. CORA HAS INSISTED THAT the three of us meet up early and that we go together to the Roma for chips. In the afternoon, I spend a few hours playing snooker with Éamon, and as we finish he produces a pack of Carroll's No. 1 and we take one each and smoke and chat with some other players.

'Hey, attention,' Éamon prods me with his elbow. 'Two class-one arseholes approaching.'

I look to the door to see Slime Sloane and Pitiful Bobby Boyd. I feel the air cool and tighten. The two arrivals see us, and stall. I am standing between the door and the booth. They need to pass me. I see Sloane's doubt. He knows we have noticed their entry, so a retreat will be a humiliation. But to proceed he must pass within an arm's length — my arm's length — and Sloane wants to avoid that. There is silence behind me in the room, and all games have paused.

'Are you two lovely boys taking me out today or what?' Cora asks, arriving in the middle of things.

'We sure are, darling,' Éamon answers, enjoying the whole show. 'That is if Johnny doesn't want to hang about and beat up these two.' So Cora wants to know the whole story, and Éamon is happy to settle into the tale as we make our way out.

'Slime Sloane,' Éamon begins, pontificating in the way he does, 'is an enigma wrapped up in an arsehole.'

I leave them, briefly, to run back into the snooker hall to get my scarf, which I had left behind. I take a long look at Sloane as I lift the scarf from the wall peg. I know he knows I am there, but he keeps his attention to the booth and doesn't turn to me.

Sloane had been in my class in secondary school, and I disliked him from the off. He was a scammer and a dealer, supplying the schoolyard with cigarettes, hash, cannabis, porn, and whatever newest fad could be bought, smuggled, and sold. Sloane was the sort who would pimp his sister; a small-time wannabe who pushed his luck to the edge. Yet he survived. He won more than he lost.

It was our first year in the secondary school when I interrupted him in the changing-room, going through pockets and bags, helping himself to whatever could be taken, while the rest of the class was on the sports field. Flippantly, he dismissed me with a threat. I approached him without comment, and threw a loose and useless punch. Sloane caught my left fist in both his hands and laughed. He didn't see the right coming. I hit him low and hard, and I felt a burst of foul breath pass as Sloane fell. He stayed on the cold floor a long time before he was able to crawl out. I would have hurt him further but for Éamon's intervention, and Sloane knows that. If I can, I keep my violence removed from Éamon's view. Sloane and I have kept a distance since. I nicknamed him Slime, and the name stuck.

Sloane's sidekick is Bobby Boyd. Boyd is a year older than Sloane, but was a year behind at school. He is tall — he is a clear head above Sloane — but is too thin, and his arms hang loose and uneasy, as though unable to find purpose. Boyd has orange hair, and orange hair is a particular thing: it looks great on a girl, but it never suits a boy. Boyd is not blessed with good looks, either — he is heavily freckled, with a prominent brow and a thick mouth. I have thought that Boyd carries an early-evolutionary look about him. It's unfair, I know, but true. The whole town knows that Bobby Boyd had a rough upbringing, that he was raised in a violent home. We all have heard the stories of beatings and abuse. Boyd follows Sloane around like a roped mule, and Sloane continues on where Boyd's father has not left off. It is a case of from the hot plate into the fire, and I have no doubt that, for Bobby Boyd, it will be from the fire straight into hell. Boyd is a born victim; he appeals to everyone's sense of cruelty. I nicknamed him Pitiful, and regret it, because the name has stuck. Boyd doesn't have much to hold onto in life. But I know he is sure of two things. One: he is sticking with Sloane, come shine or flood. Two: he is staying out of the way of Johnny Donnelly.

In the Roma, we agree on chips and fried eggs each, and three large glasses of milk. Éamon is still going, still telling Cora the full history of my encounters with Sloane, and she is loving it.

'Happy birthday, you mad fool,' I toast Éamon when the milk arrives.

'Don't be jealous, Sunshine,' he counters, and then continues on to the next story.

The rise of Ochaine

IT IS THE LAST WEEKEND OF OCTOBER, AND I SIT AND DAYDREAM AS Declan drives the red Fiat eastwards on the Carlingford Road. Dundalk falls behind to the west, the Cooley Mountains rise to the north, and, to the south, soft marsh and muddy inlets open to the bay. At Ballymascanlon, a narrow stone bridge crosses the Flurry River where the mountain river levels off to lower ground. With sharp bends, the road encounters the bridge like it might a discarded lover: a treacherous greeting at one end and a dangerous parting at the other. Passing a row of yellow terraced cottages facing the roadside and then crossing the bridge, Declan pulls the car off the main route and onto a minor country road. He drives north up through a narrow, wooded glen. To one side of the climb, the mountain river runs down the hillside while the road, bordered on both sides by a ridge of fallen leaves, turns and twists as it cuts against the fall. The rusted, molten colours of autumn line the way. We drive through greens, reds, auburns, and yellows. All the colours have a used look about them. Halfway up the mountain, the road ends where the climb crests to a broad crease. Another road offering passage east and west runs across the junction. Declan stops the car, and with a tumble of his head tosses a wordless question into the back seat.

'Ravensdale,' I say. 'Fire a right here, Declan, and plough on ahead for a couple of miles. All right there, Miss Flannery?' I ask, taking Cora's hand.

'It's nice here, isn't it?' Cora answers, finding the lock of my fingers. 'Be nice to live here.'

'Need a small fortune to buy here,' Declan cuts in from the front, steering the car east through the junction. 'Shauna has it all checked out. She prefers Blackrock, though. She has us on a five-year plan. She says in five years — seven, max — we'll be moving on out to the "Rock".'

'You're not in Bay Estate a wet week,' I say, and laugh.

'Just a stepping stone, she calls it. Shauna's got big plans, Johnny. Big plans.'

'I've never liked Blackrock,' Cora says. 'There is always a cold breeze blowing.'

'Yes, you're right there, Flannery,' I say, looking out across the stone-walled fields and farmsteads. 'Just our luck in Dundalk to have the only unappealing strip of seaside in western Europe — excluding England, of course. Blackrock deflates the soul. It's depressing. A move out there would sit somewhere between a mistake and a bad idea.'

'Shauna's not alone,' Declan defends from the front seat. 'Half of Dundalk would move there, if they could only afford to. It's a nice place and very popular. You just don't see it.'

I keep my gaze on the green hills. 'That's very true, brother — there's many who view Blackrock as a desirable address. God help them, but in that act alone they contribute to a portrait on the fickleness of human nature. People need protecting from their own wants.' I turn again into the car and throw a suggestion forward. 'So it's going to be a long way from the ghetto of Cox's for Miss Clifford?'

'Ard Easmuinn, Johnny, if you don't mind,' Declan laughs. 'Ard Easmuinn.'

'Yeah, well, whatever. I'll say one thing for her. At least she has you moving in the right direction in Bay Estate.'

He doesn't reply as I look at the road ahead of us.

'Just over this little bridge, Declan, and pull in there on your left by The Lumpers.' We stand in the midday air and watch as Declan turns the Fiat in the gravel yard of the small country pub. On the other side of the road there is a wooded rise.

'Trumpet Hill,' I say, looking across. 'That's the famous rise of Ocháine in the tale of the Táin. From that hill, Cúchulainn bombarded Medb's armies with his slingshot.'

The car stops.

'Are you sure you're all right for a lift home?' Declan asks from the open driver's window. 'I don't mind a spin out to Carlingford for you.'

'Thanks, but my daddy's picking us up,' Cora answers.

'Okay,' Declan shouts, driving off. 'I'll be in the snooker hall if you need me.'

We wave him off as the car returns to the road and re-crosses the humpback bridge, with Declan's arm raised in farewell through the open window.

'I'd say we've time for a cup of tea, Cora dearest.'

She takes my arm as we walk towards the door of the pub. 'Haven't we all the time in world, Johnny.'

'Are you coming or going?' the heavy-set barman asks as he places the pot of tea on the table before us.

'Sorry?' I ask, arranging the order on the table.

'On the walk. Are you coming or going?'

'Going. We're walking over to Carlingford.'

The barman nods and returns to his post behind the bar.

'Fair dues to you, son,' the only other customer in the pub calls across to us. 'There's very few who ever know if they are coming or going.'

I look to an elderly man sat at the bar; he is stooped over the horse-racing pages of an opened newspaper. He has paused his reading, anticipating a response, but we remain unprovoked and ignore him. When we finish, Cora carries the pot and cups to the bar.

'A fine day you picked, too,' the horse-racing reader tries again. 'God is good. There are days up there when the east wind can cut you in half.'

'Good luck, now,' I say into the pub, tidying my scarf in the Dunn & Co, and opening the door for Cora. 'If we are not back by Christmas, call for help.'

High hopes

WE TAKE THE RUTTED ROAD THAT RUNS ALONGSIDE THE GRAVEL YARD, and walk up into the mountains. A few houses are strewn along the road, and a few more are scattered on the lower hills. There is no one about, all is quiet, and the mountains above are empty. It is a fine day. The weather in the previous weeks has been everything — one hour couldn't be trusted to predict the next. That's the way it is in Ireland: the seasons only loosely perform to pattern and definition. It seems the island exists in some kind of fixed meteorological arrangement with the North Atlantic, a kind of permanent grey winter. But sometimes there are breaks in that grey arrangement; and when they come, the land lifts with deep, rich colours, and the wait is rewarded. Today it seems that the mountains and sky have conspired, have gathered and saved a few hours of sunshine, and spill it now on the hillside as an offering, a welcome, just for us.

It was Cora's idea to take the walk. It is the twenty-eighth day of the month, a Sunday, and it's six months today since the first night I walked her home. Cora insists that we need to celebrate, and so she has us out here on the mountain. We leave the road where it meets a river at a cluster of homes near Ballymakellett, and where a path veers off into the conifers of Round Mountain Forest. We climb a wooden gate to enter the forest, and as we go over I point north to the next rise.

'Doolargy Mountain,' I say. 'And behind Doolargy is the secret high valley of Dubchoire — The Black Cauldron. And it was there,

Cora, that the Brown Bull of Cooley was hidden as the desperate Queen Medb rampaged around the country in search of it. And as she searched for the bull, one by one the boy on the hill slaughtered her soldiers with his slingshot.'

'Isn't it totally mad, Johnny, that we are on the same path that Cúchulainn and Queen Medb's armies used?'

'Yes, Cora, total and all-out madness,' I answer, putting my arm about her and kissing her head.

We climb the forest trail beneath the conifers for two miles, and on the hilltop we exit into heathland. Behind us is the rise of Castle Mountain, and before us is the heather-covered hillside of Moneycrockroe. A half-mile below, a small road runs north to south through a broad upper-mountain valley. A narrow scrape of a path leads down through the heather. Almost immediately, as we step into the scrape, a hare breaks from its hidden form, rushes across us, and disappears down the hillside. Cora follows the hare and walks before me. I watch her move through the scrape: the stepping of her red boots, the hop of her arse in the blue jeans, the dance of her golden hair above the heather. Below us is a valley of patchwork greens, and beyond the valley the bare, livid rock of Ireland rises.

At the bottom, we cross a wire-mesh fence on a wooden-stepped stile, and we continue south on the road. The tarmac of the road is comforting and solid beneath our feet after the unpredictability of the forest floor and the uncertainty of the heather slope. Quickly, we come to a junction above the boggy glen at Spellickanee. Dundalk is signposted south-east through the valley of Aghameen; our path is way-marked south-west to north-east. For two miles we walk on the mountain road. To the south and east, the mountain rock of Slievenaglogh rises and shields us from Dundalk Bay. To the north and west, the high gabbro peaks of The Foxes Rock, The Ravens Rock, The Eagles Rock, and Slieve Foye cut us off from the deep water of

Carlingford Lough. Below us and between the mountain ridges is the broad, green valley of Glenmore. Wide-open grasslands fill the valley with scattered pockets of bracken, and stone walls meander to no definite pattern. A small river runs north-west to south-east along the valley floor, and a farmhouse beside a copse of woodland stands alone on the lower ground. A Táin Way trail-marker pointing at Slieve Foye pushes us off the road and onto a narrow lane.

We rest where the lane crosses the river, and sit facing the autumn sun with our backs against the metal side-rails on the flat bridge. As we rest, Cora asks that I tell her again the story of Cúchulainn and the Táin. And I do. I know it well; I must have read that story a hundred times.

'Hey, sleepy head,' I rouse her, gently, as she rests on me and the tale is finished. 'We have a mountain still to climb.'

For one mile, we cross the green valley. We cross a second valley road and continue west by climbing broad, high grasslands. Mountain sheep ignore us as we climb high along the Golyin Pass and under the rough rock of Slieve Foye. The mountain of Barnavave stands to our south. Climbing north, we mount the crest of the pass, and the deep, dark waters of Carlingford Lough now lie below us. Across the lough, the higher Mourne Mountains rise from below the water to punch tall into the clear sky. Beneath us, in the shade of the mountain, the village of Carlingford grips the rock. At the edge of the village, two elbowed grey arms embrace a piece of lough water, and spots of blue and red can be seen within the arms. From hilltop to village, a grassy trail zigzags down the mountain through scattered gorse. A grey gunboat sits in the dark water of the fjord, at midpoint from the northern and southern shores.

'The empire patrols the stolen lands,' I say, with a gesture in the direction of the gunboat. 'It claims and claims again the lands of Ireland, as if time and repetition justify the theft. But it knows nothing and it never learns.' I don't know why I do this, but sometimes I can go on a bit with that kind of talk.

'What would Cúchulainn do if he were alive today, Johnny?'

I look to her, and words and intent fly around inside me. I want to tell her. But I cannot.

'What could he do but fight?' I answer her. 'Though the people of Ireland would lock him up or have him shot. And once he was dead, we would think him a great lad. It is the Irish way. Those who challenge the ordinary and familiar are viewed as a greater threat than any oppressor. Right and wrong are unfixed: they are conditional on time and place.' I sweep one foot across the short grass of the path, as if I might etch the argument into the mountain. I take a few steps forward and gesture across the water towards Northern Ireland.

'Over there is hell on Earth.'

She looks to me; surprise is held in her green eyes, but she doesn't interrupt.

'Over there are two tribes, two peoples. One tribe are the children of neglect. They are locked in the attic and left to a neighbour's care. It is an act of abandonment. But for the other tribe it is even worse. The other people are the orphans of history. They are nobody's children.'

'That's a very sad account of things, Johnny-boy.'

'It's a very sad place,' I continue, 'so the current status must be broken, whatever the cost. What exists there is not real. One way or another, the foreign rulers must leave. And from the ruins Ireland can be rebuilt. Once freed from the unnatural, balance will be found. It's the way of the world.'

'But, Johnny, the British have rights, too, don't they?'

'Yes, sure. A right to be British? Yes. A right to live in Ireland? Yes. A right to live in Britain? Yes. But a right to live in Ireland and claim it to be Britain? No. That is no answer. They might as well claim the Earth to be flat. The children of tomorrow can never wear it. It cannot be worn. But we never learn. The history of Ireland is like our music — it circles and repeats.'

'I don't understand that. What do you mean?'

'Ireland is perpetually plagued by division. Plagued by sons and daughters who would suffer rather than raise a hand or thought to revolution. There are yet those who still question the fight that won our independence, and measure all actions against an ideal state that never existed. There are yet those who would return us to another's empire. Those, Cora, are the people of eternal compromise. Those are the people whose words have never carried anything but the death rattle of Ireland. But that is the Irish way; we are cursed to have two views on everything. This is our history, this is who we are, and this is our destiny.'

'But ...' she pauses, and I watch her as she searches through what I have just said.

'We are a divided people, Cora. There can never be an agreed Irish view on what is right and what is wrong.'

'But Ireland is a great country,' she says, as she looks out across the mountain. 'Beauty, Johnny, and magic, too.'

'Maybe. But not free, Cora. Not yet.'

She watches me. 'Sometimes when you speak of Ireland, there is something about you I don't recognise.'

'Good or bad?'

'I don't know, Johnny.'

I offer her nothing but a wordless shrug.

'You wouldn't get involved, Johnny, would you?' she asks. 'What about those terrible bombs? You wouldn't do a bad thing, would you?'

'No, Cora,' I answer. 'I wouldn't do a bad thing.'

'Those bombs.' She reaches to me and rests her hand on my arm. 'Those bombs kill people, ordinary people — men like Daddy and Éamon, girls like Aisling and me, children like Cormac and

Clara. They kill them as they wait on a parade or do their shopping. Children, mothers, fathers. You wouldn't allow that, Johnny. Would you?'

'No, Cora. I wouldn't allow that.'

'I know the cause is right,' she says. 'But then, at the same time, it's not right.'

'That's the thing about war, Cora. It's never right until it knocks on your door.'

'What does that mean, Johnny?'

'Well, it's never right until they arrive at your door and take your father away in an armoured car. It's never right until your brother or sister or husband or wife goes out in the morning and doesn't come back. War is never right, until it calls to your door. And then what do you do?'

I look to her as she lifts her head, and she looks out into the air as she forces the argument through her own sensibility. 'Anyhow,' I say to her. 'I thought you wanted us to build an army and throw the invaders out?'

'That was just talk, Johnny. I want to go to college. I want to teach Irish. I want to get married, to have children. I want to picnic on Cúchulainn's Castle and talk about Tír na nÓg. I don't want war. I don't want those bombs.'

'Yes, you are right, Cora. A bomb in a marketplace serves no cause but spite. But those soldiers must leave — this still remains a war. And it has called to our door, whether we want it or not.'

'Oh, Johnny, aren't there already too many dead?'

'The first one was too many,' I say. I walk away downhill as if I might get away from my own words, and, spreading my arms wide, the Dunn & Co catching the breeze lifting off the lough, I call out, *'They think that they have pacified Ireland. They think that they have purchased half of us and intimidated the other half. They think that they have foreseen everything, think they have provided against everything. But the fools, the fools, the fools! — they have left us our Fenian dead, and while Ireland holds these graves, Ireland unfree shall never be at peace.'*

She follows and takes my arm. 'Couldn't there be talking, to find peace?'

'Politics? A world of fantasy and fraud. It's the gathering-ground of the conceited.'

'Isn't politics how things get done, Johnny?'

'No, Cora. Politics is mostly nonsense. If you had a recording of everything any politician ever said in the history of the whole world, and you deleted all but one-thousandth of the whole, what you would be left with wouldn't make any less sense. Politics is a great lie, an endless cycle of hope and disappointment. Politics is compromise.'

'Sounds like life to me, Johnny-boy. Isn't compromise good enough?'

'No, it's not good enough. Nothing great was ever achieved by compromise.'

'What about friendship? Isn't friendship compromise?'

'No. Friendship is not compromise.'

'So what is it then, Donnelly?'

'What's what?'

'Friendship.'

'Friendship is understanding.'

'What about love? Isn't love compromise?'

'No, Cora. Love with compromise isn't love.'

'Then what is it?'

'With compromise, it's just an arrangement — a set of needs and wants.'

She is uncertain. She looks to me. Her face is full of questions.

'Love is commitment,' I say, trying to tease the thing out through my own thoughts. 'That's why a man can only love one woman.

That's why a woman can only love one man. No matter what. Everything else is just passion, or intimacy, or lust, or fun, or need, or want, or whatever. But commitment is to one and to one only — otherwise it's not commitment; otherwise it's not love.'

'Yes, I agree.' She stalls, and moves the discussion as if still trying to get a fix on the direction our words have taken us. 'What about de Valera? Michael Collins? They went to politics.'

'Two great men. But de Valera lost the plot in the end. And Collins, maybe he was the best of them all, but …well, he did leave them abandoned up there.'

'What else could he do?'

'Politics, Cora. He compromised.'

'Do you sometimes think of Éamon?' she asks.

'de Valera or Gaughran?' I ask. I know she wants to break from the uncomfortable ground we have stumbled onto.

'Gaughran.'

'Sure I think of Éamon.'

'I just sometimes think he's a bit of a lost soul.'

'He is that,' I say, happy to ride along with the change of direction. 'But he's not so bad with it; it kind of suits him. We can all lose our way sometimes.'

'*Níl saoi gan locht*,' she says. 'There's no wise man without fault. Not even you, Donnelly.' And she laughs as she lifts her head and tosses her golden hair into the air.

'I love you,' I tell her as I watch her.

'Is that a fact now? Are you sure?'

'Yes. Very sure. Only you, Flannery.'

She looks to me. Her face is now serious. 'Do you really love me, Johnny?'

I am surprised by the suddenness and the strange place from where the question comes. 'Of course I love you, Cora,' I answer, holding her and noticing a fracture in her confidence — knowing I have said too much, knowing I have frightened her.

'You wouldn't leave me, Johnny, would you?'

'No force could take me from you.'

'We will get married, won't we?'

'Yes, Cora, we sure will. On Cúchulainn's Castle.'

'Yes, on Cúchulainn's Castle, and we'll make our babies there.'

'We'll make our babies there, Cora Flannery, and we will be together forever.'

On the grassy trail high above the lough, we hold each other hard in the jubilation of our promise: togetherness forged in the power of our embrace, and relief, commitment, and happiness released into the sweet fragrance of the mountain gorse.

We walk on with lighter feet, and halfway down the mountain we stop and sit, both of us determined to slow the day and prolong the mood. I take the Dunn & Co and spread it on the grass. I push Cora down on her back as soon as she sits, and move across her, kissing her cheek, her nose, her forehead, her eyebrows, her chin, her throat. 'You are beautiful, Cora Flannery,' I whisper to her.

'Am I still a mad and wonderful thing?' she teases.

'Still unbelievably wonderful,' I tell her. 'And, yes, totally mad.'

'I love you,' she says, opening her body beneath me. 'How many children will we have?'

'Eh, maybe four?' I say, thinking this not a time for talking but for other things.

'Four? Are you mad?' It was a foolish hope. She insists on ploughing this new turf.

'Why? How many then?' I have to play along.

'Eight.'

'Eight? Are you mad?' I give up.

'Eight. Four boys and four girls. A boy and a girl for each of the provinces of Ireland.'

'You really are some lunatic, Cora Flannery.' I push her down again and draw myself across her. 'Now, if I can keep you quiet for just a moment?' I pull her jacket from her and lift the woollen pullover up and over her head, pulling it high to release her slender arms. She settles again beneath me, her face content and easy, her bright green eyes beckoning, encouraging, her golden hair scattered on the ground, her fragile neck exposed, that arc of perfection which runs from jaw to neck to shoulder, her white body beneath me against the green of the mountain, her innocent bra, white with a tiny pink rose in the middle of the two gentle drumlins, her blue jeans buttoned to her slender hips, the lip of the blue jeans loose against the taut white body, a row of silver buttons, inviting, and two red boots stretched out on the mountain. I kiss her jaw, her neck, her throat. I kiss her shoulder and down across her small breasts. I kiss the little pink rose, and down from the pink rose I kiss her, undoing slowly, one by one, the silver buttons of her blue jeans. Lower I move, and kiss her as her body arches towards me and her breathing changes. I open the fold of the fork of the blue jeans and kiss her abdomen, and move lower, a thin ridge atop soft white material, a little pink rose in the middle. I push the jeans across her hips as I kiss the pink rose.

There is movement in the nearby gorse. Something is there. We rise in a bolt, Cora quickly reaching back into the woollen pullover. I spring to the rear of the bush, and a dark shadow bursts free, a low shape running away, moving quickly across the mountain and diving into some heavy scrub. But before it disappears it turns, and I see the eyes and the grinning face.

'Jesus, what was that?'

'A fox.'

'A black fox, Johnny?'

'A black fox.'

'I've never heard of a black fox,' Cora says, recovered now from the fright. 'I'm not sure that black foxes exist, Donnelly.'

'Well, they do now, lover girl,' I joke. But I am uneasy. Something about this is very wrong. And that grinning face?

We dress and continue the walk down the mountain. Cora is oblivious to my anxiety.

'Isn't love the most wonderful thing?' she says.

'Yes, and all love is friendship,' I say. 'The ancient Irish believed friendship to be an act of recognition, an eternal belonging. So when people meet and a sudden great union is formed, the old Irish believed that this is not the creation of something new, but a subconscious recognition of something old — a finding of something pre-existing. And they were right. They called that kind of friendship an *Anam Cara*.'

'That's us exactly, isn't it, Johnny? We are each other's *Anam Cara*.'

'Yes, Cora. That's us exactly.'

'We won't hide things from each other, will we, Johnny? We will always be honest.'

'Yes, we will be honest,' I say. But as the words leave me, a heavy air enters, and I am slowed as I carry that new weight down the mountain.

It is evening, and the light is fading when we reach Carlingford. We watch as a funeral procession gathers in the village churchyard. A long black hearse and an attendant black limousine are parked before the church. Six men remove the casket from the hearse and carry it shoulder-high up the stone steps and into the dark church. Two men in dark suits walk before them. The gathering files in behind.

'An old person. A full life.'

'How can you tell?' she asks.

'Grey and frail heads stepped from the limousine. A young mother with a baby, too. Middle-aged men carried the coffin. Young adults and teenagers followed the hearse. All sad, but none broken. Four generations, and all with the shape of acceptance.'

'The last night above the ground,' Cora says. 'When you die, where do you want to be buried?'

'I don't want to be buried. I want to be cremated, and my ashes scattered on these mountains. Not on this side, though — on the other side, overlooking Dundalk Bay. It's funny, isn't it, Cora, but this side of the mountain doesn't feel like home. What about you? No, let me guess — Cúchulainn's Castle, I bet. Isn't there any part of your life you don't want to do there?'

'Nothing significant, no.'

The village is quiet, and we walk in the centre of the small road.

'Well, Cora, may we die in Ireland,' I say, taking her hand and raising the joined arms high, punching the air.

'May we die in Ireland,' we shout together, laughing.

We find a pub at the corner of the main street and enter. A grocery counter and bar are maintained in the first room. Three men stand talking, and an elderly barman with shirtsleeves rolled high on his forearms is listening from behind the counter. A push-through door and narrow corridor leads to a lounge at the rear. The place is half full: couples and mixed groups are around tables, and two men are sitting at the bar. A turf fire is burning below a wooden mantelpiece on the far wall, and a plastic bucket with coal, wooden sticks, and pieces of brown turf sits nearby. A middle-aged man, sitting on a high stool in the far corner, is playing a guitar and singing into a microphone on a stand. I recognise the tune from among Mam's favourites.

We take two low stools around an empty table against the side wall, and the barman brings the drinks I ordered at the bar. 'A gentleman,' he says as I pay. The singer begins another tune that I recognise. 'Mam would love this fella,' I comment. We have two more drinks before Cora gets up and joins the guitar player. She sings two songs. There is applause and cheering at the end of each song. 'Show-off,' I tell her, as she rejoins me. But before we go I also get up and join the guitar player for a song. Well, I couldn't let her have all the glory. 'Have you ever heard of Liam Clancy out here in Carlingford?' I ask. 'Well, if you have or have not,' I add, 'here we go. This is for Cora Flannery …'

> Red is the rose that in yonder garden grows.
> Fair is the lily of the valley.
> Clear is the water that flows from the Boyne.
> But my love is fairer than any.

I speak the words with the confident and persuasive voice that comes with having a few drinks in the belly, and then I sing, and with a wave of my arms I pull the whole room into the singing. Cora laughs.

We sit by the harbour on a low wall and wait for Cora's dad to collect us. Before us, a haloed moon rises above the dark, funnelled lough.

Lifting her gaze from the water to the night air, Cora launches a recital:

> And missing thee, I walk unseen,
> On the dry smooth-shaven green,
> To behold the wandering Moon
> Riding near her highest noon,
> Like one that had been led astray
> Through the heav'n's wide pathless way:
> And oft as if her head she bowed,
> Stooping through a fleecy cloud.

I let the fleecy cloud drift a while before I comment. 'The pensive man. Our old friend gets a mention in that.'

'We could have stayed longer, in the pub, if you'd wanted,' Cora says, re-engaging with planet Earth and turning to me.

'Enough is as good as a feast,' I answer.

'Is that a Johnny Donnelly?'

'No. One of the true masters.'

'Plato or Poppins?'

'Have a guess?'

Her face tightens as she looks out on the water. 'Poppins,' she says, and the face releases to a smile.

'Good woman, Flannery,' I tell her, pulling her into me. 'Now you have it.'

Cora looks to me.

'I think it's time, Johnny-boy.'

'Time for what, gorgeous?' I was flying a bit with the drinks and the singing, and my head wasn't in the mood for thinking things out much.

'You know — what the black fox interrupted.'

'Yes,' I say, 'the little fecker. Are you sure, Cora? You know we've all the time in the world for that.'

'Yes,' Cora answers, resting her head against my shoulder. 'I'm ready. And don't ask me where. You know.'

I laugh, but ask again, 'Only if you're sure?'

'Call for me Wednesday evening, on Samhain evening, and we'll go … we'll go for a walk. I wrote a poem for you, Johnny; I'll give it to you then.'

I kiss her, touching the side of her face with my hand. 'I love you,' I say, 'my *Anam Cara*.'

The end of the harvest

IT IS THE THIRTY-FIRST OF OCTOBER AND IT IS THE FESTIVAL OF SAMHAIN, the night that marks the end of the harvest, the night that marks the beginning of the dark months, the night when — so they say — the veil across the otherworld is thinned. Darkness has already fallen, and I cycle under streetlight. A full moon appears and disappears beyond moving cloud, but I barely notice it. I barely notice anything. My mind is on Cora, and I have thought of Cora all day.

'You couldn't bate snow off a rope today,' Jack Quigley said, and laughed. 'Whatever's wrong with you?' Twice that day I'd left tools behind. 'Only for they're in a bag, you'd lose them,' Jack said, and laughed again.

My thoughts jump from our walk on the mountain — and all that was said there — to the anticipation of the evening ahead and all that awaits us on the hill. I cycle the Ramparts Road, Distillery Lane, Jocelyn Street, Roden Place, along the pavement at the Town Hall and alongside the courthouse, through the Market Square, Clanbrassil Street, Church Street, and Bridge Street, and I am still lost to my dreams as I pedal west on the Castletown Road. I don't notice the commotion on the road ahead until I near Níth River Terrace.

Two blue lights circle halfway down the terrace, the beam of the lights running along the row of grey pebble-dashed houses. I stop and get off the bicycle. Passing traffic has slowed to a crawl and is being managed around a blockage outside the chip shop. A garda stands in the middle of the road and waves each car through in turn. Drivers and passengers strain to get a look at the disturbance. Thirty yards before the chip shop, a police car is pulled over on the wrong side of the road, facing away from me. Its doors on the pavement side are open, and a second garda stands by the rear door. He is writing in a notebook that he carries in one hand. In front of that policeman, a woman sits in the open rear door of the car, a blanket pulled across her shoulders. The garda says something, and with his pen points to the front, but the woman does not turn, and looks only to the ground. I look to where the pen points. A driverless car stands in the road before the chip shop. There is a smash in the centre of the windscreen, as if a ball had been pushed into the glass. A number of potato chips have fallen on the glass, and have slid and gathered on the rubber blade of a wiper. Some yards in front of the car, torn paper lies on the road, and chips are scattered on the ground. I look to the second blue light. An ambulance is parked on the near pavement beyond the chip shop. Passing houses five, six, and seven, I notice people standing at their doors. At number nine, a woman sees me approach, and I see her raise her hand to her mouth as she turns away.

I drop the bicycle and run to the gate of number sixteen. I glance to a house with the door open. I run to the back of the ambulance, where a crowd is grouped on the pavement. Distress pours from the gathering. I step into the crowd and move towards the vehicle: voices, light, fear, and dreadful certainty meet me as I push through. I step up to the open door. Confusion is packed into the space, and for a moment I remain unseen. Before me, in the ambulance, is a steel trolley, a gurney. And on that gurney a white sheet is pulled long. And below that sheet, what? A body? The white sheet covers the head, but I know that shape. I look beyond the gurney and see Gerry Flannery, who now notices me and moves towards me with his mouth open and calling. But I don't hear him. I no longer hear anything. For on that gurney there is a body — the white sheet pulled high, the face hidden, and at the end of the sheet, two legs showing, two feet, and on those feet, are Dr Martens boots. They are red, and they are tied in extravagant bows with green laces.

Station Road

MORNING LIGHT CREEPS AROUND THE CLOSED CURTAINS OF THE EAST window. It is Saturday, and I have no plans for the day. I look over her sleeping body to the small clock perched on top of a stack of books on the far bedside locker. It is early, and I decide to read. She doesn't move; the duvet that covers her is pulled tight, the edge tucked beneath her. From below the duvet, the curves of her small frame show. She has a good body. She is a good-looking girl. Her pretty head is buried deep into the pillow, with her fair hair — strawberry blonde, she calls it — scattered about her. She faces away from me, her pretty face pointing towards the clock above the stack of books. I sit up and adjust my pillows behind me, and I play with her hair as she sleeps.

This was her room when I came here. It is a big room: two large windows (one east, one south), a heavy oak wardrobe, a fireplace, a mirror over a grey-marble mantelpiece, a double bed at one end of the room, a chair and a long table that I use as a desk at the other. She who sleeps moved to another room when I joined the household. She moved so that I would have the table. That's just typical of her, my little Bella — there's a big heart in that small, curvy body. It was she who'd answered when I first called. ROOM FOR RENT: MIGHT SUIT A PROFESSIONAL, the classified read. 'Will a poor student do?' I'd asked as she made tea. 'A poor student will do lovely', she'd answered. The house was a lucky find; perfect, really. It sits at the station end of Station Road, the other end of which joins the main street of the small town of Ennis. The house is big: there are four of us here, and we all have a large room.

It was the beginning of 1991 when I left Dundalk. I just couldn't stay there. It was January and black and cold, and Cora was gone. Now I study in college in Limerick — I am studying to be a teacher — and to help pay the bills, I work some weekends at home in the engineering works, and weekday evenings I teach carpentry here in County Clare. It was Delaney who came good with the job here. He pulled a few strings — fair dues to him. To live in County Clare and study the nineteen miles away in Limerick, I needed a car, so the folks have gone halfers in a Renault 4. I'd always wanted one. I like the shape, that innocent functionality. It's so uncool, it's cool. 'It's a GTL,' I said to Dad, and he laughed — he wanted me to buy a Volkswagen or an Opel, and I nearly did, but that Big Robbie rummaged this beauty for me in the North. 'And what colour is it?' Mam asked. 'It's a seductive cream,' I told her, 'the colour of milk coffee that's been dipped into by one digestive too many,' and she too laughed.

They have been down for a visit, and I took them for a drive around the Burren and West Clare. Mam loves a spin, loves looking out at all the houses. Anna visits, too, and I take her to Galway, where we buy clothes and books and visit cafés. She is a fine-looking woman, all grown up and sensible. Has a boyfriend, too — Tiernan something-or-other. He's a solicitor. Mam will be delighted if that goes all the way to the altar. Anna's a good girl; what you see is what you get. Éamon and the boys come down, too; they are all fond of Bella's parties. I let the drink get the better of me at one party, and thought I was Liam Clancy again and sang a few songs. 'Have youse no homes to go to?' I roared when I finished, and Bella cheered and chuckled. It was after that party that she first arrived in my room. 'Are you lost, girl?' I asked. She didn't answer — not with words. She makes a return visit now and again. She's engaged to be married, my little Bella. Nice fella, too. Well, what he doesn't know …

I reach to the locker on the near side of the bed, and take a book from the pile. As I read, I rub the ridge of skin by my left eye. It has become a habit, the touching of the scar. I read for two hours. She moves slightly, and her hand searches behind her in the bed for me.

She finds me. 'Hey,' she says sleepily. 'I thought you'd abandoned me.'

She leaves her hand on the inside of my left thigh, tugging and teasing the hair on my upper leg. I return the book to the pile and go under the cover to her.

'Hello, girl,' I say, kissing her head.

She caresses my leg, her fingers spreading and closing. She is still facing away from me. I lift the duvet to lie close to her. She is naked. I kiss her back and her shoulders. She has lightly freckled skin — smooth, fleshy-white, Irish skin. I kiss the undulations of her spine. I caress her legs, her thighs, her hips. I touch her abdomen, lightly, with fingers spread across her little pouch belly, that little womanly rise. I pull my fingers up her skin and touch her breasts. I softly pinch her nipples, carefully, massaging the hardening points between my fingers. She works her hand up to take me, and strokes me easily with thumb and fingers. I move my right hand down, touching her lightly, gently opening the folds, finding her. I concentrate on the touch, and she pushes against me, stretches her body long, and goes silent, her breath suspended, before release. I raise my left hand to the centre of her back, and push and fold her again. She still faces away from me. She pulls me towards her. She touches herself with me, stroking her opening. She breathes heavy at the touch. I push into her. I am not in properly. I come out and I lower myself in the bed behind her. She takes me in her right hand and guides me in with the fingers of her left. It is good to be inside her. I push deep as I keep one hand on her back and the other on that little abdominal rise. She tries to keep me inside when I finish, but I fall away as the blood leaves. I kiss her back, her shoulders, her hair, and she settles under the cover, burying her head deep in the pillow.

She is asleep again as I rise from the bed, wrap a towel around me, and walk across the landing to the bathroom. I shower and return across the landing in the towel. I dress into jeans and a T-shirt, and put on a black woollen pullover that Anna has sent for my birthday. Scattered on the long table are piles of books and notepads. I settle on my chair, open a notepad, and take a pencil from an Italia '90 mug. I clear a space on the desk. I sharpen the pencil, dropping the shavings into a wicker wastepaper basket. It is one of the simple joys of life: a sharp pencil. I take a clean page and begin a letter: *Station Road, Ennis, 6 June 1992*. 'Hello Aisling, my friend,' I write. Aisling has visited, too, but she cries every time. Aisling and I have a painful bond: though we are friends, our friendship does not exist as its own thing — it is a Cora thing. She's been good with her letters, too. They all have. They all make the effort. I reach over to a biscuit tin on the long table, open it, and remove a bundle of papers. I put them on the table before me.

Bella moves in the bed. 'Are you reading those letters again, Johnny?' she asks gently.

I walk over to her, sit on the bed, and kiss her pretty face. I go down to the kitchen, my bare feet clammy on the cold tiles, and make tea and toast for us. Mick, another who shares with us, passes through on his way out. 'Are you right there, Michael?' I ask. Mick is well tired of my old joke and grumbles 'Morning' to me with an annoyed grimace. I take two mugs of tea and a plate of buttered toast up to my room. I put one mug and a slice of toast on my desk, and take the other mug and the plate over to the bed. She watches me in silence as she eats. I switch on the Philips. 'A bit of The Cure to get the day going,' I say. When she has finished the tea and toast, she reaches from the bed and takes the T-shirt that I wore last night.

She puts it on, leaves the bed, and comes over to me. I stand and kiss her, and feel her bare butt under the tail of the T-shirt. I increase the volume on the Philips on the opening beats of 'Inbetween Days'. I dance through the intro and then I sing. She joins me, and we dance, four bare feet skipping on the wooden floor. There is a knock on the door. I open it.

'Hola, Marcela,' I say. 'Are you wanting a dance?' Marcela is a cousin of Bella, and is from Valencia.

'She is here?'

'Who?'

'I know she is here.'

'Nobody here but me,' I reply. 'You have your chance.'

'No thanks. But tell her who isn't here that her fiancé is to call this morning. And then what will we say? Eh?'

'Nice fella, that Colin,' I suggest. 'A sound bloke.'

'Yes, he is,' she says with conviction, turning and marching off across the landing. She turns again. 'But you two …' She searches for a word. 'You two are … a disgrace.'

'Well,' I say, turning to Bella as I close the door. 'You ask a girl to dance, and all the abuse you get.'

Bella kisses me with a laugh and disappears out the door. I watch her go. I watch the movement of her arse below the T-shirt. She'll get a lecture from Marcela, but, like our promises to make each time the last time, it will make no difference. What was one of those triads of Ireland that Bob used to recite over the oil-store workbench? 'The three deafnesses of this world: a doomed man faced with a warning, a beggar being pitied, a headstrong woman hindered in lust.'

Well, what now, Bob? What now, my old friend? This whole world is a total fuck-up. I hold my head and push my hair back hard. I try to put it all out of my mind. I try to put Cora out of my mind. Sometimes it's easy, like it never, ever happened, and I'm fine and all is well, or it did happen and I'm okay. But it's not true, and later the whole thing comes down bigger and heavier and shittier than ever, and I just want to fucking scream.

I don't remember the fall; not really. I fell, so they tell me, and caught the concrete pavement with my head as I crashed out of the ambulance. I only remember Cora, the white sheet, and the red boots.

I lower the volume on the Philips. My birthday cards are still on the mantelpiece — I turned twenty-one a month ago. Twenty-one. I should take the cards down. I don't know why I left them up — I just did. I gather them and spread them on the table beside the letters. I sit, and one by one I read the cards again.

'We hope you are managing well', says one from Mam and Dad. Well, they are not for long statements. They struggled with the accident; they struggled to find a place for it. Up until that evening, the mantra of 'The Lord works in mysterious ways' was used with abandon to cover all that life threw at us. But that just didn't hold for Cora. In the hospital, it was all doctors-this and tests-that, but the best Dad could manage when Cora was mentioned was to blow hard, shake his head, and turn away. They were afraid that I might be damaged after the fall. 'Will he be all right?' I heard Mam ask when she thought I couldn't hear. 'You never know with head injuries.' They have been unsure since.

Another card is from Aunt Hannah. It came with a package for my birthday. The package was a blue scarf. 'Time to trade in that old rag', Aunt Hannah wrote. I gave the new scarf to Bella. I'll keep the old rag.

I lift a drawing from Clara. It is of a tall man in a long, dark coat. The man is holding the hand of a small girl. The sun is shining, the grass is green, and around the man and the girl there are flowers and trees. On the man, a blue scarf flies in the breeze. Clara was such a great girl after the accident, overlooking the chaos, ignoring all the hoo-ha.

I lift a card from Anna. It also came with a package — it was the black pullover. It came, as usual with Anna, with a list of dos and don'ts: mind your head, keep warm, study, take me to Galway soon, don't miss the tests, don't drink too much, don't do anything silly. Anna worries about me. She knows I got broken, and she tries to fix me.

I was afraid after the fall that I might have said something, have let something slip, and added chaos to the tragedy. Delaney kept a watch from the sidelines. In the end, the secret survived, and I ended up with a broken skull, a bad eye, a new look, and no Cora. The ambulance that waited at her gate that dark evening took us both to the hospital. I lived. She died.

I move my hand across the table and lift the letters from 16 Níth River Terrace. It was a difficult decision for the Flannery family — what to do with Cora when she died. All who knew Cora knew about her love of Cúchulainn's Castle, but it went against tradition and expectation — and it went against the law — to dig and to bury her there. There were only two choices: the cold earth at Dowdallshill, or the hot furnace of a crematorium. They held her ashes until I was fit to leave the hospital, and we ignored the law and buried her below the single oak as fallen leaves blew around us in a winter breeze. Aisling sang 'Táimse i m' chodhladh is ná dúisigh mé' into the cold air. When we are young, we think that death comes only at the end of life. We are wrong. I should have known better.

I put the letters and cards aside and finish my own writing to Aisling, and I write a letter to Hamburg to confirm a teaching placement for summer. I step into a pair of black trainers before reaching into the Dunn & Co and pulling the collar up around the blue scarf. I take a walk through town. I slow up while passing the shoe shop. I tap on the window. Inside, Dervla Kerrigan raises her head of red waves from where she attends the feet of a customer. 'Hello, Jezebel,' I mime as I blow a kiss across the boot-and-shoe display. Still on her knees in the shop, she straightens and shuffles her shoulders, tossing her head back. I look on her. Dervla Kerrigan has a chest that could stop an army. I nod an intention through the glass, and she receives the proposal with that dirty smirk of hers. Dervla Kerrigan is a girl for fun. Her only morning choice is silk or lace, and she carries her lingerie as easily as early summer can carry hope.

The first night, after we met in the bar of Brogan's Hotel, she took me to her house. We were still in the hallway when I pulled the clothes from her and she pushed me down onto the carpeted steps of the staircase. She lifted me out quickly and forced me between her breasts nested in the black lace. Then she swallowed me, her head bobbing below the red curls. I was rushing to a finish, unable to stop or slow an emptying, and she held her tongue wide to catch me. 'Thank you,' she said, as she looked up when it was over. The second time, we made it to her living room, but only just. I leant her over a couch, her back resting on the arm of the chair, and the front of that body arched towards me and offered as I pushed the dress up, the two white cylinders through the taut suspenders, the sheen of the black triangle, a sliver of silk before the inveigling chalice, inviting, enchanting, the slipway to oblivion. The third time, we made it to her bedroom.

I post the letters and I stop in Brogan's Hotel in O'Connell Street. Maggie is on duty, and I chat to her for five minutes before I take one of the dark, wooden booths. Over the course of an hour, Maggie brings me two large coffees with fresh cream, and I read the *Irish Times*. When I finish the newspaper, I return to my room on Station Road and read through my coursework for the rest of the day. Later, I reach into the biscuit tin and remove a sheet of folded paper. It is the

Wünderkind

'KANN ICH IHNEN HELFEN?'

I turn. It is the tall girl I have noticed before, and at this closeness she is taller than I thought, and she is lovely — so lovely that if I'm not careful I might just stare at her, dumbly, or reach out and touch her, or do or say something foolish. I pass her the peaches, and she weighs and labels them for me.

'*Danke schön*,' I say.

'*Bitte schön*,' she answers. Her face offers a kindness, but her words rush at me, and already brought unsteady by her nearness, I am blown from the course of certainty. She is young, her face has all the fullness of innocence, and her long, brown hair is swept back, where some of it has caught and hangs on her shoulder. Her mouth moves, the smile remains, but there is a question held. Her pouting mouth has pouting pink lips, with the gentle, soft, damp gleam of something. Of what? Woman? Yes, but no. It is more — a flesh pink, not a painted pink. I am staring. I am doing what I have warned myself not to do. We stand in a momentary silence, a kind of suspension of time, as I look to her, and, between her high cheeks and her high forehead, her brown eyes look to me.

I breathe. I decide to play my trump card. 'I'm Irish … I'm from Ireland,' I say, offering my hand, and she smiles a smile that is half fun and half embarrassment. She takes my hand.

'Hello, Irish boy,' she answers in the precise English that comes from German schooling. 'I am Mila. Welcome to Germany.'

We walk together to the checkout.

'A fine supermarket you have here, Mila,' I say, and I begin a rollcall of the contents of the mid-shelf: '*Brötchen, Frikadellen, Gulaschsuppe, Sauerkraut, Knödel, Bierwurst, Leberwurst, Schinkenwurst.*' There are lentils — lots of lentils. Lentils are really big here. I stop and lift a tin of lentils with cooked sausage. I tell her that I've yet to see an Irish family sit down to a feast of lentils; lentils are not so popular in Ireland. I replace the tin on the shelf, and we continue towards the front of the store as I plough a furrow of commentary up the supermarket aisle. At the checkout, I pay an older woman for the groceries, and Mila helps put them in a paper bag. I should say something. In these matters, momentum is everything. Tied to the hot flow of excitement, a cool knowledge runs through me — I might not get a chance like this again. I have to act.

'Would you like to go for a coffee, Mila?'

She looks out through the window — it is a warm day. 'Would an ice-cream be too much?' she asks.

'An ice-cream,' I say, 'would be the most perfect thing ever.'

We find an ice-cream parlour nearby, all tiles and glass, and we sit inside. All the other customers are sitting outside, and we have the place to ourselves. We order two banana-splits from a heavy Italian. The ice-creams arrive, and they are magnificent.

'Be the hokey,' I say, shaking the Italian's hand. '*Magnifique.*'

'I think that's French,' Mila comments, in a serious voice.

'Close enough,' I answer, and she laughs.

For two hours we sit and talk, chasing the banana-splits with several coffees. She tells me she is from Bremen and is staying in the Grosshansdorf area of the city with her relatives, working the holidays in her uncle's store. I tell her about Ireland and that I am teaching English here in Hamburg for the summer.

We leave the parlour and walk to the high street. It is a modern street, a new street. The pedestrian pavement is clean and broad, and there is a row of flagpoles along its length; but there is no breeze, so the colours of the German federation hang low. We pass a small drapery store with FOLLOW ME stencilled on the window. The Germans have a fancy for putting English names on their enterprises; I guess they think it gives the establishment a certain something. On the edge of the district, I have passed the Happy Cars Garage. But who am I to judge — in Dundalk, I go to the Roma for chips. We walk to the store, where I offer my hand, and again Mila gives a look that is half fun and half embarrassment.

Every day for the next two weeks I visit the supermarket, and twice each week we go for ice-cream and coffee. I have made the effort to learn a few Italian adjectives, and I shower the proprietor in glorious praise. I am rewarded: he is serving us pure art.

At the end of the second week of our friendship, we walk the two miles to the town of Ahrensburg, where we spend the evening drinking Weissbier in tall glasses, and singing German songs with the locals. The wheat beer gets the better of me, and I think I'm Liam Clancy again. I sing three songs; one is 'The Dutchman', which is the closest I can get to Germany. I finish off by shouting 'Haben Sie keine Häuser' at the gathering, which causes some confusion and doesn't go down as well as I had hoped. Afterwards we walk to her uncle's house, where we part at the front step with a handshake and her shy smile. I walk to my room with Mila on my mind. Later, as I lie on my bed, I realise that sometimes when I'm with her I do not think of Cora.

It is a late Saturday morning, and I am halfway through my Hamburg contract. I walk through the grounds of the residence and then go to my room and wait, leaving the door unlocked. Today she will call for me, and we will go into the city for the afternoon. At midday, I hear her footsteps on the tiled hallway. She reaches the last room on the long corridor — mine — and knocks.

'Hello,' I call out.

She pushes the door open.

'Hello, German girl. *Willkommen.*'

She looks around the room and absorbs the scene: a novel and a Walkman on a bedside locker; a single bed; a toilet bag on a glass shelf above a corner sink; a beechwood-veneered wardrobe with no clothes showing; a single chair; a half-dozen books on the floor; and on a small table, a beer mug with flowers cut from the garden, a cup of pens and pencils, and an open notebook beside the flowers. A funnel of light reveals the woods beyond the window.

I take the Dunn & Co from where it waits on the bed, and I put it on as she watches me. She walks farther into the room, and at the table she looks to the open notebook.

'What do you write about?'

I grimace and shrug. She looks to me — those brown eyes, those pink lips, holding the question open.

'About life,' I answer, forced into some comment. 'I guess,' I add, trying to tie a rope around the loose admission.

'Is it something about me you write?'

'Yes.'

'What about me do you write?'

'I write, Mila,' I say, moving to her, 'that you are a beautiful girl.'

I raise my hand to the side of her seventeen-year-old face as I kiss her pink lips. I have never kissed a girl as tall as Mila, and the feeling is strange.

'Irish boy,' she says to me after the kiss, and we rest our heads against each other.

'Come on,' I say after a while. 'Let's go.'

We ride the U-Bahn into the centre of Hamburg, and walk to the Rathaus — the city hall. It is a sandstone building, and the sandstone reminds me of the cathedral wall at home. As Mam says: isn't it funny the way the mind works? At Rathhausmarkt, there is a crowd gathered in a wide circle, and we push our way in to see a painted man juggling firesticks. We move on, wandering along Mönckebergstraße, where I stop to look at coats in the window display of Peek & Cloppenburg. Strolling through the streets of Spitaler Straße, Alsterarkaden, and Jungfernstieg, we follow a canal to the Binnenalster lake.

'It's a big smoke,' I say to Mila.

'This is the second-largest city in Germany,' Mila tells me. 'Hamburg is both a city and a state. The city area is seven times bigger than Paris, and two-and-a-half times bigger than London. We have much green spaces here. Hamburg has two thousand three hundred bridges. That is more than Venice and Amsterdam if you put them together.'

Somewhere in me, it registers that I enjoy her habit for relaying facts. We walk around the lake, and we take a terrace table at a waterside restaurant.

'How about lunch?' I ask, sliding the menu across the table. She has her hands clasped in her lap below the table. I lean across the table and take both her hands in mine, raise her hands to my lips, and kiss each of her open palms. She looks to me across the table with a face that is no longer half of anything, but all of something.

After lunch, we wander around the district of Saint Nikolai, passing the Hopfenmarkt and the ruin of the Saint Nikolai church. 'It is a memorial to war,' Mila says. 'It's why we leave it such as this.' I look at the bomb-damaged ruin, and then I look around to the German folk going about their business, and I think how this nation, this leading edge of our civilisation, did what they did just fifty years before. How could these people, who championed engineering, science, arts, and culture, load their neighbours onto trucks and trains, and drive them to be slaughtered? How could that possibly be?

'Do you ever wonder, Mila, about what happened here? How did it happen?'

'It was a bad time in history. We were controlled by mad people, crazy.'

It is true in some way, I suppose. But it was not Hitler or Himmler or Goebbels who gathered their neighbours, who loaded those trains. It was bakers, cobblers, factory workers, teachers, musicians, and carpenters. How the fuck did that happen?

We cross to Alte Deichstraße, and wander on to Speicherstadt, past vendors of rectangular pizza slices, and stalls of sandwiches topped with cold-smoked and pickled fish. We take a city commuter bus to Landungsbrucken on the River Elbe, and hold each other as we look out across the vast harbour. Below us, tourists are boarding the barges of Große Hafenrundfahrt and Fleetfahrt for harbour and canal boat-tours. I wonder how it is possible to organise so many ships, freight containers, and people. We take the bus back into the city and find a bar, the Anno 1905, across from the Holsten brewery, where we sit for hours drinking glasses of Lübzer Pils, Holsten Pils, and Franziskaner Hefeweissbier.

In the late evening we leave the bar and head towards Saint Pauli. Busloads of elderly tourists pass us, and crowds meander outside theatres showing *Cats*, *Phantom of the Opera*, and *The Little Shop of Horrors*. We slow as we read the billboards, and then we push on with the crowd into the Reeperbahn. The streets here simmer with the curious and the intent. It's as Mam says: people are strange. People travel for an assortment of motivations, and find their own fold of comfort in odd places. Among the restaurants, bars, and clubs, we pass window displays of sex-shops and brothels. Ushers entice, bargain, and plead outside strip-clubs. Girls and boys proposition passers-by for trade. We walk through the Reeperbahn like two spinsters at a wedding, inhaling every scene and occurrence. When I briefly stop to gawp into a shop window, I am separated from Mila.

A girl approaches me. She is good looking, her blonde hair is tied in a Grecian braid, her pretty face and clear skin show above the pulled collar of an American college jacket, and her arctic-blue eyes lock and hold me to her. I think she is simply being friendly and saying hello, but she is selling sex. I am embarrassed by the revelation, and quickly apologise and walk away. Homeless tramps and addicts, slumped on the pavement edge, beg with polystyrene cups offered for alms. I watch as passers-by not just ignore them, but fail to see them. I look for Mila and find her.

'Let's go,' I say, and we walk back toward the city centre. We find a bar, and later we find a club, where we stay and dance until morning. At four-thirty, we take a taxi to the Fischmarkt. As light rises over the harbour, we wander around the stalls — the freshly caught fish, the smoked eel, the imported fruit and vegetables, and the bric-a-brac. The bus tours that passed us on the way to the Reeperbahn the previous evening have reappeared, and the bleary-eyed curious join the crowds of all-nighters and the market traders. I hold Mila close to me as we make our way through the mob. Heavy men manhandle heavy, wide pans over hot burners, where pieces of potato are fried and served with egg. Through the morning air, the smell of hot fried potato entices our hungry bellies, and we order a portion each. As day brightens, we ride the U-Bahn home to Grosshansdorf.

'I shall come to you, Irish boy,' she says, before she falls asleep on my shoulder in the train. 'I shall come to you.'

In Grosshansdorf, I leave a tired girl at her uncle's house, where I kiss her face and her pouting soft pink lips. I return to my room, and I lie on my bed and think again on the Nazi thing. How did it happen? How could a thing like that happen? I don't know the answer. I guess that, like it or not, this is who we are. But I do know one thing. The only way to stop a Nazi was to shoot him. That's how the battle played out. It took bullets and guns and bombs to stop them. All the peace-talking didn't work — only war saved the rest of us. As sleep comes, I wonder, *What am I doing? Where am I going?* I wonder … but I am too tired.

My summer in Hamburg passes, and it is now mid-August. Throughout my days here, I think again and again on how tyranny and massacre happen. And I think on why, at times, some people don't fight. I wonder why this happens, even when sometimes the number of the oppressed is many and the oppressor is few. Why the obedience? Is it fear? Sure, oppressors, generally speaking, have the weapons. But why be afraid of getting killed, when you're going to die anyway? I don't understand it. I try to figure it out, but I don't find an answer. Why, at the very end, as they walked in neat, ordered lines to their death, didn't the Jews throw themselves at their guards? Why not fight? What was there to lose? Why didn't slaves rise against their masters? Okay, some did. But they were the few. And why didn't the starving Irish of the famine fight for food from their English landowners? Why didn't they just fight, whatever the risk or cost? I would. I'd fight. I'd have to, because I couldn't take some bastard chaining me, starving me, or ordering me into a neat line to kill me. I'd throw myself against it. If we don't do that, then what are we? Isn't it more than just a right to fight? Isn't it a duty? But so many people don't. And perhaps it isn't fear at all, but desperate hope — a hope that no matter how bad things are, they remain somehow better than they could be, and that there is yet a chance for a reprieve and survival. Isn't that mad? Isn't hope a fucker?

These weeks here with Mila have been a blessing, but my teaching contract is finished and I am leaving. Stefan, a taxi driver, collects me from the residence. Mila stands on the grass, feeding the remnants from my cupboard to the birds. Stefan puts my two bags into the car as I kiss Mila goodbye and we hold each other. I tell her I shall come again to visit her. She tells me, again, that she will come to me.

It was Stefan who collected me when I first arrived in Hamburg and who gave me a German lesson as we drove to Grosshansdorf. Most of the time I had no idea what he was talking about, but he didn't give a damn, because he kept the flow going for the whole trip. 'Well, Stefan', I said then, laughing, feeling confident and philosophical, and thinking anyway that he didn't understand me. 'Life is just all-out madness, absolute all-out madness.'

As we return to the airport he asks, 'So, *mein irische Freund? Deutschland, gut?*'

'*Sehr gut*, Stefan,' I answer, and I quote a verse of a drinking song that I learned in the pub in Ahrensburg. '*Aber, alles hat ein Ende; nur die Wurst hat zvei.*' — 'But everything has an end; only the sausage has two.' He takes up the tune immediately, and we motor towards the airport, laughing and singing loudly to the road.

'*Und …?*' Stefan asks as we lift the bags out of the rear of the car, indicating where we came from with his head.

I nod and say nothing.

'*Die Liebe?*' he laughs, patting me on the shoulder. 'Love: just all-out madness.'

Line of sight

I AM CROUCHED BEHIND THE GRAVEYARD OF CROSSMAGLEN. IT IS LATE August, and in the clear light of evening I have a line of sight down to the village square. I've had misses since Cora died. I shouldn't have tried so hard; I know that. I took risks. Delaney said it was too soon, that I wasn't right, that the planning wasn't great. But what about focus and all that stuff, I told him, and, anyhow, wasn't it all good practice? So I went ahead.

I have spent two weeks preparing for this location. I have been back and forward from gun to target three times — twice on a bicycle, and once walking with a stick and dressed in an old coat and cap. The day I walked, I borrowed a dog from the county pound in Meath, and returned it the next morning to another in Dublin. I have yet to be stopped when on a bicycle or when walking a dog. A dog can be fierce useful for unearthing any SAS units dug in and hiding; so, oddly enough, can the curiosity of cattle — a grouped long stare is a warning, and I am careful to monitor bovine behaviour. I abandoned a shoot last month when a herd of Holstein dairy cows paid long attention to a briar patch below an ash tree in a distant ditch. And I am careful, too, not to let my own location be recognised by inquisitive livestock.

I scope the pavement at the Northern Bank. Delaney had a volunteer meander there today, and I know I have a clear shot. I am ready.

There is no hunting like the hunting of man. So says my friend Mister Hemingway. These words revisit me, and I have to chase them away and rid my mind of everything other than the senses.

I have the gun set and the scope fixed — 'Dope the scope', the American called it. I have one shot. I have allowed for the elevation and bullet drop. I have allowed for the temperature and humidity. I have calculated for spin drift. I know the range, and today the gods are with me and the wind is low. What breeze there is, I have allowed for. So far I have had eight shots — all misses — and nine aborts. Today I will take the shot, and I will not miss.

I practise my routine. Safety off. Deep breath. Let half out. Hold. Crosshair. Crosshair. Squeeze the trigger.

Four soldiers approach the bank through the village square. Soldiers one and two move in and out and through the reticle. I count them through. I put the spotting scope down and look through the scope on the rifle. The eye that was damaged in the fall is my left. I scope with my right. How lucky was that? Soldier three passes through. I am fixed on the corner of the wall. I wait on the last soldier. I know he will pause, and I am aiming to where that pause will be. I relax my breathing as soldier four enters, the scope moving right to left towards the crosshairs. I begin to exhale a slow breath. I count him across the mil dots of the horizontal: four, and three, and two, and ... He goes down on his haunches to cover the rest of the patrol as they step onto the road to check a lorry. I breathe in. I adjust. I let him settle for two seconds, and I put the crosshairs on his folded body. I exhale another slow breath. I squeeze the trigger. Boomph! I absorb the short recoil of the Barrett, allowing my shoulder to be beaten back an inch to dampen the punch. I remain low on the gun, and I keep watch in the scope. I watch the shockwave through the air. I see pink spray. I see soldier four pop and splatter onto the Northern Bank's wall.

Mila

In the early morning, I drive home to Ennis, and every hour the radio news tells of the soldier killed in Crossmaglen. I go in by the rear door. Bella is in the kitchen.

'Hello, stranger,' she says, her back to me as she prepares breakfast on the counter.

'A cup of tea and two slices will do lovely,' I say, passing behind her and tapping her arse.

'You have a visitor.'

I stop.

'She arrived at the door yesterday, all flustered, the poor thing. I let her in to your room. This is for her — you can take it up.' She turns and faces me. 'She's very pretty. And young, isn't she?'

'Yes,' I answer. 'She's very pretty.' What can I say?

I take the tea and toast, and knock on the door of my own room before I enter. The room is dim, with a soft diffusion of light that filters from the curtained windows. She moves in my bed.

'Hello, German girl,' I say, making space for the breakfast on the bedside locker.

'Irish boy,' she says, and I see anxiety fall away from her as she sees me. 'I told you I would come.'

I lift her hair from her face and kiss her soft, pink lips.

'Yes,' I say. 'Here, Bella has sent this up to you.'

'She's nice, isn't she?'

I sit on the edge of the bed and watch her eat. When she finishes,

I kick off my trainers and climb in beside her. She rises from the bed and walks to the corner between the two windows. She faces the wall and, slowly, piece by piece, she removes her clothing: the socks that she wore all night, the loose top, the pyjama bottoms, the white bra. She turns to face me. In the gentle dust of morning shadow, she stands before me. Her skin is dappled with light that seeps from the curtain edge. In shades of grey, beauty is cast in the corner of my bedroom. Nothing that exists in the universe, nothing, is as beautiful as woman. I look on her tall frame — her head held high, her dark hair, her neck, her shoulders, her arms, her breasts, her belly, her long legs. I leave the bed and go to her and touch her. I kiss her face. I kiss her neck, her breasts, and I kneel down as I kiss her warm belly, her legs, her thighs. With her hands sliding by her sides, she pushes the white knickers down, stepping from them as I push her against the wall.

The next morning, we pack a picnic into the Renault and drive north from Ennis into the patchwork limestone of the Burren. At Mullaghmore Mountain, we leave the small road and park the car. I take the picnic and a blanket from the back seat, and we walk to the mountain over fissured ground. We stop and sit by a lake under the mountain, the still water clear in the cradle of the grey-white stone.

'It's like we are on the moon,' Mila says.

'It is that,' I agree. Around us is one hundred square miles of rock.

We picnic on the blanket by the water, as two mute swans watch us from beside a reed bed.

'I wonder, will they eat bread?' she asks. She rises and walks towards them, and throws pieces of bread that float on the clear water, but she has to retreat before the swans approach. We drink hot coffee that I pour from a Thermos, and I tell her we are sitting on the bed of a sea.

'That was a long time ago?' she asks.

[*143*]

'Yes, hundreds of millions of years. It could drive a man mad just to think about it.'

After the picnic, we drive through the village of Kilfenora and on to the small town of Lisdoonvarna. I explain how every year people come here to a matchmaking festival: men looking for a wife; women looking for a husband.

'Why don't they try the pub, or the supermarket?' she asks, and as she asks she gives me that look — that look she gave me on the first day — and I see her again in that aisle among the *Brötchen*, *Knödel*, and *Schinkenwurst*, the German girl, almost as tall as I am, but young, her face with all the fullness of innocence.

Leaving Lisdoonvarna, we take the coast road north to the village of Ballyvaughan. The road meanders along the jutted Burren coast, with the Atlantic Ocean on our west and the grey-white rock on our east. At Ballyvaughan, we take the inland country road back to Lisdoonvarna, and from there we drive out to the ocean's edge at Doolin, where ferries take tourists to the Aran Islands. We park the Renault on the verge of the road and we walk along the pier. The wind is blowing, and below us the sea crashes onto the shore. We find a pub at the top of the pier, and we order bowls of hot chowder and brown bread. A lone teenage girl plays a fiddle in the front bar. A coach-load of tourists arrives, and they gather around her. The girl stops playing and begins to sing. I walk to the front bar, where I stand watching her. She sits with her fiddle held to her chest like a little girl holding a favourite doll, and her long, orange-red hair falls down by her white face. I stare at her mouth as the words leave it. The tourists applaud as she finishes, and she puts the fiddle down on the seating and walks to me.

'Hello,' she says.

I realise I have been staring at her. 'I'm sorry,' I say. 'That song ...'

'That's okay. Some songs do that.'

'It reminded me of someone.'

'So I see.' She pauses. 'I'm Aoife.'

'Aoife …' I reply, still confused by the place the song has taken me.

'Aoife Jensen.'

'Jensen?' I look to her now, to the pale-blue eyes in the pale skin.

'Yes, my father is from Denmark. Came here to West Clare on holiday, met my mother, made me, and stayed.'

'A Norse and Irish mix,' I say. 'A powerful blend. Just like the old days.'

'Yes,' she laughs. 'Just like the old days.'

'I have to go,' I say, glancing away. I take her white hand in mine. 'Goodbye, Aoife Jensen. Tell your dad he made a beautiful girl.'

We leave the pub in Doolin, return to the Renault parked along the verge of the small road, and drive south to the Cliffs of Moher. We walk out along a narrow path. It is evening, and the few remaining tourists are leaving. We reach the cliff's edge and stand behind a slender wall of stone plinths. A wind is blowing. Below us, the blue-grey ocean pounds against rock. I look from the water to the girl. Her jacket billows in the wind, and her hair flies around her. In this place, the ocean has travelled from the American continent. That's a long way, so the air itself has had the time and space to be rid of impurities. It arrives here clean, and I feel like I can breathe and gather all the shit in my head, and pack it into some shape I can get a hold of, and throw it up and away into the passing air rushing from sea to land; and just for a moment, I am renewed and free. I stand behind Mila, and hold her tightly as I kiss her head. We run back along the path to the car, relieved to get out of the wind, and we drive on along the ocean's edge to where the coast softens to sand and grassy dunes at Lahinch. We stop at a small general-store for petrol and groceries, and then we drive home.

Samhain

I AM AT HOME WITH THE DONNELLYS. LAST NIGHT, I WENT TO THE OAK tree and I sat on the low wall. This morning, I walked through the town. The Sunday gathering has convened, and in my distraction I have missed my exit, and I now sit among them at the kitchen table as the soup is served.

'Did you see the head on Rose Hamill this morning?' Mam asks, throwing the question across the table like a hopeful gambler rolling the dice. 'First up to communion, she was, brazen as anything.'

'Aye, himself wasn't far behind,' Dad responds, pulled from a daydream. 'No shame at all. Came over and shook my hand on the way out.'

'They're not coddin' anyone but themselves, them two,' Mam continues. 'And those young ones moping about on the steps again? Can they not go in and sit down like civilised beings? Outside like a bunch of dopes with the whole town gawking at them. God Almighty, is it too much to ask?'

'I see that Joanne has the new place opened,' Dad says across the table to Shauna, speaking of her sister who has opened a clothes store. 'It must be exciting for her.'

'She was always a great one for the fashion, that one,' Mam adds.

'Four years in college is a long time to waste to work in a shop,' Shauna replies.

I look up, provoked by the pouring of bitter water on the enterprise.

'She'd be better off going out and getting a job like the rest of us,' Declan joins the pouring. 'She'll never make anything out of that caper.'

'And you know who else I met on the way out?' Dad asks, before continuing without waiting for an answer. 'The bould Sam McComish. He says his youngest has got a start above in the brewery.'

'That was some stroke to get him into the brewery,' Mam says. 'The bould Sam, he's deadly.'

'They had pull there,' Shauna interjects. 'Herself has a brother above.'

'Well, that's them finished,' Dad says. 'That's the last one settled. And you won't believe this, but Sam's after taking the redundancy bundle from the job, and they are moving out to Lanzarote for six months every year. Lanzarote? Wherever the hell that is. The world's gone mad.'

'She was always shifty, that one,' Mam says. 'That'll be her idea. She always had notions. Where is Lanzarote, Johnny?'

'Spain,' I tell them. 'Well, it's an African island that belongs to Spain.' And Mam and Dad shake their heads in astonishment as if I have confirmed that the bould Sam McComish and the shifty one are moving to the Amazon jungle or Mars.

'And Father Woods is putting together a trip to Knock,' Dad tells, moving on from the Lanzarote news. 'I said we'll go. It'll help fill the bus.'

'I'll let Hannah and Eddie know,' Mam says. 'Put the four of us down for it. It'll be a day out. Will you come with us, Johnny?'

'Will I come on a trip to Knock?' I ask. 'Are you mad? No thanks.' And everyone laughs.

'There's the rain on,' Dad says, as the first drops tap against the window.

The Sunday conversation continues as I drink tea and retire to my own thoughts, and I think of the girl below the oak tree.

Barnacles

FROM DUNDALK, I TAKE THE EARLY BUS TO DUBLIN. I WILL TAKE THE last bus back to Ennis so I have the whole day in the city with nothing to do. There's magic in that. I have a coffee to kick the thing off and then I visit the bookshops. I walk around with no plan or direction. I have a fast-food lunch, which I regret like I always do: it only ever fills with a sense of dissatisfaction. In the afternoon, I visit the National Library, just to get a feel of the place, and I do the same in the National Gallery and the museums. And then I go to a pub.

I order a pint of porter. It's not my favourite. In fact, I don't really like it, but I'm feeling all Dublinish. I sit at the bar and lift a book from my backpack, and I'm in the third chapter when she mounts the stool beside me. She, too, orders a pint of the black, and she, too, lifts a book from her bag. The book is all Post-its and notes.

'You know what his dad said of them?' I ask her, 'the first time he learned of Nora?'

She turns to me and shakes her head.

'He said, "She'll stick with him."'

She laughs, and a laugh early on is an important thing: it kind of sets the deal up. We read on, slipping the odd comment sideways, and when I order a pint each we put the books on the counter.

She is an American student, all the way from Pittsburgh, USA. Pittsburgh. I wonder what a place like that could look like, and she is spending a month in the city doing the book thing. She's all groovy and cool in the way that girls with a comfortable heritage can be:

edgy without any edge at all. But she is nice, really nice, and though she is intense about the book and stuff, I cannot help but like her. Girls!

At the end of the second drink, I have a decision to make. I put my book into my backpack. I put the Dunn & Co on over the blue scarf, and I pull the collar up.

'I have a bus to catch,' I tell her. 'The western ocean calls. Can you hear it?'

She smiles through our disappointment. It's a funny thing how you can miss someone you didn't know an hour-and-a-half before. But it is true, and I don't try to hide my own regret. I lean over and kiss her, and then I go.

In the midweek, I have an afternoon off, and I take the Renault to the coast, and I sit on dark rock and run my hand over barnacles as, onto me and onto Ireland, the Atlantic rolls.

A Christmas carol

IT IS CHRISTMAS, AND I AM IN STATION ROAD. MILA HAS GONE TO Bremen for the holidays; Bella, Marcela, and Mick are gone, too. I am alone. On Saint Stephen's evening, I walk to Brogan's Hotel, where I stand at the bar and drink beer. The place fills, and I feel a hand on my arm.

'Hello, lover-boy.'

I turn — it is Dervla Kerrigan. 'Hello, Jezebel.'

We drink together in the packed bar, and later we go to the nightclub in The Queens Hotel, and afterwards I take her home to Station Road, where I lie her down on the double-bed until morning creeps around the curtain of the east window.

The slanted rain

IT IS THE FIRST DAY OF FEBRUARY, AND THE CHIEF SITS FACING ME IN THE small front room he has used as his study for forty years. Delores — she, too, now in her seventies — taps the door before entering, and leaves a tray of tea and biscuits on the low table between the two armchairs.

'It's great to see you again, Johnny,' she says to me. 'It's been too long. You're looking great anyways.'

'You're looking great yourself, Delores,' I say. 'There's no stopping you.'

'Away out foreign, he tells me he's been,' she says, turning towards her husband. 'Germany. Isn't it well for the young these days — they have the world at their feet. God, I remember when you came here first, Johnny, such a sweet boy, all fresh and eager, and no arse in your trousers.'

I am often struck by the difference in the couple. She is relaxed with her way and her tongue, and he is all collar and tie, articulate, pedantic, annoying.

'Fifty years next year,' she says to me, nodding at him. 'Fifty years, Johnny. I could have been in and out twice for murder, and still be a free woman.'

'But what fun you would have missed,' I say.

'It has been no fun at all,' she says, indicating across the room. 'Look at the state of him — it was like marrying a straitjacket. I've been a martyr. I'm not joking, Johnny. When my time is up, there will be a corridor of angels to greet me at the gates of heaven.' And she leaves the room laughing.

'She hasn't lost it,' I say, as she disappears.

'She's a holy show, John. You couldn't let her out without a chaperone. Still, we all have our crosses.'

It will be ten years this year — since I was twelve — that I have been coming to this room. First I came to learn. Then I came to talk. And then I came to speculate, to commit, and to plan. I was in my first year at secondary school when the history teacher told us to write an essay on twentieth-century Irish history. Any topic we liked, he told us. He gave us one week, and asked me to stay back the day we handed them in.

'Now then, young Donnelly,' he said, holding up the three foolscap pages and reading the title, '"Britain 10–Ireland 0."' 'Would you care to explain this scurrilous article?' And so I did. I explained how ten IRA prisoners had died on hunger strike, and how it meant nothing and gained nothing. 'But what about status and the right to wear their own clothes?' he asked. 'It doesn't matter what they wear,' I told him. 'They will still be in a British prison, and British soldiers will still be on Irish streets.' 'But it hardened public opinion,' he suggested. 'It brought attention to the cause. It opened doors.' 'Attention fades,' I told him, 'and nothing changes, but those men will still be dead. And, by the end of it, people stopped caring — they got used to the dying, the big marches and protests were falling away, the black flags were torn and fading. And it opened no doors worth entering.' It was quite a speech; I was only twelve. But I was on a roll, so I kept going. I lifted my head and looked into the grey eyes. 'If they had waited and gone out and shot just one soldier each, instead of sacrificing themselves on a useless battle in prison, there would be ten more of us and ten less of them.'

He looked at me hard. 'The word is fewer, John. And ten fewer of them.'

The private lessons began the next week. 'Shows great potential', he wrote to Mam and Dad. 'He must be encouraged.'

At first it was all talk. Then he let me help on some minor missions — moving guns and ammunition from one hide to another. It was just the two of us; he was careful to keep me apart from the others, careful to avoid bringing me into contact with any other volunteer. 'Never attend a march or a funeral,' he told me, 'and never sign your name to anything. Do you understand why?' I told him I did.

Later, we made some attacks of our own. I was fifteen when we first killed together. It was an attack on an informer and his special-branch handler. We shot them both. I knew Delaney worked with others, too, especially on the bombs, but he kept me removed from all that. For years, we prepared our battle plan, and the plan involved getting the gun. And then in 1988 he lost two men, his two bombers. He never told me what happened. He never told me about that stuff; I learned it all on the News. His focus hardened on me after that. I told him that if he got the gun I would take ten of them — one for each of the hunger strikers — and put some right to that wrong. He got the gun. And when it came, and the plan was ready, we agreed to thin the contact, to bring no attention upon us. We set up our operation, our communication, and our means. The mouthy American came to train me, and afterwards we couldn't let him go.

My code name became Cúchulainn. I call him Chief; he likes that. 'They know about me, of course,' he told me. 'It'll be a heavy file. I'm too long in the game. But they must never know about you, John — absolute nobody. Not even our own side; especially our own side.' He told me how he wanted to do things differently; how, by introducing a sniper into the battle, he could make it happen.

[153]

'You must take great care,' he warns me again today. 'SAS units are floating around like waste in a sewer. There's a big push for information. MI5, as well as the Special Branch, are running their own touts; people in the town have been approached.'

'Informers, the scourge of Ireland,' I say, and turn to look out at the weather. Outside it is wet, and the wind drives the rain in hard angles against the window. 'Nothing in Ireland is straight,' I continue. 'Even the rain falls at a slant.'

He turns and he, too, looks out at the weather.

'They can't be tolerated,' I continue. '*Is i ding di féin a scoileann an dair.*'

'It is a wedge of itself that splits the oak,' he translates, and he gives me that thin smile of his. I watch him, knowing I have him on this one: *Is i ding di féin a scoileann an dair* is an Irish phrase the Chief himself had taught me years ago.

He tells me to relax, that the Devil himself doesn't know who the shooter is, but he cautions me again to be careful. He tells me that there are two IRA sniper units preparing in South Armagh, that there is a Belgian FN, and maybe another couple of Barretts on the go.

'Maybe?' I ask him.

He ignores me. 'They will shoot all before them, John, and most likely won't hit a damn thing. Still, it's good cover for you. They are planning to shoot out of cars, vans, trucks, horseboxes, everything. They have a platform built into a 626. But their scouting is useful, and they are finding good, dead ground for us. We'll let them plough ahead with their efforts — it'll keep the Brits busy, it'll give us a clear run, and we'll sneak in under all the noise. We're going along nicely now.'

I drink my tea, and lift a biscuit off a white plate. I tell him I have seen Sloane and Boyd around town selling *An Phoblacht*. 'There is no need to include people of that sort,' I tell him. 'It doesn't do the movement any good.'

[154]

He laughs at my annoyance. 'But there is a need. An army is in need of its foot soldiers. They cannot all be generals. They cannot all be champions — some need to be laid down as foundation for the common good.'

I don't agree that this should include Sloane and Boyd, but I say nothing.

I turn to the near wall and look on a copy of the 1916 Proclamation of the Irish Republic that hangs there. It is an aged print encased in a simple wooden frame. The print has dropped on one side, and so sits at a slight angle within the frame. I have long noted that it is the only thing in this house or about Delaney that is not perfectly neat and aligned, but I know it is also the only thing Delaney possesses that belonged to his father. Apparently, the print has been off-square since it was first mounted, and I guess the Chief feels it's not for him to change it. People can be peculiar about stuff like that.

Irishmen and Irishwomen: In the name of God and of the dead generations from which she receives her old tradition of nationhood, Ireland, through us, summons her children to her flag and strikes for her freedom … We declare the right of the people of Ireland to the ownership of Ireland, and to the unfettered control of Irish destinies, to be sovereign and indefeasible. The long usurpation of that right by a foreign people and government has not extinguished the right, nor can it ever be extinguished except by the destruction of the Irish people. In every generation the Irish people have asserted their right to national freedom and sovereignty … We place the cause of the Irish Republic under the protection of the Most High God, Whose blessing we invoke upon our arms, and we pray that no one who serves that cause will dishonour it by cowardice, inhumanity, or rapine. In this supreme hour the Irish nation must, by its valour and discipline and by the readiness of its children to sacrifice themselves for the common good, prove itself worthy of the august destiny to which it is called.

How many times have I sat here and read those words?

'Are you sure you want to go on?' he asks, reeling me back into our conversation. 'You've done your bit already. You've made your mark.'

I shake my head and brush some biscuit crumbs off the Dunn & Co, and we talk about Ennis and Germany before he questions me again.

'There would be no harm, John, in quitting now. Thatcher is gone. There's talk of peace; things have changed.'

'Nothing has changed,' I reply, and he silently nods.

I tell him I'm near set to go again, but I don't tell him more. I never tell him much in advance of a shooting. I never phone or write. I seldom visit. When I am ready, I let him know what I need, and when and where. He takes care of supply and transport. When I need a car, one will be waiting. When I need a bicycle, one will be waiting. If I needed a fish or a goat, one would be waiting. I find the target, the route in, and the route out. I have a reserve exit plan in place. Getting in is no good if I can't get out; we have enough bloody martyrs. He is the only one to join me on a mission. If he needs to get a message to me between contacts, he will intercept me. It was his idea that I take the apprenticeship in the engineering works. He said that the training, facility, and location would provide opportunities. He was right.

I say my farewells and leave, and, as I walk away from the Chief through the slanted rain, I think again to that wet day in the woods — the first day he let me kill on my own. I had been walking alone, pushing through heavy weather, the day he intercepted me in the street.

'Time to fly the nest,' Delaney said as I sat into the car, a different car to the Chief's own. And a different car meant action.

'A unit has been spotted above in Ravensdale Forest. They're watching the road.'

'Why are they watching the road?' I asked, and he ignored me as if he hadn't heard the question.

'Who spotted them?' I asked.

And this time, to buffer my anxiety, he answered.

'A man walking a dog.'

'A man walking a dog,' I echoed. 'Isn't it always a man walking a dog? Like all those abduction victims you see on the television, always found by a man walking a dog. Never a woman with a dog. Never a man on a bicycle. Always a man with a dog. Funny that, isn't it?'

'John,' Delaney said to me in that schoolmaster's voice he used when needed, 'settle down and concentrate.' Then he told me what we would do, and, as he unrolled the plan, I heard the schoolmaster's voice falter, and I felt an edge of excitement about him, and I saw some dilution in his normal cool rationality. I knew why. British soldiers anywhere on the island were a call to war for Delaney; but British soldiers south of the border — well, that was something else.

'They might know they've been spotted, Chief,' I told him. 'They might be gone.'

'They might,' he answered, before turning to me, his grey eyes full of intent. 'And they might not.'

We drove on for a while without talking, and I went over the plan in my head.

'You have what you need,' he said to me, with a glance into the back seat.

I reached back and lifted a knitted blanket — the type you'd leave in a car for a picnic — and I saw my Armalite. It was the right weapon for this job: it was easy to handle, it didn't mind the rain, and it wouldn't let me down. 'So it's just me and you, friend,' I said to the gun. I was excited; I had to force my breath and nerves to relax. But I wasn't afraid. I was sure of the ground. I was sure of the gun. I was sure of me.

'They're not expecting you,' he said to me after we agreed the plan. 'And you'll be on home turf. You know the ground well — it's where you walk that hairy dog of yours.'

'How do you know where I walk my dog?' I asked, and he ignored me again as if he hadn't heard the question. I laughed. I knew that Delaney kept a very close eye on me.

We drove to Anaverna at the south-east edge of the forest. 'There will be at least two of them,' he warned me. 'Perhaps another two not far off. Find the southernmost man and take him. And do not get spotted from above. And watch your back. And know your routes out.'

'Yes, Chief,' I told him.

I took low cover as the car rolled away, and I waited for one hour before moving. Then, carefully, I worked my way to the area where the man with the dog had spotted the soldiers. It took another hour to crawl there. *I hope he was one of us*, I thought, *that man with the dog. And I hope he is a good one — you can't be sure in this war*. I considered the terrain that I knew well, and I calculated where I would lie if I wanted to watch the road. There were options, but I knew which one I would choose: it was a knob of moss-covered rock surrounded by a thicket of tall pines, where I often sat as Che ran rabbit trails through the trees. If the soldiers were here, they would be among those pines.

Low on my belly, I worked my way in a slow arc to approach the rock from the east. I moved slowly; by the time I got into position, another two hours had gone and the low light of the grey evening was failing. I checked my watch, and knew that Delaney would now be busy on the road below. I had thirty minutes to find a soldier, kill him, and get out.

It took twenty of those thirty minutes to find him, and I was lucky. There are no perfect edges in nature: no straight lines and no concentric curves. And there is no black. The purpose of camouflage is to diffuse shape and colour, to break the symmetric form of the human body into the uneven randomness of the surroundings. This he did well, and but for the antics of Delaney below, who must have drawn his attention, I would never have seen him. But he made one mistake, one minute movement that brought my attention to that place, and then I saw it. It was a small crescent, no bigger than three inches by two. But it was a perfect curve, and it was black. And I knew what it was — it was the heel of a boot. I watched the heel for five minutes, and still I could not find his shape on the ground. But then he moved again, and I found him.

He was above me, near the higher rock; to make sure of the shot, I would have to stand. If the second soldier turned in time, I would be in the open. I worked my way to the nearest pine and took my chances. I stood up, fired three quick rounds into the body on the ground, and then dropped as fast I could and ran at a low crouch down through the trees. Shots exploded behind me, and bullets smashed through wood, but none into me. I jumped into a ditch I knew was there, and returned fire, and now I had the advantage. Though he was on higher ground, if the second soldier was to follow he would have to come through the sunken amphitheatre that led down to the ditch, all of which was covered from below. He could work his way down tree by tree; but that, too, would still give me the opportunity to take him. I knew he would not come. I hammered a dozen shots into the forest, and then I worked my way along the ditch, south and east, to meet up with Delaney.

'And?' the Chief asked, as the wipers cleared a view through the rain.

'I got one, and I left one. I didn't see any others.'

'That's my boy,' he said. 'It's a great day when we get one of those bastards. You did well, John. You did great.'

I nodded to him, but I said nothing.

'We won't hear of that one on the News,' he told me, as he dropped me off in town. 'The Brits will never acknowledge a loss south of the border.'

I waved him off and continued on through the rain.

I was on my way home from school that day, the day when Delaney picked me up for the attack in the forest, the day I first killed on my own. I was sixteen.

I walk through the rain the short distance from the Chief's house to the Market Square. I look across to the bench outside the courthouse before continuing north through Clanbrassil Street, Church Street, and Bridge Street, turning east at the bridge and walking along the river. To the south are the cold and windy school sports fields I used to avoid by sneaking away with Éamon to the snooker rooms of the CYMS; and to the north, oystercatchers, herons, and gulls feed in the mud. I think about him as I walk, the Chief.

Once, I asked him why he got involved, and he told me. It was 1920. It was mid-morning, and in a field outside the village of Toomevara, his father was digging a drill for potatoes. Inside the rented cottage, his young mother added a cut of turf to the fire and brought the flame ready for the pot. In a cradle in the corner, the three-month-old infant slept. The conception came before the marriage, and the young woman's family had relieved themselves of shame and responsibility by ejecting their daughter from the townhouse in Thurles. But the young mother was happy. She had a good man and a new baby boy, and the small cottage was a world away from the pious formality of the town. She was preparing the pot when a shot rattled the window and ran off over the land. In a panic, she scampered across the field to find her husband dead across the shovel. She heard the jeering from the road and looked up to see two Black and Tans waving their arms and rifles as the patrol truck drove off.

She moved to a tenement in Dublin, where she took a job cleaning and cooking. She had nothing to give her child but her selflessness and her insistence on his receiving an education. She drilled the boy on history, geography, mathematics, writing, and spelling. She worked day and night to put him through college, and it was the justification of life itself when he qualified as a teacher. He took her with him to Dundalk when he met Delores and married. 'At least she had some comfort in the end,' he told me. 'At least I could give her that. But, John, I'll tell you this, it was no life she had, only a substitute for a life torn away by that flying bullet.' He never forgave the British for that single shot across the potato field, and he dedicated his life to revenge. 'He probably never saw the truck approaching on the road,' Ignatius Delaney said of his father. 'He would not have heard the shot. He wouldn't even have known he'd been killed.'

He never questioned why I wanted to do what I do — not after he read my essay. We both knew that I was drawn to the battle as surely as an infant is drawn to its mother's bosom, as surely as a songbird must sing, as surely as a dropped stone must fall. From the age that I could know anything, I knew that I would fight for Ireland. A boy can give himself to cause long before the world would suspect him of vocation.

I continue along the river until I reach the port. I stop and sit on a stone bollard along the quayside. The tide is out, and I look across the wide estuary to the Cooley Mountains. The grey mud is broad, and, here and there, pockets of scrub and marsh grass have claimed some banks and islands. A single ship tied to the harbour awaits the evening tide. Beside it, on the quay, a tall, steel crane is locked and shuttered. Behind me, an old pub is long closed, the doors and windows shuttered behind bleached and unravelling plywood. The grain store is closed. I take a pack of Carroll's No. 1 from my pocket and light a cigarette. I gaze down at the mud. A purple BMW drives into the port and turns at the pub. It slows to a stop alongside me, and I hear the electric motor as the window drops. It is Callan, the owner of The Cooking Pot.

'Hello, young Donnelly.'

'Hello, Mark,' I say. 'Are you lost?'

'I wouldn't jump in there,' he suggests. 'You could be stuck in that mud for hours before the tide would take you. It'd be a slow end.'

'I'll keep that in mind,' I say.

'A sound man,' he says, and he drives off.

'Arsehole,' I call after him, as the BMW turns out of the port.

I leave the port, return along the river, and walk west on the Castletown road. I am cold and wet as I sit under the single oak. I look at the ground. I go to speak, but don't. What do you say to the most beautiful girl in the world who is two-and-a-half years dead? I walk down the path around the mound, through the fosse under the bare beech trees, and down the pebbled path covered in the fallen leaves of the previous autumn. I see her face as we danced, as I grabbed her two hands and swung her as we spiralled down to the gate, with leaves, pebbles, and two red boots flying through the dappled air. I climb the stone stile at the round pillar and walk into town. I slow at the corner of Castletown Cross, where the country lane meets the main road, where she thanked me for telling her those simple things.

I walk to Níth River Terrace, and I knock at number sixteen. As soon as the door opens, I step inside.

'Let me in quick,' I say, as I hug Aisling. 'It's freezing out there.'

'In beside the range with you, Johnny,' she says, ushering me in, 'before you catch your death of cold.'

[162]

I stand in the kitchen near the range cooker as Aisling adds two heavy pieces of wood to the fire box that already glows.

'I thought you got rid of that old coat?' Aisling asks, as I hang the damp Dunn & Co on the back of a chair.

'I kept it for a rainy day.'

'You are a holy terror, Johnny. Where's that mad car of yours?'

'Sometimes I need to walk and let the air in.'

'Let's get the tea on first. Then you can tell me all.'

'Thanks, I'm parched. I thought you'd never ask.'

'You only just got here,' she laughs.

'I'm only coddin'. So is it Doctor Flannery yet, or what's the hold-up?'

'Not yet, Johnny. Why don't you come and see me in Dublin? You should. You can stay for a while, if you like. We can go places, do stuff.'

'I might just do that.'

'No doubt you are hungry, Mister Donnelly.' She winks, and moves a large, heavy, grey-metal pot over the hot plate on the range.

'God bless all in this house,' I say, lifting the lid and taking a peep at a lamb stew that already begins to simmer. 'You Flannerys make the best stew on the Mississippi. What would I do without you?'

'We're not on the Mississippi, Johnny. How's all the family?'

'Same as ever,' I reply, pulling a chair near the stove and sitting. 'Still gathering on the Sunday. Peter, Declan, and the two wives; Anna brings Tiernan now; Aunt Hannah, of course. Eddie, too. Mam makes the pot of soup. You'd wonder at the stuff they think to talk about — it seems they grab at the nearest things to fill the spaces. I give it a skip as much as I can.'

'If you ever lost her, you'd all miss that soup.'

That's the thing about Aisling — she can come out with clever things, as if she has given all these matters a good examination and

[163]

has diagnosed some remedy, before administering the medicine in slow droplets.

'You haven't taken the German girl home then?' she asks, raising an eyebrow.

'No, not yet.' I don't ask how she knows. I guess Anna must have told her.

'They're all well, anyhow,' I continue. 'Still talking the same talk. Why is it they do that?'

'Do what, Johnny?'

'You know, talk about whoever isn't there, and bring unkind thoughts into unfavourable comment.'

'That's just harmless gossip, Johnny. We all do that. That's how many people fix their place in life. That's how people work. That's how families work.'

'Not this family here,' I protest. 'And harmless, I don't know. It doesn't seem right. People can choose to be positive or negative with words. We all have that choice. It is a choice.'

'It's not too wrong. Not everyone sees life as if it is being played out on some giant stage before them. Not everyone judges life from a distance.' Aisling turns and looks to me. 'Not everyone sees life as a poet, Johnny. Not everyone is a dreamer.'

'Is that me, Aisling? A dreamer?'

'Maybe.'

Ah, but a man's reach should exceed his grasp,
Or what's a heaven for?

'Let me guess,' she asks. 'A friend of yours?'

'A friend of Cora's, actually. She was a devil for the poetry.'

'You two were well matched.'

I look to Aisling and, without thinking, dispense a few lines of

Kavanagh into the space between us:

> I gave her gifts of the mind, I gave her the secret sign that's known
> To the artists who have known the true gods of sound and stone
> And word and tint. I did not stint for I gave her poems to say.

'Exactly,' she says, and smiles.

'You know, Aisling, all the great things in life begin as dreams and aspirations. It's what makes us human. It's what took us out of the trees. Can you imagine when that first ape took to walking through the savannah? Just imagine the abuse he took from the high branches. *Look at that eejit go*, they would have said, *making a show of himself, trying to stand up straight like a fool.*' I do an impression of an ape getting on its feet and looking out over tall grass.

She laughs. 'That's an impressive impression. But then you mightn't have found it too difficult.'

I threaten her with a wooden spoon that I lift from a dish beside the range. 'Careful there, Flannery, or I might have to deal with you.'

'Did you know I'd be here today?' she asks, letting the humour drop. 'Is that why you called?'

'Yes.'

She sits beside me, and we are silent as we wait for the stew to finish heating, secure in each other's presence now the admission has been released, safe now in the knowing. After a while, I get up and take two bowls out of a cupboard and put them on the table.

'C'mon,' I say, 'let's sample this Flannery stew.'

We sit in the kitchen until evening, and I don't leave until she sings for me.

'Don't forget Dublin,' she calls as I go.

I walk into town and visit Frank Boyle. Frank has settled down with his girlfriend, and has bought a house. He takes two cans of beer from the fridge.

'Great value out at the border,' he says.

He shows me around the house: the tidy living room, the matching furniture, the new sofas and the cushions, the video player, the study full of boxes and no books, the bedroom and the fitted wardrobes. I sit on a chair in the kitchen, and drink the beer from a glass.

'Galway Crystal, that,' he says. 'Nice, isn't it?'

'Yes. Lovely.'

I used to enjoy calling on Frank. Teenage Frank moved with a kind of bounce, and he spoke with energy as if he was trying to throw his words over some sort of height. His talk was filled with the latest music news; it was all Ian Dury or The Cure or The Pixies. But things have changed, I guess. We were such great friends, the four of us: Éamon, Conor, Frank, and I. Big Robbie joined us late. We spent the time together. We talked on the important details: school, the first division, the top forty, the hassle at home; the wish for a flat of our own, for money, for the weekend, for women. So many times we did nothing, but we did it together — the trips to nowhere, the football in the street, the bags of chips, the buying of clothes and records, the first few pints, and then the next few, the discos and the fun on the dance floor, the sweat-soaked shirts dumped on the floor for the mothers to revive for the next week, and so much to say. And I would stay in their houses and they would stay in mine, and we would talk and talk and talk. And as I sit at Frank's kitchen table, I know the years have passed. Not many, but enough.

I thank Frank for the beer, give my wishes to the girlfriend, and leave.

The price you pay for empire

IT IS MID-FEBRUARY. I AM HOME AGAIN, AND WE ARE IN THE COOKING POT. We are all there: Éamon, Big Robbie, Frank, and I. Conor is home from London, and introduces Sebastian, Kate, and Flossie — three English work friends he has brought with him. We drink beer, we tell stories, and we sing songs. We try to remember the songs we wrote in Conor's room, with Conor playing the guitar, Éamon writing down the lyrics, and Frank doing his funny dance. We sing the few bars we can remember of each tune: 'Crossmaglen Maggie', 'Jenkinstown Joe', and our favourite, 'I'm originally from Annagassan, but I'm all right now.'

I hear a call as someone enters the pub: '*An Phoblacht — Republican News! An Phoblacht — Republican News!*' I turn; it is Slime Sloane. It is a weakness in the IRA that they allow arseholes the glory of association. Are we that desperate? It is a flaw that proves time and time again to be fatal, and it fucking annoys me. Sloane doesn't see me. I look behind to see that only Bobby Boyd is keeping cover at the door. I rise quickly and take the back of Sloane's leaning leg. As he falls I catch him, turn him, march him to the door, and throw him out onto the pavement. Boyd has already scarpered.

'You'll pay for this, Donnelly,' Sloane says, as he rises. 'You're a dead man.'

I walk to him, grab him, and talk into his ear. 'I don't think so, Slime. Good people haven't died for dickheads like you to ride the bandwagon. Now fuck off.' Well, what can I say? I know I should have ignored him, but this guy just pisses me off. He's too much to take.

I return to the group and relieve the tension by telling a few school stories of Sloane. Later, as the drink settles, there is talk of Britain and Ireland, of colony and rebellion. I don't contribute much. After the politics and history, we leave the pub and go to a nightclub, where we dance until early morning, and afterwards we sit in the small lounge in the hotel. Sebastian has had too much to drink and is unwell. Conor and Frank help him to his room, and then they go home. Kate and Big Robbie have disappeared, and I am left alone with Flossie. She is a big, chatty girl with big blonde hair and big red lips. She is all talk, she is all curves, and she is all flushed flesh. In the absence of others, desire — which has peeped from the shadows all evening — steps forward. I stand and I take her by her hand, and we ride the elevator to her room. The door is still closing as I push the blouse over her shoulders, as she unbuckles me, and I am lost to the pleasure and the frantic hunt. I push her across the carpet. I fold her meaty body over the bed as I take her from behind.

'Hello, English girl,' I say, as I come out of her and run my hands down her shoulders, her back, and her hips, her raised arse offered and ripe.

I ease between the two halves of the round as she takes a quick breath, and as I enter, the breath catches in her throat before suddenly leaving her.

'Jesus Christ, Johnny,' she says, when I finish and roll onto the bed beside her. 'You might have asked.'

'Well, chicken,' I say, as sleep takes me, 'that's the price you pay for empire.'

A question for Anna

'ARE YOU GOING TO THE DOCTOR? WHAT ABOUT THOSE HEADACHES? Are you looking after yourself, Johnny? Please be careful with the drinking.'

I am at home with my sister. Anna worries excessively about my head. After the fall and the hospital and the burying of Cora, it was Anna who attended to my convalescence at home. For Anna, like most, my broken head was easier to deal with than my broken heart. With my head, she felt that she could do something tangible, say something useful, help. But my heart? I'm not sure about repairs for that kind of stuff. I think some broken things cannot be fixed.

But in many ways, I am a new man. In many ways, I am not the person I used to be. Just days ago, the surface of my skin was covered with a completely different set of cells, all of which have since died and flaked off. Just months ago, I had a completely different bundle of red blood cells flowing through me. Constantly, my body regenerates, replacing old cells with new ones. I am not alone. I am not superman. This renewal is shared with the rest of the species. But my brain is different. Not different from the rest of the species, but from the rest of my body. At birth, my brain came fully equipped with one hundred billion nerve cells. That's a lot of cells to get your head around — literally. There are more cells in my brain than there are grains of sand on the long beach at Schilling Hill. Again, I am not alone. Again, I am not superman. This wonder, too, is shared with the rest of the species. The same can be said for pitiful Bobby Boyd —

and that really is difficult to get your head around. And because the human brain is so complicated and has so little capacity to regenerate it is vulnerable to the effects of damage. This I learned in the hospital as doctors spoke of 'acquired brain injury'.

'It's not just the injury caused by the initial trauma and the action of the brain inside the cranium; the damage from bleeding and augmented pressure within the enclosed skull can indeed be more consequential,' said the doctor to Kathleen Donnelly. *Oh, sweet hallelujah*, I thought. 'Whatever the injury,' the doctor continued, 'the material, cognitive, and behavioural effects can be multifaceted and complicated and may, I suggest, require monitoring and treatment.' Mam nodded away to him like a buck rabbit doing the business, but the doctor might as well have been speaking Japanese.

I didn't need any monitoring or treatment. I just got better quickly, and everyone kind of forgot about my head and moved on with the other things that people move on with. Everyone, except Anna. Everyone, except Anna and me.

'Do you ever wonder, Anna, about how our brain works, about how we come to think the things we think?'

'Do you mean you, Johnny? Or the rest of us?'

'I mean us all, Anna.'

A nun in the park

I AM AT HOME IN DUNDALK FOR THE WEEKEND. IT IS DRY AND IT ISN'T TOO cold, and in the early afternoon I sit with Clara and watch television.

'Hey,' I suggest, 'let's get the bikes out and go for a spin.'

Within five minutes, we are on the Ramparts Road and heading for town. We take Distillery Lane, Jocelyn Street, and Roden Place. We cycle along the pavement at the Town Hall, on alongside the courthouse, and on we go around the benches of the Market Square — where I can't help remembering Cora — and on into Clanbrassil Street, and north to Church Street and Bridge Street, and there we turn east along the river. The tide is in, and the water is high and wide. I pass Siobhán McCourt, who is out running — she does this athletics stuff — and I stop and chat, and she insists on joining our modest adventure. So she sits on the bar of my bicycle and teases me, and we continue as a threesome to the park. We decide to go in and let Clara cycle around; it will be safer than the roads. A nun is entering the park as we reach the gate. She greets us all and says hello — I know her, as she is part of the same rosary militia as Mam. We return the greeting with smiles, and allow her to enter before us, and I watch her as she goes away from us with the light load of certainty carried in her gentle stride.

To fight life's battles, the Irish have two weapons in their arsenal. The first of these is the Mass, which is used as a kind of marker for any beginning or occasion or end. There are Masses for arrivals, weddings, and funerals — although I've never really understood the appropriateness of a Mass for a funeral, when the recently deceased gets but a brief mention in an event that celebrates another thing altogether, although nobody seems to mind but me — and there are the peculiar Irish Masses for the opening of a new football field, or club or community centre, or a new bus, or a fishing boat, or a factory, or anything at all. At school there were a gazillion Masses for all kinds of stuff: beginning of term, end of term, mid-term, for those students beginning, for those students leaving, for visitors, for exams, for more exams, for all the important saints, for all the Irish saints, for holy communions, and for confirmations. It was mad stuff altogether. And then there is the House Mass for no particular reason at all, other than a change of scenery perhaps. It's a bit of a travelling road-show, that one, like the Mission Mass that travels parish to parish and carries a bite, and lets the priests go those extra few yards into ecstasy and deliver the threat of damnation. And there is the Annual Novena, when half the country descends on Saint Joseph's for nine days, with Masses running around the clock, and stalls outside selling everything but Coca-Cola and popcorn. The Irish would be lost without the Mass.

The second weapon in the national arsenal is the rosary. This is a very useful weapon, as it can be carried concealed, needs no preparation, and can be whipped out pretty much anywhere and without any notice at all. The Mass is for everyone, but the rosary attracts the fundamentalist in the way that any kind of communal chanting seduces the vulnerable. Mam is a big fan, and belongs to a group who gather in Saint Joseph's to pray for the sins of the world and to end all vices, heresies, wars, vanities, and misfortunes through the intercession of miracles, the Celestial Court, and the abundant, divine mercy of God. You couldn't make it up, and I have to admit that it does add to Mam's vocabulary. The nuns of the local convent attend this group, and Mam has them around to the house every month. I try to avoid being home for these visits, as the thing can descend in no time from a cup of tea and cake to Mother Marys and Sacred Mysteries, and it's not good to be caught up in those.

I salute the nun as she walks away on the left path to circuit the park clockwise, and we pedal right towards the bandstand. We get off the bicycles, and I sit with Siobhán on a bench while Clara plays behind us in the bandstand. Farther along the path, on another bench, a woman sits alone. There is a dishevelled look about her, and beside her is a supermarket shopping-trolley filled with plastic bags.

'Parks attract the oddballs,' I tell Siobhán. 'As do churches and libraries. I think what attracts them is the opportunity to sit somewhere.'

'But I run in the park. And I go to the library. And I even go to Mass on an occasion. Are you calling me an oddball, Donnelly?'

'Not you, McCourt, no. But you know the type — men who talk to themselves, and women who keep cats.'

'Women who keep cats?'

'Yes. Not the woman with a cat or two, or even three — though three is borderline. But the woman with half-a-dozen or more. You know the type: troubled, unbalanced.'

'That's all right, then. But I can get troubled myself, now and again. And I need a bit of rebalancing, if you know what I mean.'

I laugh. 'Siobhán, you are ...' I look to her face, where her eyes are wide open and her mouth carries that seductive draw of hers. 'You are some lunatic.'

'Yes,' she says, rising, 'but that's what you like about me. Go on, admit it, Donnelly. You have a thing for me, don't you? I know you want me — I see it in your eyes.' And she runs off to chase Clara around the bandstand.

And she's right. That is what I like about her. And, yes, I do think of her. And, yes, I do want her. But that's normal, isn't it? I sit and

[173]

daydream in the park until I feel her approach again behind me.

'All right,' I say, raising my two hands. 'I admit it. There are times when I see you there in Saint Joseph's, when I'd love to bundle you into one of those confession boxes and slide the curtain. Or, even better, stretch you out on the altar and worship that lovely body of yours.' And the thing is said as I am turning to give her my own dirty smile, and it cannot be unsaid or withdrawn, though I try. But it is too late. And the best I can do is to kill the smile, but even that is too late.

There is nothing to say now but the obvious. 'Ah, hello, Sister Immaculata, it's yourself.'

She gives me a look that the devout reserve for the worst class of sinners, and she bolts away, and I see that within the first stride the rosary beads have been released from concealment as she departs with another intercession to pray for.

Broken skies

DELANEY WANTS A CHAT, SO I AM HOME AGAIN AND ON MY WAY TO THE house near the town centre. Beneath a broken sky, I take a walk through Dundalk. I pull on a Carroll's No. 1. I realise that these streets are etched into my earliest memories. I remember it was here that I walked with my grandmother. She was a great woman. She was born with all the good things: she was beautiful and warm, her only nature was kindness, and she was full of hope. But martyrdom is a cloaked jester. It pushes as many as it pulls. It allures and it deceives, it wears many forms, and to its charms many fall. Anna McMahon — my grandmother — was one who fell.

She was a pretty girl. Not just pretty, but she had a special quality that some girls have, though in each it can be different — girls can be tricky and slippery. I have a photograph of her as a girl, and she had a touch about her that was beyond Ireland. With her dark hair and her Spanish skin, she carried an allusion of other lands. She was a reader as a young girl. 'That one always has her head in a book', she told me her father would comment to others, he prouder of her reading than he was of her beauty. She read everything she could find in the town. She read of other worlds, and she dreamed of escape. She wanted love and adventure, but what she got was a baby in her belly and marriage to Charles Reynolds. She was just sixteen years old.

It broke her father's heart that Anna ignored his desperate pleading. He begged her not to take with Reynolds; he warned her that Reynolds offered nothing but a false hope. But Anna was hungry for a journey, and she was too young to see the shallow depth of Reynolds's charm. She let him take charge of her dreams, and Charles Reynolds erased those dreams from her life. He lost his charm, and she lost her hopes, as he took to the drink and she took to survival. She bore him twelve children, and love and adventure became very distant shores. But she refused to let Reynolds rob her of her intelligence, though he set about it as if it were his life's purpose.

What escape Anna managed was confined within the town of Dundalk. She studied the town's story and streetscape, and years later she transferred this to me. When I was young, she took me for walks through the streets of the town as she delivered tender lectures, hard facts of history wrapped in a soft tale — who lived and who had lived, who had done what and who had done what to them, the injustices suffered here, and the battles for Ireland there. She knew every street and building, and she had a story for them all. She never tired of telling the same yarns, and I never tired of listening. In the olden days, she would say, townsfolk spent their days here around market stalls and fairs: 'There was great comings and goings altogether. But there would have been a lot of horseshit about. I mean real horseshit. Not the kind your grandfather comes out with.' And we would both laugh at that. She told me that joke a hundred times. I could see it all then, as if I walked that market myself. I can see it all now. But those days, like Granny Reynolds, are gone.

Boggy fields

I AM ALONE WITH MY BOOKS IN STATION ROAD, AND AS I READ I RUN MY left index finger along the scar by my left eye.

It's all falling apart now, Bob says.

'It is not. We remain on target.'

Target? What target? What are you on about?

'To free Ireland.'

He laughs. *Ireland is free.*

'Not all of it.'

Depends what you mean by free, then. Is life in Leitrim so much better than in Fermanagh?

'That's not the point.'

It is the point. It's just not your point. Isn't that the truth?

'Ireland has a right to its own self-determination. All Ireland.'

Self-determination? Well, you'd know all about that. Ready to kill again, are we? Have you no shame?

'Shame for what?'

Not for what. For who.

'Cora didn't understand the necessity of battle. Maybe that comes with having a pure heart.'

Is that a fact? And what about your heart?

'Fuck off, Bob.'

It is late February. I am in Crossmaglen, and the gun is set. I am ready. I have given the time and labour to master the elements of my craft

— my other craft, sniping, not carpentry. Delaney drilled me through the training, and he drilled me again and again and again. 'The ability to shoot,' Delaney said, 'will make you good, but knowhow in the field will make you great. And it will keep you alive. Nous, cunning, and field-craft will win the day over gullible squaddies. You be the fox, John, and those soldiers will be chickens in a henhouse. You just wait your moment, and some stupid bastard will always leave a door open.' And so I learned how to invade the enemy, how to get inside the range, how to find ground and to know that ground, how to survive in that ground and maintain the shot, how to observe everything, how to absorb everything, how to see without being seen, how to mask the attack, how to plan the escape, and how to get away. I learned that how to get in and how to get out are as important as any other thing, and that without this preparation the best shot in the world will not succeed in what I do. And, at all times, I have options on a way out. I have read of German snipers in Normandy who shot from church steeples — and with great effect — on the attacking allies. But those snipers made a fatal mistake: they left only one route out — down the steeple — and when this was eventually choked, the German was dead. The Japanese snipers shooting from trees made the same mistake. I studied their mistakes. I studied everything; I studied long. And, in this pursuit, I was a good student. 'Don't make second place', the American told me. 'Second place is a body bag.'

I take the shot, and a pink spray bursts into the morning air.

It is lunch time on Saint Patrick's Day. In every village, flags are flying, children are marching, pubs are full of drinking and singing, while I am lying in the mud of Forkhill waiting on the lead of a patrol to move towards the junction of Church Road and Bog Road. Finishing a conversation with a local, he steps into the crosshairs. And I kill him.

[178]

It is May, and I am at the long table on Station Road, helping her with her study.

'You don't love me,' she says, my German girl.

'I absolutely love you.'

'Not like her. You don't love me like you love her.'

I hold her in the bed that night as she sleeps on me. I hold her body and I touch her hair and I kiss her head. But how do you love someone more?

In early June, I take her to the airport in the Renault, and she returns home for the holidays.

A bullet to the brain is a dramatic event. The body can go mad. An explosion of electrical signals can blast the limbs into a frenzy — the body flailing, trashing, and leaping — before the eternal silence. I saw a body do that on a shooting with Delaney, and since then I aim only at the torso. It is bigger target, and there is less drama. But today the memory revisits, and I am forced to push it away and clear my thoughts of everything but the present. It is late June and I am in Newtownhamilton. Below me, a British army private looks out over boggy fields. I see his face in the scope, how relaxed he is — he has just shared a comment with a colleague. He doesn't see me. He doesn't know he will never see anything again.

Cause

I am in the Donnelly family kitchen.

'Why do they kill? For what cause? For Ireland, is it?' Mam stalls mid-motion, the peel falling into the basin, the bright, naked flesh of the potato glimmering under the running tap. She isn't talking to me. She knows I am there, but her speech is addressed to the radio news-report. 'Another soldier shot,' she continues, now looking out through the kitchen window. 'Another boy to go home to his mother dead. Another boy to die in Ireland. And for what? Nothing? What difference will it make?' She shakes her head. 'Who would shoot a soldier? And why? For us? What good could that possibly do? Who would do such a thing? Who would do that?' She blows a long breath and shakes her head again. She draws the blade across the potato, and another strip of peel drops to the basin as she lets the enquiry fall.

I watch Mam in the way she watches me. I guess that's what mothers do — the watching thing, the wondering. It goes back to my very arrival, Mam's watching. Mam frequently tells of my birth; she says it was too unforgettable.

It was 1971. It was early morning, and she knew she was fading. Her pain had long since breached the walls of impossibility, and as hope fell away she held only to prayer. Exhausted, she asked God to help. And as first light broke the final dark hold of night, I was born. Mam considers the birth a miracle; but, again, that's what mothers do, I guess. Mam considers us all to be blessings from God. There were disappointments: five times she felt the cramping and the blood

[180]

flow in the early weeks of pregnancy. The babies, when they came, came in two bursts of two. There was just over a year between the first two boys, Peter and Declan. And five years later, Anna. The first three were all summer babies; I was born in the spring. Mam says that there were moments in that long night of delivery when she was sure she was going to die. Yet she still remembers the light of the morning. It was, she says, a beautiful day to be born. And, after me, there were no more babies and no more pregnancies: the doctors took her womb.

Mam tries to keep a devout home; she tries to send her children off into life with at least some religion in us. I try not to break that delusion — what would be the advantage in that? Mam manages a frugal household; the poverty of her childhood has never left her. I know she wished better for us than for her. I know she has tried to ensure that her boys and girl do not surrender hope and childhood for a factory punch-card.

Mam's own mother was softer, more at ease with the world. 'You can take that gassun anywhere,' Granny used to say of me. 'An answer for everything and the lure to go with it. It is Orpheus himself we have among us.' Mam has never quite known what her mother meant by that.

Yet Mam has been curious about me — I guess she never could make me out. Enough times, she has seen the withdrawal to contemplation; she has seen the daydreaming. I hope she thinks they are as harmless as the private ramblings of Dad. It is a blessing for her not to know better. It is a blessing for her not to know who would shoot a soldier.

I get up from the table and leave as Mam pulls a familiar tune from her head, and I am closing the kitchen door as Kathleen Reynolds begins to sing.

Among bramble and weed and moss and stone, I wait and watch the foot patrol approach the village. I am ready. I will wait for the last soldier to cross the gable-end of the low cottage, and there I will kill him. Behind me the falling sun is dropping to green hills, and below me the golden light of evening raises the village as if offered by the gods.

It is July, the month when the lost tribe of the empire decorates itself in the remnants of colony, and parades to the beat of yesterday's drum. Banners of settlement and plantation are unfurled and aired: it must be a painful thing to be lost just a few steps from home. Of course, it isn't home; nobody there wants them either. Their only homeland is the crumbling bridge of the union. And as we attack and break that bridge, these settlers — who barricade themselves from this land and people and culture — wither and rot and ferment and drown in their own poison.

Orange and red and blue will fly, the bunting of an allegiance to an entity that no longer exists. But no monarch or statesman salutes their lonely parades. Who would want that? Who would want them? The only cheer and applause is their own. And each step they take is a step on the road to extinction.

I cannot be seen. From any distance, the old stone wall carries nothing but an ancient mark. The wall is long broken, the fallen boulders scattered, and here and there the twisted wood of gorse, haw, and hazel bursts through the stone. Across the fields, where once gates stood, are empty spaces; cattle move freely on the hillside. Where stone has fallen and cattle will not graze, the wild weed of Ireland has taken refuge: nettle, thistle, foxglove, and fern embrace me. It cannot be told where ground ends and where I and gun begin.

I watch the soldiers spill from the field. In three groups of four, they move toward the village; overhead, an army of rooks gathers in growing numbers in the falling air. I know every distance and journey: from the cottage it is a four-minute hike to the sanctuary of the barrack's high steel-gate. The soldiers move quickly, quietly, and, in the silence, anxiety hangs about them like a putrid air. The final effort of a patrol is a concoction of elation and vulnerability. This, too, I know.

'*Was du ererbt von deinen Vätern hast, erwirb es, um es zu besitzen,*' I have read from Goethe. 'What you have inherited from your forefathers you must first win for yourselves if you are to possess it.' I know this; they don't. So they can march all they want, and carry all the colours they want, for the ground beneath their feet is green. Always was; always will be.

I am patient. Success is a dependant of the time taken, so I have devoted time to it. From time and observation, I have forged knowledge; one by one, I have learned the things of the earth. I try not to daydream. It is the most difficult of all the disciplines, but Delaney has taught me, has insisted, not to let the mind wander. So when thoughts of the unreal invade the real, I take to studying that which surrounds me in the fields of South Armagh.

The first soldier of the last group of four reaches the cottage, seeks the defence of the cottage gable-end at his back, signals to his comrades, and takes the corner low with his gun raised. Soldier two follows. I ease the safety on my Barrett to off. I steady my breathing as soldier three takes the corner wide, crossing from the near ditch, turning, twisting, covering front and back as soldier four bolts to follow. I know that the last soldier must cover the patrol from a rear attack. I know that the soldier will pause before taking the corner. I breathe in. Soldier four runs along the cottage wall. I breathe out. Nearing the turn, he stalls, rolls on his heels, pushes his back against the stone, and twists with raised gun to the rear fields as the air explodes and a loud fracture tears across the valley as if the land itself has been whiplashed by an unseen giant.

[*183*]

The soldiers plunge to the ground, and fight to bury themselves into the very earth, before a pause, before they rise again in jabbed increments to cover the western hills in wide, frantic sweeps with their rifles. They call to each other, their voices choked and rushed, as fear grapples their windpipes. Twelve names ripple through the air in the village street. Twelve names: eleven voices. They find him — his torn body on the ground, his flak jacket punctured and useless against a projectile that smashed blood, sinew, and bone deep into the stone of the cottage gable wall.

The alarm is raised. Reinforcements will pour from the barracks, roadblocks will cover all exits, and helicopters will sweep the countryside. But it is too late: I am gone.

Oisín and Niamh

IT IS SEPTEMBER, AND SHE IS LEAVING ME. I STAND BEHIND THE HIGH airport fence and watch her as she walks across the tarmac and boards the airplane.

'It can't be worked,' Mila said, the evening she arrived back in Ireland, just two days ago. 'You can't be worked. You will never love me like you do her.'

I pleaded with her to stay, to give it another go. I said that I would try harder, that I would build around her. But it was over. We both knew that she was right. Yesterday we drove to the Burren, parked the Renault under the rocky layers of Mullaghmore, and walked to the lake. We threw bread to the swans, put the blanket on the ground, and drank coffee poured from a Thermos.

'I'm sorry,' I said.

She didn't say anything. What was there to say?

We lay together last night and I held her close, and kissed her hands, and kissed her head. I awoke in the morning to her scream — we'd overslept, and we were late. And so we grabbed her bags and ran, and I drove to the airport door, and she ran for her flight. There was no time for goodbyes, no futile gestures, no final words.

I drove out around the airport, and I watch her now through the perimeter fence as she enters the airplane and disappears from me. I hold the wire with my fingers stretched, and I see her, the German girl, almost as tall as I am, young, her face with all the fullness of innocence, her long, brown hair swept back where some of it has caught and hangs on her shoulder, her mouth slightly pouted with full, pink lips. And between her high cheeks and her high forehead, her brown eyes look right at me.

It is three years today since she died. I drive to Dundalk, and allow the dark evening to invade on the east wind before I walk to the mount. I gather broken wood to add to the kindling that I have brought with me. I wonder where she is? Could someone as great and beautiful as Cora Flannery be just gone? Or does she exist in a somewhere else? It's what we do, isn't it? We create make-believes to give ourselves hope against the misery of the obvious. They provide a false hope; we know that, but we believe it anyway, like Cora believed in Tír na nÓg. Or is that different? I don't know. I think about that for a while, and as I do I remember the first time I heard the story.

'What is Tír na nÓg, Granny?'

'Tír na nÓg, Johnny, is our Irish otherworld. It is the land of eternal youth. They say it is an island somewhere off the west coast. They say it is home to the Tuatha Dé Danann, the first people of Ireland. In Tír na nÓg, there is no sickness and no death, no sorrow and no pain. There is only youth, beauty, music, and happiness. But Tír na nÓg can only be reached by invitation, and whoever goes there can never return. Will I tell you the story of Oisín and Niamh in Tír na nÓg?'

'Yes, please, Granny,' I asked her, my two feet swinging.

'And so it begins. Are you listening?'

'I'm listening, Granny.'

'The leader of the army of the Fianna was the great Fionn Mac Cumhaill,' she said, embarking on the tale. 'With Sadbh, the daughter of Bódearg, the King of Munster, he had a son. The name of this boy was Oisín. The boy grew to be handsome and to be a great warrior. He was also a fine poet and spent many quiet days writing. One day, Fionn and Oisín were hunting by the lakes in Killarney when a mysterious cloud approached over the water. From the cloud a magnificent white stallion appeared, and on this stallion was a beautiful, golden-haired young woman. The girl was Niamh Cinn Óir, daughter of the sea-god Manannán Mac Lir, and she wore a striking cloak of green silk. She told Oisín who she was, and added that her father was the King of Tír na nÓg. *Away with me*, she said, *to the land foretold, of peace and plenty, where none grow old. Away with me to the land of song, of beautiful things, where none do wrong.* No one could refuse an invitation to Tír na nÓg, and so Oisín joined Niamh on the white stallion. *Fear not, Father*, he said, *I shall return and bring you news of this adventure.* Fionn watched as Niamh and Oisín disappeared into the cloud which moved away and dropped below the horizon.

'Tír na nÓg was everything Oisín could ever have dreamed of. It was a magical place; there was music everywhere, people laughed and sang, and strange, plentiful crops filled rich fields. Niamh and Oisín were very happy together and they had three children.

'One night, Oisín dreamed of Ireland and the Fianna, and the next day, thinking of his dream and remembering his promise to his father, he asked Niamh if he could go back to visit his homeland. Because she loved him so, Niamh agreed; but she had a great fear of his journey. So Oisín returned on the white stallion with a warning from Niamh not to dismount onto the earth of Ireland.

'Oisín was delighted to see the green hills of Ireland once more. But he was concerned when he noticed that the great forests were missing and that the people were much smaller than the men of the Fianna. He returned to familiar places; but these, too, he found strangely different, and no one that he had known could be found. Only when he questioned someone did he realise that during his decade away in Tír na nÓg, three hundred years had passed in Ireland. 'Oisín was greatly saddened. In his sorrow, he continued his tour of

[187]

his old lands. One day, he came across some men struggling to move a large rock with iron bars, and knew this work would have been easy for the men of the Fianna. He approached the men, leaned down, and moved the rock with one hand. But as he did this, the saddle-strap broke, and Oisín fell to the ground. As soon as he touched the ground, the handsome young warrior became an old, dying man. Quickly he told his story to the men, and later they took it to a scribe to have it written down.

And that is how we know of Tír na nÓg,' Granny said, kissing my forehead, easing the embrace, and rising to attend her pots on the scullery stove.

I light a fire under the single oak. In the fire, I see a girl with eyes the lightened green of an August meadow. I see a girl with pale skin and golden hair. I see a girl with red boots tied with green laces.

'Is the fire to please the gods?' Aisling says, walking across the mound. 'Or to damn them to hell?'

'Gods? I thought one God made us,' I say to her, as she sits on the low wall. 'Don't you believe anymore?'

'I believe still. I believe for her. Cora had great faith.'

'She believed in Tír na nÓg, not God.'

'Isn't that the same thing?'

'Maybe. I haven't thought of it like that before, although that makes sense if you think in that kind of direction. But isn't Tír na nÓg the land of eternal youth? The land where nobody grows old and nobody does wrong, a kind of heavenly paradise invented by the early Irish, like other early peoples who came up with similar ideas of another life beyond this, an afterlife, a better life? And do you know something, Aisling? I think it might exist. I think Tír na nÓg is where we all go in the end, in the very end, as death takes us and the body stops and the mind closes. In that very last moment, we all retreat to our own Tír na nÓg. We all fall to a construction of our memories and dreams, a mixture of all the love and beauty experienced in life, imprinted with our greatest hopes. We are only there for a fraction of a second, if measured from this world, but as that fraction of a second is the last fraction of a second of our life, we are there forever. It's not real, of course; not really real, if you know what I mean. And it won't matter, and we will never know whose version is right: yours, or Cora's, or mine, or my Granny's. But, I think, in the end, we all go to Tír na nÓg.'

'And where is God in all that, Johnny-boy?'

'God? What god? Your god, the Christian God? That kind of a god doesn't exist, couldn't exist. Don't you think, Aisling, that this whole religion thing comes from some innocent prehistory, when nobody knew anything, so they made up some consolation thing and believed it? And now we — who do know something, and because what we do now know isn't good, isn't what we want — fool ourselves into the same damn consolation, believing that those guys from prehistory, through some power or magic or intuition that we have now lost, knew something, and that they were right all along.'

I look out into the dark evening.

'Isn't it all too simplistic? Isn't it all too un-fucking-believable? The only way a god makes sense is if you believe too many answers and don't ask too many questions. And I can't be with all that praying and stuff, all those rules and sins. I can't take that shite.'

'The church and God are two different things, Johnny. Don't confuse them. Are you near conversion yourself yet? Has there been an incident on the road to Damascus you want to tell me about?'

'No, nor on the road to Ennis, neither. I'm still an atheist. I don't believe in any of it — it's all a load of crap. The whole thing is nothing but a fantasy, a kind of madness. It is nothing but simple need. No, I don't believe in any of it — thanks be to God.'

She laughs. 'That's my Johnny. But I won't give up on you just yet.'

'What is the church anyway, Aisling, but a hierarchy to the vanities of men? The higher you go, the finer the robes, the taller the hats. You couldn't make it up. The whole charade is incredible.'

She laughs. 'There are many churches, many faiths, and the faults of any church are the faults of man, not God.'

'If there is a God,' I resume, 'why is *He* obsessive about devotion, about praise, about worship, about belief? Why does *He* place the highest value on belief? Why must people believe? Why would God be jealous?'

'Those assumptions are the delusions of man. It is our tribal instinct — we organise ourselves around an us and a them. We've taken God down to our level.'

'An us and a them. That makes a lot of sense, Aisling, I'll give you that. But if God does exist, why must *He* be a he? Only a woman could have given birth to the Earth. And only a woman could then let it be. Men can't do that. Men are compulsive adjusters, manipulators, developers. Men take something and make something else from it. They want to force elements and shapes to their own will; they are not capable of clean creation. There's only one thing men can make from nothing.'

'What's that, then?'

'War.'

'Well, I guess most don't think it through, Johnny. The church is as vulnerable to the weaknesses of man as you and I. The absence of the church has led to no utopia — only to the neglect of the individual. Show me the ideal churchless state, if you can.'

'A vigorous defence, Aisling Flannery. Fair dues to you. Yes, idealism and extremism are the default remedies of man. But they only lead to tyranny. And that's a sad thing, isn't it?'

We stay until the fire dies. I lift a burned ember from the ashes and let it cool in the grass. When it has cooled I lift it again, wrap it in my handkerchief, and put it into the pocket of the Dunn & Co. We leave the mount and walk down to Níth River Terrace, where we drink tea and talk, and later she hugs me as we part.

'Cora had something extraordinary,' I say to her as I leave. 'It was as if she still carried an ancient way, as if it was born with her.'

'Cora was a special girl. She was Ireland made flesh.'

'Yes, I have thought that, too,' I say. 'Maybe it was Ériu, or Danu herself, who walked a while among us.'

The distance of fall

IT IS THE SECOND OF NOVEMBER, AND I AM IN NEWRY WITH THE BARRETT. It is said, by those who read and speak and teach and preach about war and battle and all that stuff, that snipers are a kind apart: that we don't play by the rules, that we are solitary players in a team sport. Well, perhaps that is so. I don't play, and, anyhow, I don't know what the rules are. Rules aren't drafted by those who lie in cold ditches and put bullets into strangers. But, then, this is no sport, and I don't care what they say. I bring fear and confusion to the enemy. This is my role. With this gun, I will take ten lives. I will level the score. And I shall be independent. There is as big a threat to me from this side as there is from the enemy. My survival relies on concealment and self-reliance. My success depends on cunning, patience, fortitude, observation, and accuracy. Delaney has taught me well. I shall remain calm. I shall maintain attention to detail. That is, of course, if I don't go mad. There is that risk. I laugh, quietly, and settle.

I found an old booklet on sniping in the library in Dublin: *Rogers' Rules of Ranging*, from 1757 — it wouldn't have been called sniping then. *Don't forget nothing*, it begins. *Have your muskets clean as a whistle. Act the way you would if you were sneaking up on a deer. See the enemy first. Never take a chance. Don't ever march home the same way. Take a different route back.* Well, whatever they called it, not much has changed — that's still good advice. Rogers, I remember, did go on to add: *Let the enemy come close enough to touch, then let him have it. Then jump up and finish him off with your tomahawks.* Well, what a way to finish. He must have been some lunatic altogether.

I have read, too, of Simo Häyhä. When Russia invaded Finland in the winter of 1939, Simo took to the snow and the woods with his rifle. One by one, he killed over five hundred Russians. Five hundred and five confirmed kills by one man and one gun. He used only an iron sight to keep low. He compacted the snow in front of the rifle so as not to give himself away, and he kept snow in his mouth so there would be no vapour. With these small methods, he took all those Russians. And every time he got in, he got out. Simo Häyhä: the greatest lunatic of all.

Then there were the Germans. Under Himmler's orders, there was a snipers' programme and code: *Fight fanatically. Shoot calm. Your greatest enemy is the enemy sniper. Outsmart him. Become a master in camouflage and terrain. Survival is ten parts camouflage and one part firing.* That's about it, all right; that's the secret wrapped up there. But that's the Germans for you; it's no surprise that they got it right. Well, I have read their programme and code, and I have learned their lessons. *Vielen dank, Herr Himmler.*

The American once spoke to me of Marine Sergeant Carlos Hathcock — 'Gunny Sergeant Hathcock', he called him — a docile young man from the cotton fields of Arkansas who found the theatre of the jungle of Vietnam to be his calling. Hathcock stuck a white feather in his bush hat, put his eye to the scope of a sniper's rifle, and took ninety-three Viet Cong lives. War can do that: it can change a lapdog into a wolf. And it isn't about the killing; it is just that the job fits.

I clear my mind and focus on the gun. Today is a long shot. I am eleven hundred yards from the target. That's thirty-three hundred feet; that's a long way. It is the longest shot I have tried. At this distance, neither he nor I can look on the other with the human eye. Only through the scope do I see him. Delaney says that now I am showing off. Maybe he's right, but who cares? I measure the range, the elevation, the temperature, the humidity, and the wind speed. I calculate my scope settings, but he is so far away I need to allow for the curve and rotation of the Earth. For this shot — as well as field-craft and marksmanship — I need to be a mathematician. This stuff really can blow the head off you.

Through the scope, I watch every detail of the patrol. I select my target. I watch his movement, his pace of step, his gait, his habit of fixing his collar with his left hand. I watch how far and how fast he bends over to speak with drivers of cars he is stopping and checking. Some hardly bend at all and remain upright and stiff and speak to drivers from an arm's distance. Some drop to their haunches and speak to drivers face to face. Some bend and get close. He bends. He bends and chats, and that is a mistake. He gives me what I need most: he gives me time.

At this distance, the round will take two seconds to travel from gun to target. That gives the target time to move. I have two choices: either I need to calculate where the target is going to be after the shot and aim there, or I need to take the shot when I guess the target is in a static position. His bending and chatting give me the advantage.

I look to my notebook to confirm the calculations. The round will leave the rifle at two thousand eight hundred feet a second. Gravity then plays a part. At three hundred yards, the round will drop seven inches. At six hundred yards, it will drop sixty-eight inches. At eleven hundred yards, the round will drop three-hundred-and-sixty-nine inches. That's over thirty feet. That's the arc of trajectory the round will take, that's the distance of fall, that's what I allow for, and that's what I calibrate into the scope. I adjust for the crosswind from the south-west. It is consistent between me and the target, and there are no intervening or contradictory crosswinds and no major buildings providing a wind shadow. Although the round will slow, it will still be travelling at one thousand feet per second when it hits the target. At that speed, and with this calibre round, the bullet will not just go through him — it will rip him apart.

A car stops, and he bends. I put the crosshairs on him. I take the shot.

It is mid-November, and I am on my bed reading in Station Road.

You're going great guns now, Bob says, as he sits at my desk. *I suppose you think you are a great fella.*

I ignore him.

It is late November, and I visit Delaney.

'Word has it that there is a new leak,' he offers. 'Myself, I think there is a British operative living in town — someone under cover. A brave man, but that would make the most sense. Though I have no idea who he is, or who he is talking to.'

'Any word on who's the tout, Chief?'

'Not your concern, John,' he answers. 'Stick to what you're good at, and let others take care of that.'

'Just curious,' I lie.

It is December and cold, and I am near the village of Keady. I have the gun readied on an eight-man army patrol. I am caressing the Barrett to the step of a lance bombardier. I stay on his stride and I count myself down: five, and four, and three, and two, and one, and ... His steady pace has killed him.

I am in Ennis, and walking home to my room on Station Road. Delaney intercepts me, and walks alongside.

'I have him,' he says. 'Another SAS superspy wannabe. For queen and country and the glow of the battalion spotlight. Where do they get these clowns? But it will be for our tomorrow, John, that he will give his today.' Delaney stops and looks to me. 'He's working out of the snooker hall, pumping it for all it's worth. He's running under the name Baldwin, says he's a returned emigrant. The naivety of their eager foolishness is almost enchanting. But he must think he is making progress: he's staying, and he seems to have some weekend meet thing going. I'm going to leave him in place — there's no danger to us in there — and I'll start feeding him to our own end.'

'Who's he pumping?'

'Not your concern. You leave this alone. Anyway, what would anyone there know? It would be nothing but bluster; it would be all blow. Best stay away from there for a while.'

'Well, I don't play much now; just the odd game with Éamon or Declan. Sloane and Boyd are regulars there, though.'

'Stay away from those two fools, John, do you hear me? Let them be. They know nothing, and can do no harm.'

'All right, Chief, I hear you,' I lie. 'But touts have to be taken out. And in full view. It's the only way to stop them. We need to make a declaration. Anything else is playing their game.'

'I've made a decision, John. And we will all abide by it. It behoves us to take maximum advantage of all potential. You are to stay away from that place, and that's that.'

Behoves us. What the fuck does that mean? I watch the man below the trilby walk away — there will be a car waiting in another part of town — and I wonder why he came all this way to tell me not to do something.

It is a weekend in mid-December, and I spend the afternoon and evening in the snooker hall. I play a few games with Declan, and after he leaves I play on my own. Sloane and Boyd come and go, but they don't stay when they see me.

'Who's this chap that's fairly new here?' I ask Jimmy, the man in the booth who has managed the snooker hall for the fourteen years I have been coming here. 'The chap who plays regular, but is someone you'd never seen before a year ago?'

'I'd have to think about that one, young Donnelly,' Jimmy answers, sucking his lips into his mouth. 'Leave it with me.'

Later he approaches. 'Just couldn't think until he walked in. Dark-haired chap, table four. Moved home from England. Baldwin, his name is.'

'Good man, Jimmy,' I say. 'And, Jimmy,' I add as he goes to walk away, 'not a word.'

'Understood.' He nods and returns to his post behind the counter. I watch him go, and he turns to me and nods once more before continuing with his work.

I play for another hour and then leave. I cross the street, and I stand in a back alley where I can watch the snooker-hall door. I open a fresh pack of Carroll's No. 1, and I wait. Just before ten o'clock, he leaves and walks towards the carpark at the rear of the nearby hotel. I hear a car door open and close. An engine starts, and a car drives off.

It is Sunday evening, and I am again in the alley across from the snooker hall. Again, just before ten o'clock, he leaves and walks towards the carpark at the rear of the hotel. I stay in the alley. I hear a car door open and close. I hear no engine. I wait. I hear the door open and close again. He must be coming back. I wait, but nothing. *Shit, what is going on?* I risk walking out into the side street and I keep close to the wall of the hotel. A couple of drunks are sitting on the steps of a service entrance, a bottle of cheap wine on the concrete between them.

'All right there, our-fella?' one of the drunks asks, and I see he is about to rise and approach me. I look to him, and he retreats to the step.

I approach the carpark. I see a dark outline in a car. It is him. He is parked in the far corner, in the shadow of a high wall. I look above me to see that the car is out of view of the hotel security cameras. He bends forward and I see a second outline; someone is with him. If they turn, they will see me. I draw back. After twenty minutes, I hear a car door open and close, and an engine start. I walk into the side street as the car drives away from me. I look around, but whoever got into that car is gone. I run into the snooker hall and note who is and isn't there. Sloane and Boyd are missing. It must be Sloane; it must be that slimy bastard.

I am in the Imperial Hotel café reading the *Irish Times*. It is the Saturday before Christmas, and the streets of the town centre are full with shoppers. The hotel, too, is busy and I don't notice her enter.

'John Donnelly, isn't it?'

I look up. It doesn't take long to place her — not many have the look of Loreto Delaney.

'Johnny,' I say. 'Your father is the only one who calls me John.'

'Broke from the same stone you two are, though you both hide it well, for some reason.'

I don't say anything. Loreto Delaney had already moved to America when I first started visiting the Delaney home, and I only met her there once.

'Yes, John, Mother tells me everything. His star pupil, you were, Mother says. He had high hopes for you.'

'Sorry to disappoint you all.'

'You don't disappoint me, darling.' And she sits down across from me and unbuttons her coat. I am remembering the one time we met. The dark coat she wore then has been replaced with one of a new design. Her black hair is cut to a neat bob, and surrounds her powdered white face. Her fiery-red lipstick assaults me with her every word. There is a fragrance in the air, a sweet mix of carnation and vanilla.

'What is that perfume?' I ask.

'Bold, aren't you?' she answers. 'It is *L'Heure Bleue*. By Guerlain. French, of course.'

'How's California treating you?'

'I'm getting divorced. Infidelity, it's a messy business, John. I just need a break, so I've come home to Mother.'

'I'm sorry for your troubles.'

'No trouble, really. The pleasure was all mine. The trouble is all his.'

'So how is Mother?'

'Absent, to tell the truth, John. The two of them are away in Tipperary for a few days. Left me all alone, the selfish buggers. Isn't it just fine that I have you now to mind me?'

And she gives me that look, that same look she gave me all those years ago when I met her as I walked home from Mass in Saint Joseph's.

We have lunch together in the hotel restaurant where we drink Margaux — her insistence — and she tells me about California.

'I'd love to go to California sometime,' I confess.

'You must, darling. You simply must come to visit me.'

After lunch we move to the hotel bar, where we order another bottle of Margaux from the restaurant, and the dark evening has already rolled in when she suggests that I walk her home. Arm in arm, we walk the short journey to the redbrick house near the town centre. She leaves the curtains open, so the street light filters through the window blind, and she shows in yellowed tones above me, naked, as she pushes down on me.

'Just to walk me home, you were,' she says, as she drives her fingernails into my chest. 'Just to walk me home, you bad boy,' she continues, as she pumps with intent becoming fury, her hips crashing down on me, her black bob flying, *L'Heure Bleue* in the air — French, of course. 'Just to walk me home, John Donnelly. You are a bad, bad, bad boy.'

It is Sunday evening. I am in the dark alley across from the snooker hall. I have a black woollen cap rolled back on my head. I have a half-full wine bottle in the pocket of an old coat I got in a charity store. In the other pocket I have the Glock.

I know they will meet. People are susceptible to habit — it helps to keep things simple and tidy, but it can also help to get you killed. I wait. Just before ten o'clock, he leaves the snooker hall and walks to the carpark at the rear of the hotel. I hear a car door open and close. After five minutes, I hear another door open and close. I pull my black woollen cap down low on my head, and I move. I walk into the side street and quickly walk to the carpark. I reach into my side pocket and remove the bottle of wine. I enter the carpark staggering, and drift towards the far corner. I see two people in the car. I think I recognise the shape in the passenger seat. It's that fucker, Sloane. I approach the car. I drop an empty can of Coke that I'm carrying, and start to kick it around the carpark. I sing the song of a drunken man — all long, whiny notes, and joined and incomprehensible words. I drift nearer and nearer to the back of the car as I kick the Coke can through the carpark. I see that he watches me in his rear mirror. I drop the wine. It crashes on the ground. I raise my left arm and cheer. The driver door opens, and the Englishman steps out.

'Fuck off, mate.'

I turn with the Glock raised, and I hold my arm straight and level as I shoot into the centre of his chest. He falls back into the angle of the open door and the car frame. He is holding on to both, his mouth is moving, but he is falling. I put another round into his chest, and walking to him I put another through his head.

I walk quickly to the passenger door. Sloane is rigid with fright.

He stares straight forward. He does not look at the dead Englishman, and he does not turn to me. I pull the door open with my left hand and raise the gun quickly to Sloane's head. He pisses himself on the passenger seat. I have to get a look at the bastard's face one last time. Countless good Irishmen have died or have been imprisoned because of touting bastards like him. Sloane was always going to try to sell too much. It ends now. I drop my head as I shoot.

After, as I walk away, I see him again and again and again. He was trembling with panic and fear, staring blindly forward and calling for his mammy, my mammy. It wasn't Sloane. It was Declan Donnelly, my brother.

Three cheers for Johnny Donnelly

It is the end of December, and I am in Crossmaglen. As I wait, I try to put Declan's head out of my mind, so I try to remember the words of the songs I wrote with the boys, and I am singing 'Crossmaglen Maggie' as a guardsman walks into the scope.

It is New Year's Eve, and I am at home in Dundalk. In the early afternoon I walk to Seatown, where I sit at a bar. After two beers I move to another bar, and after more beer I move on to another. *You wouldn't do a bad thing, would you?* I hear those words again as clear as I heard them on the walk over the mountain, as clear as I heard them when I stepped out of the alley and walked towards the hotel carpark, as clear as I heard them in Keady, Newry, Newtownhamilton, Forkhill, and Crossmaglen. *No Cora,* I told her on the mountain, *I wouldn't do a bad thing.* I have killed eight with the big black gun, and where are we? Where am I? I have almost done what I set out to do. And what now? I have no fucking idea what now.

I move on to town and sit in another bar, and then another. The Chief says there is a push for peace. But we both know a ceasefire will finish it; there will be no way back for a generation. A ceasefire will suit them more than it will suit us. It always does. They will reclaim the roads, and from there they will infest the communities. The war will be cut off at the throat; it will suffocate. Republican leaders are pushing for a political settlement. Bastards. It's more of the same — another turn of the wheel. They grow old and they tire of the struggle. They'll settle into the administration of the very thing they fought against all their young lives. The only fight left in them is the one among themselves in the rush for office. The wisdom of maturity, they will package it, their self-delusion. But wisdom is earned only by the very few, and it has nothing to do with maturity. Their kind of wisdom is just the absence of battle; it is the loss of the will to fight.

I order another beer. Two girls approach the bar, and I sneer thickly to the nearest. She tells me to get lost.

'How perfectly ironic,' I say to her. 'I couldn't get more lost.'

Both girls look at me. *Yes, have a good look now; roll up, roll up, and take your fucking tickets.* They move off to the other end of the bar. I call to the barman for that beer. There is chaos at home: Mam is hysterical. Dad is distraught. Declan mugged and shot dead along with some poor Englishman — shot dead for a few pound, shot dead by a drunk looking for cash. The police wouldn't let them see the body. They asked me and Peter to identify him. How mad and cruel is that? Mam says she will never get over it, that she just wants to die with the shock of it. 'Why would a drunk have a gun?' Dad asks. 'What in the name of God is the world coming to?' Anna has been crying ever since. People came from everywhere to sympathise; I didn't know most of them. They all shook my hand — the same hand that held the Glock, the same hand that shot Declan.

I hear a voice: *Pissed his fucking pants, mate. Pissed his fucking pants.* I look across to bottles of whiskey on the back shelf of the bar, and I see Bob watching me from the glass between the Powers and the Black Bush. He doesn't speak. He just stares at me. *You think you know something, Bob? You know nothing. You think you have answers? Who the fuck are you, anyhow? What did you ever do to make a difference? You're not real, you're nothing but a gobshite, a total fucking gobshite.* Where's that beer? Cora wanted to teach Irish, to marry and have children, and to picnic at Cúchulainn's Castle; Declan wanted money and a move

[203]

to Blackrock. Well, that's what Blackrock can do to a man. It was never a good idea. The English have always been able to buy a few Irish — that transaction defines us all. Mila wanted me to love her. It shouldn't have been difficult; she is a beautiful girl. But I fucked it up. Only a fool would let a girl like that go. She offered all; I gave her next to nothing. Aisling wants me to see her in Dublin. I don't think that I can go there — that would be just too fucked-up a thing, wouldn't it? Funny-boy Frank wants a new car; he's not so funny anymore. Éamon is still trying to find Éamon; it could be a long search. Big Robbie wants a drink, and then another. And Conor just wants someone to love, someone to go home to. Good old Conor, the only one to step through it all and come out the far side still himself.

I leave the pub and walk home. I pass Saint Patrick's Cathedral. I stop under the arch of the sandstone gateway, and I piss on the wall. Bless me, Father, for I have sinned.

Good man, Johnny.

I step into the churchyard to see Bob standing above me on the plinth of the cathedral, his two arms held wide in the green overalls, the red rag hanging loose from the pocket.

Well done, Johnny Donnelly. You did it. You showed them. There's a holy exodus of the British from Ireland — the great army of her majesty is in full retreat. Many are dead from your hand alone. You killed them. You killed them all. Well done, Johnny, you have saved Ireland. You are up there now with Cúchulainn the mighty. Fair dues to you. Three cheers to you, Johnny; three cheers for Johnny Donnelly. Hip Hip Hooray, Hip Hip ... No, wait. Hold the bus. The British are still here. Everything is as it was. Nothing has changed; nothing at all. Johnny, Johnny, Johnny.

I walk on. I pass the Georgian townhouses in Roden Place, the railed steps and brass nameplates of doctors, dentists, and solicitors. I approach the junction with Chapel Street, where the Home Bakery sits on the corner, where Mam still queues on a Saturday morning for two French loaves and an almond ring, and, every so often, a chocolate or pineapple cake. I change my mind and decide to return to Seatown for more beer. I walk out on the road. I don't look. I don't want to look. I don't see the car. Well, maybe I do.

The pure in heart

IT IS NOT A TOTAL BLACKNESS, BUT A DENSE AND DARK FOG. THE FUNNEL of light is remote and distant; but, though the light is weak, I know she is with me.

'Easy, Johnny, do not worry, I am here.'

I hear her voice, a clear voice, like music — every word a note. And that voice? Cora? But Cora is in heaven. I can't be in heaven, can I? Maybe purgatory? Maybe Mam's rosaries have won an indulgence? Good old Mam. A shadow crosses through the fog. I reach out. I touch her arm. Her arm moves, gently, slowly, and her hand takes my own arm, and I feel it as it moves down to my hand, stopping to cradle my fingers and thumb.

'I did a bad thing.'

'Do not worry, Johnny. I shall stay with you.'

But I cannot stop. I have to let it all out. And I do. I keep talking, and the hand that holds keeps holding.

There is only silence when I finish. Her touch leaves me, and I am not sure if she is still there. Then I feel her again as she touches my arm and as her hand moves down to take my hand.

I try to look up to her. But as she stands over me, I can only see her shape and not her detail. 'Are we in heaven?'

'Maybe, I don't know. Maybe Ireland is heaven?'

'I hope not,' I say with a heavy effort. 'If it is, we are all doomed.' And I feel a kind of falling away as if I have stepped onto non-ground.

'Tell me something,' I say, as I fall. 'Have you ever met Sister

Josephine up here?'

'Sister Josephine?' she answers. 'A right funny nun she is.'

'God help him.'

I hear Aunt Hannah.

'God help us all,' I hear Mam reply. 'Of all the things to do in the world, you'd think the one thing he wouldn't do is step out in front of a car.'

'Was he drinking?'

'No, I don't think so. Still, you never know. Who could blame anyone for turning to drink after what happened to Declan.'

'Did he ... ' Hannah hesitated. 'You know ... do it on purpose?'

'I don't know, Hannah. I never did know what that boy was thinking.'

'Who knows what anyone is thinking, when the truth be told. Is Mister Delaney still waiting outside?'

'No, Hannah. I sent him and Anna home. He never had to try too hard for people to love him, this boy. He hadn't to try at all.'

'He never did get over that girl. Such a thing to happen. Who could have thought we would see so much tragedy? I'm driven demented by the whole thing. I declare to God but we won't be right again after these terrible weeks. God help us all.'

'Straight out in front of the car, he walked. Straight out, they said.'

'Will you give over, the two of you?' I call out.

'Jesus, Mary, and Joseph,' Hannah exclaims. 'Are you awake, son? Are you all right? I thought you were out cold.'

'I was. It's a miracle.'

'Still a smart alec,' Hannah says. 'Well, that's good to see.'

'Where am I? Have I died and gone to hell? Will I have to listen to you two forever?'

[207]

I see Mam look to Hannah with raised eyes and then slip out of the room.

'There's been an accident. You've been run over, Johnny. But you're alive, thank God. Haven't we all had enough tragedy for one lifetime?'

There is no answer I can give to that, so I don't comment. Mam returns with a doctor.

'Good morning, Mister Donnelly. How are you feeling?'

'Hello, Doctor. I've no idea how I'm feeling, to be honest. What's the damage?'

The doctor looks to the two visitors.

'You'd better not ask them to leave,' I tell him. 'The curiosity would kill them.'

With long and uncommon words, he tells me that I have a broken arm and a broken leg.

'You are a lucky young man,' he says. 'You must have nine lives.'

Many lives, actually, I think, but I say nothing.

'There is no apparent head trauma,' he continues. 'You were a bit delirious last night. Because of your history and your condition, we kept you under observation; but just at the point of your greatest anxiety, you had a visitor and you settled after that. The nurses kept a very close eye on you. We moved you here this morning.'

'A visitor?' I ask.

'God Almighty,' Hannah says. 'But I can't handle this at all. He's rushed into ICU, he put the heart out of us all, poor Anna and Mister Delaney and that Flannery girl are beside themselves all night out in the corridor, and he's in there chatting up the nurses. Pretty young things, were they? That'd be just like him, a complete scoundrel. Probably got them running bringing him tea and toast, too, knowing him.'

Anna visits in the afternoon.

'Well?' she says.

'Well, yourself.'

'So what happened? Were you drinking, Johnny? What have I told you?' She sits beside me on the bed and lifts a piece of toast from the bedside tray.

'What's wrong, Johnny?'

'Nothing. Just a bit of an accident. I'm fine, really.'

She pauses, and I look away; and in her sympathy, I guess, she lets that enquiry go.

'And what happened with Mila? She was such a lovely girl.'

'She slipped from my charm.'

'Well, this should put an end to your gallop. You have to be more careful, Johnny. And no more drinking sessions. Do you hear me?'

'Yes, Anna.'

'I got engaged, Johnny, last month. We were going to tell everyone at Christmas, but then … you know, it didn't seem right. It doesn't seem so important now.'

'It is important. I'm very happy for you. He is one lucky man. When's the big day?'

'Not for a couple of years — don't know when exactly. You wouldn't miss it, Johnny, would you, my wedding?'

'No, Anna,'

'You better not,' she says leaning into me, holding me, suddenly sobbing. 'So don't go walking out onto any more bloody roads then.'

Later in the evening, Conor Rafferty visits.

'You better not have come all this way for me, Rafferty.'

'I was just passing.'

'Stick your head out the door there, will you, and see if the tea-lady is about, and ask her to bring us a pot of tea?'

'Will you feck off, Donnelly,' Conor protests. 'I will not.'

Nevertheless, the tea-lady is summonsed, and we enjoy tea and toast together.

'Don't ask,' I warn. 'It was just a bit of an accident, and let's leave it at that.'

'I wasn't going to. By the way, Flossie sends her regards.'

'Well, if you insist on knowing,' I tell him, 'I was fluttered drunk. And that's the whole truth of it.'

'I didn't insist on anything,' Conor defends. 'By the way, I'm driving down to Ennis tomorrow with Anna. We're collecting your things. You will need them at home — you won't be back there for a while, Johnny. I'm sorry.'

'Thanks, Conor. Always the thoughtful one. Say hello to Bella, and tell her I'm fine and not to worry. Tell her I shall come to see her when I can.'

The tea-lady arrives with the wheelchair that I'd asked her for.

'If anyone asks, you didn't get it from me,' she says.

'Right you are,' Conor replies, confused.

Conor helps me out of the bed and into the wheelchair, and we set off around the hospital as I tell him of our mission. We search the corridors and waiting rooms before making a tour of the grounds. We don't find her. We pass the morgue where Peter and I identified Declan as he lay on a steel table beneath a bright robe. I look to the cross on the morgue door.

'I have an idea,' I tell Conor. 'Let's go back inside.'

'What idea?' he asks.

'Just a mad guess.'

We reach the hospital chapel. Conor pushes the wheelchair through, and he leaves as the heavy door closes behind me. It is a small chapel, five pews each side of a central aisle. She is kneeling in front of the altar.

'Why was I searching for you?' I say, rolling towards her. 'Did I not know that you would be in your father's house?

She stands, turns, and steps into the central aisle.

'Have you come to ask me not to tell?' she says as I near. 'Not to tell those things you told me?'

'No, I'm not worried about me. I'm worried about you, that I gave you this thing. I'm sorry.'

'Isn't it too late to be sorry?'

'I'm not sorry for what I did. I am sorry for you, that I gave you this burden.'

'Thing? Burden?'

'Killings, then. Do you prefer that?'

'I prefer none of it,' she says hard, but then immediately softens. 'Will you tell me something, Johnny? Tell me about the beginning? How did it all start?'

'I don't think I can do that.'

'Please, Johnny?'

So I begin with the hunger strikes and the useless sacrifice of it all; how it angered me, and how I was determined to act and to make a difference; how I wrote the essay as asked and handed it to the teacher; how I began the visits to the teacher's house for the private lessons; how the conversations grew, evolved from observations and comment to plans and intent; how there was no great epiphany, no one moment of decision, no beginning; how it was just as it was meant to be — that I was born for the battle, that I was ready-made for the gun.

'But you were just a boy,' she says. 'What was it about those soldiers?'

And I tell her about the checkpoint and the standing in the cold rain and Mam's shopping scattered on the road, and I tell her about the big black gun.

'Tell me about the first killings.'

And I tell her about the .303 and the three long years of learning and then the Armalite, the Kalashnikov, and the Heckler & Koch, and how I spent a year on each and how I took them all into action, with some actions successful, some not. I tell her of the early attacks with Delaney. I tell her of the wet day in Ravensdale, the first one on my own, and then the others. But that, for me, it was all preparation for the big gun.

'Tell me about the American.'

I tell her about the gun coming, and about the training, and how we went to a remote island because we couldn't use the regular grounds at Ravensdale or Inniskeen. How, at the end of it, I remained on the island as Delaney stalled the boat halfway to the mainland. How it took a single shot — no loose ends, Delaney insisted. How the American was wrapped in chains and dropped in deep Atlantic waters.

She asks that I light a single candle, and I watch as she kneels on the first carpeted altar step below a high cross.

'Do you pray for him, the American?' I ask.

'Yes. I pray for him. I pray for you. I pray for that teacher. Tell me what you did with that gun.'

And so on it goes. I tell her about the Barrett, about what it could do, how all the training had been for it, how I planned to bring fear to the enemy, to change the war; and, one by one, I tell her how I killed in South Armagh. I tell her about Forkhill, Newtownhamilton, Keady, and Crossmaglen. And after each telling, she asks that I light a candle, and I watch as she kneels and prays. 'Blessed are the peacemakers,' she says, 'for they will be called children of God.'

'They were not peacemakers,' I tell her. But she ignores me.

'Tell me about the Englishman.'

I tell her about the waiting in the dark alley, how clearly I heard Cora's words as I stepped out into the side street and walked to the hotel carpark. How there were two people in the car, including that fucker Sloane, I thought. How the driver door opened and the

Englishman stepped out. Fuck off, mate, the last thing he ever said. How I walked quickly to the passenger door. Sloane rigid with fright. How it was not Sloane. How it was Declan, my brother.

'Blessed are the poor in spirit,' she says, 'for theirs is the kingdom of heaven.'

'There was no spirit in what they were doing,' I tell her. 'No spirit at all. Only greed and betrayal. *Honra y provecho no caben en un saco*, as the Spanish proverb goes. Honour and money don't belong in the same purse.'

Once more she ignores my protest and asks that I light a candle, and once more I watch as she prays.

'Tell me about Cora.'

'Please don't ask me to do that.'

But she insists — and the righteous ground is not mine to defend — so I tell her about the girl with golden hair that fell in soft waves over one side of her pale face. I tell it all. And I tell about how we walked that last day together on the green mountain; how we sang in the pub; how we went home in her daddy's car; how the next time I saw her she was dead.

'Cora was a special girl,' she says.

'Blessed are the pure in heart,' I tell her, 'for they will see God.'

I light a candle for Cora as Aisling Flannery kneels and prays at the altar.

Aisling

THE FOUR MISERABLE WEEKS OF FEBRUARY HAVE PASSED. FEBRUARY IN Ireland is cold and wet and grey, and the only succour to be found in the month is that it is not January and that the days begin to lengthen. Patches of spring can occur, but they are passing rather than permanent, taunts rather than hints, and without determined attention these small freedoms can go unnoticed. The first ten weeks of the year in Ireland are a challenge to mood and spirit; depression hangs heavy in the cold, damp air. Our national day in the eleventh week is a celebration of survival.

I have healed: my leg and arm are again strong. Well, almost strong — or, as my dad says, *Enough to be getting on with* — and in the eleventh week I pack the Renault 4 with two bags. A half-dozen books rest on a blanket on the rear seat, and Aisling Flannery sits beside me in the front. Eddie and Hannah stand by the garden wall while Mam forces a bundle of sandwiches and a flask of tea through the open car door.

'You didn't need to do that,' I say, and I salute Dad, who watches from the front porch.

'Right you are, Son,' he calls. 'Mind how you go.'

I look to Aisling, who is studying a road map. Aisling's hair is dark, and her skin is infused with honey and sunshine — I don't know how that has come to be, how she can have skin like that. There is so little direct sun in Ireland that we have evolved with a skin mostly free of pigment, so we might capture what little light there is; but Aisling hasn't, and the result is a total blessing. And her eyes? Aisling's eyes are pure poetry, for they are the rustic gold-speckled brown of the fading fern of autumn.

'You are some lunatic,' I say to her, and her face brightens. I reach over and take her hand.

Conor Rafferty says that the Flannery girls were God's special creation, that He made them with His own hands, that they had a unique purpose, that they came straight down from heaven. But somehow God got distracted, took His eyes off their placing, and they ended up in Dundalk. Maybe he's right. It makes sense to me — I mean, if I was to believe in God and all that stuff. How else could it possibly be? Cora Flannery had golden hair, her eyes were green, and her skin was pale; but there are times when I am with Aisling, and I am off-guard, or my attention is elsewhere, or I lose myself, and just for a moment I forget things and I think that she is Cora. It passes quickly, this kind of moment, but when it passes it leaves damage — it's a fucked-up kind of feeling.

We are on our way to London. Aisling has a two-week break from college and has the free use of her cousin's bedsit in Chiswick while her cousin, a newly qualified biologist, is away in Boston on a course.

'Will you come?' she asked me.

'To the heart of the enemy?' I answered. 'Sure.'

My only doubt was my Renault 4 — it's a long drive for the old girl. We decide to take a chance with the car and to take our time with the trip: three days to get there, a week in London, and three days to come home.

'To her majesty's great and glorious realm we go,' I say, 'Rule Britannia.' And we leave, throwing goodbyes behind us.

'How far will we go today?' Aisling asks.

'How far is salvation?' I ask her.

She looks down at the route. 'I don't see it here on the map.'

'What about happiness and contentment?'

She looks down again. 'No, I don't see them either. But that's the problem with maps, Johnny — they sometimes don't show what's straight in front of you.'

'Let's decide en route,' I say, and with that resolution she settles into her seat.

We drive to Dublin and take the afternoon ferry to Wales, and it is evening and dark when we arrive in Holyhead. We decide to stay there for the night, and we find a small bar-hotel near the port. I had asked Aisling to keep an eye out for something with an inexpensive look about it. This place fits the ticket.

'One room or two?' I enquire, as we lift a bag each from the Renault.

'That I'll leave to you, Johnny-boy.'

Up until I stand at the reception, I don't know myself what I shall ask for. I settle on one.

'What's the point of two?' I say to Aisling as I take the key. 'That would only be a waste of money.'

'Well, we shouldn't waste money, Johnny,' she says, holding my arm as we climb the stairs to our room.

We wash and return to the bar for dinner. The bar is empty, but for two men sitting by the counter and a middle-aged man in a crumpled, dirty-grey suit sitting alone and reading a newspaper. We take a table by a burning coal fire. We order fish and creamed potatoes.

'Have you any Margaux?' I ask the barman. I don't know why I ask for Margaux — the thought has just rushed at me.

'Never heard of it.'

'Well, thanks be to God for that,' I tell him. 'I didn't want it anyway.'

We order a bottle of white wine, the cheapest the hotel has, and the barman leaves us, carrying a doubtful frown.

[216]

After the meal and the wine, we return to the room.

'What side of the bed do you want?' I ask her.

'I don't know.'

'Okay then,' I say. 'You take the left, but don't be sneaking over my side just to get a crafty feel of me.'

She laughs and marches off to the bathroom to change.

The whole performance is ludicrous. This journey — for us both — is an awkward crossing, and we are like two nervous teenagers fumbling our way into courtship.

She returns through the dark room and enters the bed. I hold her hand, but in the night I know that I have pulled her close.

'I think you might have tried to seduce me when you were asleep,' I say to her in the morning.

'I did not.'

'I think you did. It's nothing to be ashamed about. It could happen to any woman.'

'I'm sorry, Johnny. And you being real nice and minding me so well, holding my arse all night.'

I laugh and rise from the bed.

We have coffee in the hotel bar, and afterwards we walk along the main street and buy newspapers. We leave Holyhead and drive to Bangor, and stop for petrol and tea and a fried breakfast, and thus fuelled we push the Renault south and east through wet, green valleys on the A5, through the grey-stone villages of Betws–y–coed, Corwen, and Llangollen, and then through the small town of Chirk, where the colours and architecture changes, before crossing into England near Oswestry.

We decide to stop for the night again, and so drive into Shrewsbury and book into another cheap hotel. We wash, and sit and read our newspapers, and later we walk around the medieval town centre and eat in a small Indian restaurant at the end of the high street. After the meal, we return to our room in the hotel, where I hold Aisling as she sleeps on me.

'England's not so bad, is it, Johnny?' she asks when we wake.

'Not bad at all,' I reply, remembering our walk the previous evening. 'They have been careful to preserve their history, I'll give them that.' Shrewsbury is a beautiful town, and I haven't seen such urban care and sensitive development in Ireland. We are poor planners, and Irish towns are exhibitions of our inadequacies.

'Everywhere has a history, Johnny,' Aisling says, holding me. 'Everywhere and everyone.'

Aisling's words are echoes, and I pull her close and kiss her head. But I know that we are not alone: I know that every word between us is carried by the ghost of Cora.

We leave Shrewsbury in the mid-morning, pointing the Renault towards London. Approaching Birmingham, the traffic builds on the multi-lane motorway. Our little car is surrounded by huge, roaring trucks that all appear to have the need to get somewhere fast.

'This is more like it,' I say. 'I knew England would be a hell hole.'

She laughs, before going quiet for some minutes. 'Do you think we have a future, Johnny?' she asks. 'Together? Are we the future?'

'Yes, Aisling.'

'And you won't go back to war, will you, Johnny?'

'No, Aisling,' I tell her, though I am unsure of either answer.

We stop at a service station for lunch and to give the Renault a rest. We buy sandwiches and coffees, and stand in the cold air. It begins to rain, so I run to the car for the Dunn & Co and scarf, putting the coat over Aisling and wrapping the scarf around my own neck. Aisling turns and kisses me, and I am unable but to remember the first kiss with Cora as we sat on her garden wall as she, too, was draped in the Dunn & Co coat. I stand close to Aisling, and she rests against me as we eat and drink and watch the motorway traffic come and go.

We make it to London, and after some route misadventures find our way to Chiswick, stopping in the high street for a quick look. Though it's in such a big city, this place has the look and feel of a village, and it immediately appeals to us.

'I like it already,' I tell her.

'Yes,' she says. 'Me, too.'

Arlington Gardens is a tidy avenue of large Victorian townhouses next to a village green, and we park in the drive of number seven. The house has been divided into five bedsits, with Aisling's cousin's on the first floor. We enter a large room with a bay window that has a view down the avenue to the green. A double bed is on the near wall, a kitchenette with sink is built into the far-right corner, a grey-marble fireplace below a gilded mirror is on the right wall, and a writing desk and bookshelves align the left. Beyond the bed and before the window, there is a pink couch.

'You know something,' she says, 'it's not unlike your room in Ennis.'

'I forget sometimes that you've been to Station Road. Thanks again for getting my stuff — that was good of you and Conor. And you got to meet my Banner friends.'

'Well, they all seem to be very fond of you,' she says, though she and I know she speaks only of Bella.

'Yes,' I tell her. 'They are a simple-enough lot. They are easily pleased.'

'Is that a fact now, Donnelly?'

But I don't allow the enquiry to go any further. I move to her, and kiss her mouth and then her face and her neck, pushing her back onto the bed, where I untie her boots and pull away the socks, kissing the arches of her feet and her ankles, unbuckling her jeans as she fights to get the duvet across her. I untie my own boots, kicking them across the room, and I join her under the duvet, where we undress

[*219*]

each other and I kiss her body, and I kiss her face and her mouth as I enter her, and she holds me tightly as I slide on the edge of a glorious madness. In the night, between sleep and awareness, she pulls me to her and I enter her slowly, and I stay inside her, barely moving, and I am somewhere in some sort of dreamland.

We stay in Chiswick for a week and do all the things tourists do in London — except for visiting the royal attractions, which would have been a step too far for any decent Irish republican. In the evenings we walk along the river to Hammersmith Bridge before returning along the high street. We drink beer in the Robin Hood and Little John bar, where we meet Irishmen from every corner and creed. And it is here that I notice a strange paradox: all that separates us Irish at home is abandoned in the English capital. And I don't know why. Maybe it is because to the English we are all the same anyway: we are all Paddies. Or maybe, and more likely, the relocation is a good excuse for the Irish to relieve themselves of a useless weight.

At the end of the week we return by the same road, stopping again in Shrewsbury and Holyhead before taking the ferry home to Dublin, where we spend a day in cafés and bookshops, and we sleep that night in Aisling's bed.

I am walking on a rutted and unkempt road. High hedges fold in from the sides; blackthorn, hazel, hawthorn, and elder reach into the roadway and long shoots of bramble bow from ditch to ground. A shaded tunnel is formed by the growth, and I shiver as a bitter breeze blows through me. I see brightness ahead — some sort of a clearing— and I rush to it, but the bramble catches and rips as I go. I pull the bramble from my legs and arms, cutting my hands and limbs as the hooked thorns grip and tear. I break into the clearing to see an untidy hamlet of decrepit cottages. A terrible silence hangs in the breeze. I approach the first two cottages. The doors are open, the cottages are cold and empty, and a rotten stench clings to everything. Burned, broken pieces of furniture lie in fireplaces long unused. I see nothing but abandoned desolation, and the sick patina of damp death is layered on everything like a pox. There are a half-dozen cottages at varying angles around what at one time must have been a hamlet square. The square is now a thicket of thistle, nettle, dock, and ragwort. Saplings of birch and ash and oak rise through the weed. I go to every cottage. All have the same cold and empty neglect. I try to look past the hamlet into the land, but there is nothing to see but grey fog. A single drooping willow rises from an embankment at the end of the hamlet, and I walk to it through tufts of wet, rough grass.

As I near the willow I see a shape on the ground by a mound of earth. It is a woman: a filthy, dishevelled woman, barely covered by clothing of dirty, torn rags. Her hair is clumped with mud; her face is creviced and littered with weeping sores. Her small body is but lumpy bones wrapped in a thin, grey, broken, skin. Is she dead? I approach her and see that a tin can is tied around her neck with some rough cord. Slowly she moves her head towards me. She is alive. She faces me. Her eyes are colourless and blind, and when she opens her mouth, her teeth are a rotten yellow and black.

'*Líon mo chopán,*' she says in a coarse choke.

'What?' I say. 'Sorry, I don't speak Irish. *Níl a lán Gaeilge agam.*'

'*Líon mo chopán,*' she repeats, before closing her eyes and exhaling a long, wheezy breath. Her left arm falls into some sort of a pit beyond her, and then her body slides towards it. I rush to her and catch her, and I am holding this frail, human mess of grey, creviced skin over lumpy bones when I look down. The pit is some eight feet long by perhaps three feet wide, but it is dark and deep, endlessly deep, and as I look into it I am pushed, and I fall into that deep darkness and I am rushing down past sides of black earth. I fall a long way before I feel a hold on me, and I am suddenly caught and suspended as I near my crash with the bottom. My vision clears, and I can see through the blackness and I can see movement below me. I stare around me, and look across a vast space. Down here, the walls of black earth cannot be seen, and the pit appears infinitely wide in all directions, and in all that space there is a great mass of writhing, naked, human bodies. They are all alive, all their faces are contorted in agony and terror and madness, and they are all screaming. Great swells, like great ocean storms, move through the mass, and waves rise and fall, bringing other bodies to the top and pulling the top bodies down to some awful depth. Many see me above them, and point and roar and curse and spit and reach to pull me down.

'No,' I shout. 'Please, God, no.'

And I am lifted away and up with an almighty force.

By the pit's edge, I lie on the muddy embankment by the frail, dying woman. She has her hand on my chest.

'You wouldn't do a bad thing?' she asks. 'Would you, Johnny?'

'Cora,' I shout.

I wake up to find Aisling holding me.

'It's just a dream, Johnny. It's all okay.'

I don't sleep for the rest of the night. I can't. What was that about? Where was that? And who was that? It was so real. Was that Cora?

'What does *Líon mo chopán* mean?' I ask Aisling in the morning.

'"Fill my cup". I think it's an old Irish expression for "Come fill my dreams". Why?'

I don't tell her. *Fill my cup*. That's mad. What could that dream mean? And was it a dream at all? But as I ponder, I begin to think that it wasn't Cora I met. I mean, not only Cora. I think the whole thing was Ireland. But, what would that mean?

It is the late afternoon of the next day when we arrive back in Dundalk.

'We'll go to visit Cora, if you like,' Aisling says, sensing a new mood about me.

I think about it, but I can't get it to fit right. I leave Aisling and the Renault at Níth River Terrace, and I walk alone to Castletown Mount. I am unsure what to say to Cora. How do I tell her what I have done, what I do, with her sister? And all this after I preached the mighty sermon to Cora that a man can only love one woman, that love is commitment, and that commitment is to one and to one only? And, as I walk to her, I wonder if anything I said was true.

Pilgrimage

I SEE BOB BY THE GATES AS I AM LEAVING CÚCHULAINN'S CASTLE. I GREET him as I jump down from the stile in the stone wall, 'The dead arose and appeared to many.'

Ha ha, he answers. *Very funny.*

'Long time no see, old-timer. Did you get lost?'

Me? No. What about you?

'Totally,' I answer him. 'I thought you'd disappeared on me.'

I am disappeared. I don't exist at all. You do know that?

'Is that a fact now? Can you prove it?'

He just nods and asks, *How was the trip? How are things with the other Flannery girl?*

'The trip was mighty, Bob, and things are very good with the other Flannery girl. But Cora said something once when we spoke about this old war of ours. She said, "I know the cause is right. But then, at the same time, it's not right." I know now what she meant. That is how I feel about Aisling Flannery.'

All the same, Bob says, looking at me with one eye wide open and one partly closed, like some sort of lunatic inquisition, *it didn't slow you down too much.*

I laugh and Bob laughs, and we walk together towards Castletown Cross, where the country lane meets the main road.

The next day I decide what I shall do, so I sort out the finances — I am still on sick-payment since the accident and can survive well if I spend cautiously — and I go to see Aisling. I leave the Renault with her and she thinks me crazy, and I make a plan and buy boots and gear and stuff and a lightweight tent, and then I pack a rucksack and leave Dundalk, walking north. It is the first of April. It is April Fools' Day. Bob strides along beside me.

'All right there, old-timer?'

I am fit to burst, Johnny. We are on our way now, son. 'Does the road wind uphill all the way? Yes, to the very end. Will the day's journey take the whole long day? From morn to night, my friend.'

'It'll be a long road,' I tell Bob.

It will make new men of us. Reinvention is better than cure. 'Shall I find comfort, travel-sore and weak? Of labour you shall find the sum. Will there be beds for me and all who seek? Yea, beds for all who come.'

I look to him and laugh.

I have no definite route to follow — only a loose plan to walk around the island. And why? I'm not sure. I'm not sure of anything anymore. Am I looking for something? I don't know. I don't think so. Am I trying to lose something? I don't know that, either.

Approaching the border, I pass Peadar Neary's farm, a thirty-five acre strip of useless, boggy, land that straddles the frontier, and has thereby — by fortunate alignment of geography, politics, and differing tax regimes — created a fortune for the landowner. To create wealth from such a poor inheritance requires a special talent, but it is something that men like Peadar Neary are made for.

Neary commands the local IRA battalion in an area where no real law exists, and his business is smuggling livestock, fuel, cigarettes, alcohol, and any current or popular merchandise. In part, Neary's enterprise is a result of my own efforts: police, army, and custom officials will not patrol the northern border through fear of being shot — by me. And, well, that hurts. Neary is all that is wrong in the IRA: the corruption, the intimidation, the self-serving, and the profiteering. Delaney insists

[225]

that Neary is a necessary ally. Better in than out, he says. Delaney says that Neary's expertise and cunning serves us well for the moving of men and ammunitions, and that Neary would do what he does in any case — that the smuggling and swindling would occur with or without the war. Delaney insists that it serves the greater good to have him within the walls of the movement, and that Neary's reach is limited. Maybe. But it still hurts.

Neary is an odd-looking man with an unusual build and gait. He has a large, heavy torso, but he has short legs. As a result, he walks with a hurried, forward leaning, with his little legs struggling to keep up. His prominent chest is thrust forward below a dark, inquisitive, and suspicious head that bobs about in constant alert. As a result, as a boy, he was called Pigeon. But when he was fifteen he put an opposing footballer in hospital — apparently, for over-enthusiastic and defamatory use of the reference — and no one has called him Pigeon since. At least, not to his face. That he could play football at all with the handicap of such a physical construction was early proof of Neary's determination, a quality he has since put to profit.

Peadar Neary is married to Conor Rafferty's aunt, and together they have produced a boy called Ciarán. And everything that is bad in the father is good in the son. How can that be? I don't know. It just is. Conor insists that the boy takes after his mother, and so is a product of the good Rafferty genes. And, once more, I think that Conor may be right.

Ciarán Neary is four years younger than his cousin, and I only got to know him during my last two years at secondary school. Conor made sure to take care of the young boy in the schoolyard, and so Ciarán spent many of his breaks with us. He was a sweet kid, and I saw the same innate kindness in him that I knew in Conor. Although Ciarán was an athletic boy — he was a talented footballer — he had the gentleness of Conor about him. And along a border territory like this, and with a father like Peadar, that can lead to vulnerability. I was forever concerned for him.

I haven't seen Ciarán for some time, so I call into the farm. An imposing, large, two-storey house sits on the southern end of the land, and is entered through two tall, stone pillars, and approached on a neat gravel drive that circles a fountain that fires spurts of water high in the air. There are no gates between the pillars. Everyone in the area knows of Neary's role in the IRA; his success, and his intimidation of the local community, depends on it. So having no gates is his show of having no fear.

'Johnny Donnelly,' Ciarán shouts as he opens the door. He is thin and pale, and though he is delighted to see me and hugs me in welcome, there is an absence of that sporty and joyful bounce he always moves with. He does his best to be cheerful, but I see he carries the weight of hidden troubles, and I know something is wrong. We settle to tea and toast in the kitchen as we catch up, and I tell him of my plans for my walk and I let him get to his tale in his own time. It is two pots of tea and over an hour later when we get to the story.

'I was working the Sunday stall for Daddy, at the Jonesborough market,' he tells me. 'You know, where we sell the sweets, biscuits, and lemonades.'

I nod. There isn't a trick that Peadar Neary doesn't pull in his drive to squeeze every profit possible from the border, and any minor goods that can be bought wholesale in the north and retailed to southern customers for a return are sold at the market. Mam is a great supporter of the Jonesborough fair, convinced there are bargains aplenty to be had there. But then, so is half of Dundalk. And they all overlook the fact that they are thereby responsible for the racketeering that allows hoodlums like Peadar Neary to prosper and bully.

'Then, about two years ago, the market got a new stall,' Ciarán continues. 'It was a mother and daughter. They were from Ethiopia, and had made their way here via England. The father had died in Africa, and they met with a bad man in England; he did bad things to them, so they came here to get away from him. It was a priest over there — a friend of Father Brian, our local priest — who suggested they come here. And the market attracted them; it was a chance to start over. Father Brian gave them a small house in the village. Can you imagine that, Johnny? To escape the hunger of Africa and a violent man in England, and then to end up here? Some people have no luck at all.'

We both laugh at that.

'The girl is Demeku. She was fifteen when they came. Jesus, Johnny, she was the most beautiful thing I ever saw. Father Brian gave them some money to get them on their feet — he had spent years on mission work in Africa, and he said he felt obliged to look after them. I think he thought they were sent from God, and I think he fell in love with them both. It wasn't hard to do. Father Brian asked me to help our new arrivals get settled, to sort out the house, and to set up a stall in the market. I sourced Ethiopian goods through England: beads and woven bags, rugs, shawls, and scarves. It was great. And I spent every possible minute I could with Demeku. I loved her from the moment I saw her. And she loved me, too, Johnny. She really did. Mad, isn't it?'

'Mad stuff altogether,' I tell him.

'Everyone thought that we were just friends, that I was just helping them settle. But we made plans, you know, silly stuff — that we'd run off together, or go to college together, or open a shop or a café together. She was learning to weave here. She has a great eye for that stuff. I like it, too; I love the feel and detail of the cloth. We wanted to open our own business.'

'So what happened?'

'One day, five months ago, Daddy caught us together.'

'Together?'

'Together. You know.'

'And?'

'And the next week, she and her mother were gone.'

'Gone where?'

'Nobody knows. Father Brian and I have been looking for them since. Two months ago, we each got a postcard. The cards came from Ethiopia.'

'That doesn't make sense.'

'I know,' he answers, now crying. 'It makes no sense at all.' But both of us knew that it did.

We stroll around the house. All the rooms are large, bright, and expensively furnished.

'There must be great money in a small farm these days,' I say to Ciarán, and he brightens as we both smile.

In the centre of the house, behind a wide front door with the family crest carved into the wood, there is a large, tiled, open space — more a grand atrium than a domestic hallway. And in the middle of this space there is a glass cabinet some four foot square and seven foot high. In the glass case, and on a single glass shelf just below eye level, there is a football with scribbled markings.

'Daddy's pride and joy. Daddy is football mad. This is a match ball of the 1967 European Cup final. The year Celtic won — the Lisbon Lions, they're called. He paid over a hundred thousand for it. It cost more than the house. It has the signatures of the entire team. And no one has a key to that cabinet, and no one cleans it, but him. Not even Mammy touches it.'

I stay another hour with Ciarán, promising to help find Demeku, before I return to my walk north.

Tailor made for a solution with that gun of yours, isn't it? Bob says, as

[229]

I stroll away from the farm. *I bet you can't wait to put a bullet into Neary.*
That would solve a lot of things. And you can be the hero and bring the girl
home. Mind you, Neary, like him or not, is one of your own. It'd be another
slide on that slippery slope.

I ignore him and walk on.

'If you were sitting at home reading a book,' I ask Bob, after we
walk across the border into Northern Ireland, 'and a madman burst
in and attacked you, would you be wrong to fight?'

No, Bob answers. *Such acts are governed by the laws of nature.*
Everyone has a right to protect self, family, and home from attack.

'If you were living peacefully in a country and it was attacked by
an invader, would you be wrong to fight?'

I suppose it is the same thing, so the same laws of nature must apply.

'Isn't right and wrong a matter of opinion?' I continue. 'And isn't
it all down to time and place?'

How do you mean, son?

'Well, those who fight invaders are heroes. But that label only
survives if the invader leaves or loses. If the invader doesn't leave or
lose, the hero of today is tomorrow's rebel. And tomorrow's rebel is
next week's criminal. And next week's criminal is next month's terrorist.
Those are very different labels for the same act, and the only difference
is who wins, the passing of time, and who's doing the labelling.'

Yes, but these are the labels of man, Johnny. God will judge who was
right and who was wrong.

'God? God help us all from God. And even if there was a God
everyone would be dead before anyone knew anything. In the
meantime, like now — when we are still alive — how do we know
when to fight? How do we know what is right?'

I don't know, son. I think we are governed by the laws of nature, that
we are born with values, just as we are born with arms and legs, that we all
know what is right and what is wrong. But history tells another tale.

[230]

Through familiar country, I walk north to Newry, and I pitch the tent by the canal — the same canal we drove alongside on the day we were stopped, the day the gun went into Dad's mouth. That night, I think about Ciarán and Demeku, and how bastards like Peadar Neary get to be what they are, and do what they do, because of what I do. But I'm not sure of what I can do to help, so I push it away, trusting an idea will come. On the second morning, I continue north and east through the high, pointy rock of the Mourne Mountains to a forest park in Castlewellan where Mam and Dad used to take us for summer family picnics, and I stop beside a lake and eat lunch under a great, twisted oak. Afterwards, I walk through the trees and around a silver-grey castle, and then, as the rain falls, I decide that I've venture enough for the day and so I make camp. In the morning, I leave known terrain to march north. I walk to Downpatrick, where I stop and pitch the tent, and search for the grave of Saint Patrick; in a small graveyard in a hillside grove overlooking the town, I find a large stone slab inscribed 'Patrick' among the McCartans, Maxwells, and Olpherts. The next day, I walk on to the port at Strangford, taking a small, blue ferry over the narrow water to Portaferry, and from there I head north up the green peninsula through Portavogie and Donaghadee, staying in bed-and-breakfasts, or pitching the tent if it is dry and clear.

After a week, I arrive in Belfast, where the inner-city residential street pavements and walls and lampposts are decorated in tribal colours. Among the rows of tightly packed terrace houses, murals to the fallen and the fight adorn every end-gable and facade. But the more affluent outer suburbs I walked through were mostly free of such declarations. Tribalism, it seems, belongs predominantly to the poor.

'Would you look at this mess?' I say.

Love and pride, Bob says. *They are two blind bastards.*

I look to him. 'I don't approve of that sort of abrasive language, old-timer.'

Yeah, well, he answers. *We tend not to be so puritanical when we're dead.*

I find a hostel near the city centre, and go to bed early and read a novel I select from a small collection left there by former guests. I leave Belfast before dawn. I walk again through the inner-city areas denoted by ethnic colours, and see how the markings intensify at the tribal edges and fences, in the same way that wild things urinate at the reach of their territory. But the colours and markings here are flags of insecurity; the tribes of Belfast have no solid ground beneath their feet.

The din and grind of a powerful motor approaches — the growing growl loud in the quiet city morning, foreboding, threatening. I keep a steady, easy pace as an armoured-police Land Rover passes and continues away from me, the heavy sound hanging about the street long after the vehicle has gone. They would have taken no notice of me. To them, I am just another curious tourist, one of the many that the city attracts, here to sample the conflict and to bring home photos of murals and barricades and burned-out cars. The police do not see me as their most-wanted. Camouflage, as the Chief so often has told me, does not necessarily mean hiding.

I leave the city and spend the next few days walking to the north-east corner of the island through Carrickfergus, Larne, Carnlough, Cushendall, Cushendun, Ballycastle, and the whiskey village of Bushmills. I take the distillery's last tour of the day, and try a couple of samples before I leave.

'I understand the attraction of whiskey,' I tell the tour guide, putting an arm around him and holding the sample high. 'I appreciate the intricacies of the making; I value the joy of the single malt.' I take a sip and pull a sharp face. 'It's just that I don't like whiskey.'

That night I lodge in the home of a retired British army captain, and in the morning I am offered kedgeree for breakfast. I have never heard of it, but a breakfast of curried rice, smoked haddock, and boiled eggs is too good to pass up. It is as delicious as it is odd.

'Learn that on service in the Raj, did you?' I say to my host, joking.

He laughs as he pours himself a mug of tea, and then he joins me at the table and gives me his full military history. *If only he knew,* I think as we talk.

My legs are suffering — the joints and tendons are sore and tight, especially in the mornings, and the pain is getting worse day by day. My host notices me hobbling from the breakfast table, and insists on binding each of my knees with wide bandages.

'It isn't just the impact from the walking, my good man,' he says. 'Though it is that, too. But it's the new and unusual weight on your back that has distorted your centre of gravity. The body will take some time to adjust. Keep these on for a few days. Carry only what is necessary, drink plenty, and take it easy for the next week or so.'

He gives me a box of col-liver oil tablets as I pack to go. 'Take a couple of these every day,' he says. 'They should help. And, yes, I learned that, too, in the Raj.'

'Thanks, soldier,' I tell him as I leave, and he waves me off.

I think about things as I go. How an enemy soldier is welcoming and kind, and how one of our own is self-serving, racist, and cruel. How Neary banished that girl. How he didn't want his only son married to an African. How he broke his son's heart, and didn't care. How he didn't want the local shame and ridicule. And I think on how I allow him to do it. But what can I do about it?

Two weeks have now passed on the island walk, and I leave Bushmills with a full belly and strapped legs, and stroll the two miles to the Giants Causeway and watch tourists scamper across polygonal slabs of basalt rock. It is raining and cold, and the sea spray stings as I turn west to walk along the top of Ireland through Portrush, Portstuart, Limavady, and on to Derry, where I rest for three days in a hostel reading newspapers and novels, and drinking mugs of hot coffee. The binding and the rest have worked, and my legs are fine, and in the fourth week I walk back into the Republic, into Donegal, camping in Newtown Cunningham before continuing my pilgrimage into the grey town of Letterkenny —where I don't stop — and march north again into the Fanad Peninsula to stop and camp by the water's edge in Ramelton. I sleep long into the day, and the next mid-afternoon I continue north along the long shore of Lough Swilly. I arrive in the village of Rathmullan, and book into a bed-and-breakfast as the sky clears of cloud. After I shower and rest and eat, I walk on the shore as the evening cools and darkens, and a million stars prick through the night.

'That's a lot of stuff up there,' I tell Bob. 'And it looks permanent and static, doesn't it? As if everything has its place in the world. But it is not static. Everything is moving at speeds we humans can't really get a handle on — our heads aren't designed to make a shape out of it. Seeing something is only the beginning of knowledge.'

I leave the strand and walk to a stone pier. I tell Bob that it was from this village that the O'Neills left Ireland during the Flight of the Earls, abandoning Ireland to English rule. I tell him, too, that it was in this village that the English built a great stone battery to protect Ireland from the French — a thinking, I insist, that was beyond madness.

Maybe the French would have been as bad as the English? Bob suggests. *Who can know?*

Maybe he's right. Who can know? Though I doubt it. The stone battery still stands, and we walk around it as I tell him that it was in this village, too, that the English held the great Irish republican Wolfe Tone. That makes three English follies launched against the Irish in this small village which nowadays threatens little more than quiet fishing or a weekend retreat for the undemanding.

What was that you said about seeing something being only the beginning of knowledge? Bob asks.

In the morning, I leave Rathmullan, walking west through green hills, and in Glenveagh park I spend a sleepy afternoon resting in the open air by a long lake that glistens and sparkles under a sky of scattered woolly-white clouds and patches of blue. I camp beneath a broad pine; and the under the light of a moon that stoops through one of Cora's fleecy clouds, I look across rippling water that stretches away through a valley that some giant has scooped from the mountains, like a sort of impossible inland fjord. That night, I dream of Ciarán and Demeku running, hand in hand, by a blue ocean. And I watch as Ciarán lets her hand go and turns to wave to me. But when he turns again, Demeku is gone, and he is alone in an empty place.

I rise from my camp at Glenveagh and walk west towards the coast, camping again in Gweedore before heading south through Dungloe and Glenties, camping here and there as the good weather holds, before arriving at the port at Killybegs, where I make camp by the sea. The next day, I rest and sit on the harbour wall and watch the work of the port.

My nights, this week, are increasingly laced with dreams of Ciarán and Demeku. I have sent a message to Delaney, and he arrives to sit beside me on the harbour wall. I tell him Ciarán's story.

'She could be anywhere,' Delaney says.

'She isn't anywhere,' I say. 'And she isn't in Africa. Neary is all about control. She is somewhere he can monitor — somewhere he can act if he needs to.'

'They might not make it together,' Delaney says. 'It doesn't always work out.'

'Not our call, Chief. We have to help.'

'And why should we do that?' he asks.

'Because I am asking, and I haven't before. And because Neary behaves like he does because we allow him to, because we make it possible. And because if we don't do anything, that boy will go through the rest of his life lost for that girl. He is nineteen, Chief — the same age I was when I lost Cora.'

I let that line settle on the surface for a while before I whip the hook home.

'And the same age your mother was when she lost your father.'

Delaney leaves, and I sit and watch the fishing boats come and go. He returns in the afternoon.

'They're in Scotland. And Peadar has them warned not to come back, or to make any further contact.'

I expected this of Neary. I have a plan made, and relay it to Delaney.

'Put your best man on it,' I tell him.

'You're my best man.'

'Your next-best man. And make sure he doesn't report to Neary. Pick someone in England. And give them enough money to make a good start.'

Delaney laughs. 'Anything else?'

'No, Chief,' I tell him. 'That will do for now.'

And Delaney rises and leaves without a goodbye.

I leave Donegal, pushing on south. Some days, I walk fifteen miles; some days, twenty-five; other days, only ten. Another week passes as I walk through Sligo and Mayo to camp at the edge of the ocean on Achill Island. There is something about the Atlantic coast of Ireland that is right, like a sort of jigsaw piece that fits and closes a puzzle I carry around in me. I breathe here like in no other place. It is here I feel the gravity of home ground.

I am on the road to Westport, and in the early morning I am leaving a sleeping village into a land of moss-green, purple, and brown. Birds call though the gentle air. I pass the village school, empty and silent now, but how easy it is to imagine the noise of the schoolyard: the running and chasing, the shouting, the freedom of children's laughter. I look on the hand-drawn posters and paintings that cover the lower half of the windows. Beyond the school and the yard, I notice a handball court. It is a large concrete structure — some thirty feet wide and sixty feet long — with a high wall at the back end, two pitched side walls, and one open end. It's a simple game, handball. As I consider the game, I remember the mornings I used to climb the wall of the tennis club with Anna, when we'd play with the added joy of knowing we shouldn't have been there and were getting away with it. I enter the schoolyard and walk over to the court, where a small, black ball that must have been left behind in the dark of evening lies by a side wall. The pull is too great. I look back to the school and the village. The only movement belongs to crows. I remove my backpack and coat, take a few shots, and decide to give myself a game, Ireland versus England — every first and second shot alternating, country to country, and the first to seven will be the winner. After a while I am really getting into things and calling the score. It is a close game. At five–five I get, perhaps, too excited, and am now calling a commentary on every shot.

'A tight match here in the Westport Arena,' I call, 'between the English champion and the young Irish challenger. The crowd are on their feet and cheering every shot. It could go any way.'

It goes to six–six. I am sweating and breathing hard.

'Hold on to your hats, this thing has gone right down to the wire. Who can hold his nerve now? Who can take glory? Will it be the resolute Englishman or the brilliant young Irishman?'

I serve and call the play.

'Tension now in the Westport Arena as the Englishman pushes his opponent into the side wall with some brilliant play. But the Irishman recovers. Fantastic. The Englishman drives the ball to the side again. Surely this time he won't get there? But he does! He does! I don't believe it. And the crowd go wild. What a match! The Englishman now drives the ball hard down the middle. Is this it? No, the Irishman recovers again and stays in there. He just won't give up. Again the resolute Englishman tries, but this time the return pushes him to the side. He gets there, but only just. The court is open. The Irishman smashes the ball down the open side. The Englishman can't make it. Or can he? No, he can't. He can't. Victory to the young challenger! Victory for Ireland! And the crowd are on their feet. The noise is incredible.'

I go for my coat and backpack. Two boys step out from behind the court wall.

'A great victory for Ireland,' the first boy says to me, his arms folded across his chest.

'Yes,' the second boy says, stretching to look past me into the empty court. 'Especially against the English. They're very resolute.'

'Fantastic,' says the first.

'Brilliant,' says the second.

'I don't think we have ever seen anything like it,' the first boy says, his arms falling and his body beginning to shake. 'Not here, anyway. Not in the Westport Arena.'

In the late evening, I pick the car up in Westport — the car the Chief has provided — and drive to Dundalk. In the morning, I make the calls. Delaney's man has Demeku and her mother by a phone box in Glasgow train station. The man has given them instructions and cash, and then he has left. Father Brian has taken Ciarán to Dublin Port, given him the money from Delaney, and told him to wait by a certain public phone. And Father Brian, too, has gone. It is better that both men don't know any more — then, no matter what, they cannot tell.

And it is only now that I choose a location for Ciarán and Demeku to meet. I choose the furthest point from trouble that I can think of.

I make the first call to Dublin. I tell Ciarán to take the early ferry to England and then to travel south to Bournemouth, and to be at the town hall at midnight. I ask him for something to tell Demeku, to calm her, to convince her to go.

There is silence as he thinks.

I wait.

'A wanza tree,' he says. 'We spoke about getting married under a wanza tree, like the one in her home village. Tell her, we will dance soon under a wanza tree.'

'I'll do that,' I tell him. 'And don't worry, Ciarán — he won't be coming after you.'

'Why are doing this, Johnny?' he asks.

'Because I have to,' I tell him.

I make a call to Glasgow, telling Demeku to travel south to Bournemouth, and to be at the town hall at midnight. I tell her that they will dance soon beneath a wanza tree.

I make a third call.

It is still early morning, and the phone rings for some time before it is answered.

'What?' a gruff voice snaps into my ear.

'Hello, Pigeon.'

'What the fuck? Who is this?'

'At midday today, Neary, I'm coming to knock on that silly front door of yours. And then I'm going to piss in your fountain.' I put the phone down.

I drive to the forest, five miles from where I will shoot from, and I dig a deep grave.

At ten o'clock, I am in position, and the gun is set. I am ready.

At a quarter to twelve, Neary opens his front door wide and steps onto his front porch, just I knew he would. Bravado, from men like Neary, is predictable. I watch through the scope as he stands with his arms folded, and with a face of contempt and challenge glaring out through the stone pillars to the country lane that leads to the farm. I also see the two men in a Toyota Corolla that's parked off the main road, and the other two men in a Mitsubishi Pajero that sits in his backyard. I settle on the gun. I find the porch in the crosshairs and move slowly onto the target. I proceed through my routine. Safety off. Deep breath. Let half out. Hold. Crosshair. Crosshair. I squeeze the trigger.

I leave the car on a quiet street and I take a bus to Dublin. And from there I take a train back to Westport to resume my walk.

The following morning, I make the last call.

It is early again, but this time the phone is quickly lifted.

'Hello, Pigeon.'

'You fucking bastard. You fucking, fucking bastard. You shot my football. It's gone. It's totally fucking gone.'

'You will not go after the boy,' I tell him. 'Or the girl. Or the mother. Or next time ...'

'You fucking, fucking, fucking, fu ...'

I put the phone down.

You did good to bury that gun, Bob says to me, later in the day. *Is that the end of it?*

'That's the end of it, Bob.'

Well, that itself, Johnny, he says. *Well, that itself.*

To whom we belong

I AM IN THE BLEAK LAND OF CONNEMARA. HERE, THE EARTH IS THIN AND poor. The place has a wide air and an empty colour. At a crossroads, I remove my boots and socks, and rest on a stone wall. A gentle breeze soothes the heels and toes. An old woman approaches from the south on a broken road. She is walking slowly, pushing a black bicycle, and is dressed in a long, black frock and a black top. A black shawl is draped over her shoulders, and a black scarf covers her head. She stops when she reaches me, and lifts her face. I look into eyes that, despite her weathered age, are the bright green of a sunny harbour.

'Do I know your face?' she asks.

'Unlikely,' I reply. 'I'm a stranger in a strange land.'

'There are none of us strangers,' she says, and then asks, '*Cé leis tú?*'

I only know the meaning of her question because it is something Cora used in her attempts to teach me Irish. And I think it an odd thing in itself that I remember it at all — I have a brain that has been specifically engineered to repel the learning of Irish. But this phrase I know. It means, 'To whom do you belong?' How do I answer that?

I look to her. 'I don't know if I belong to anybody. I'm a bit of a free spirit.'

She laughs. 'We all belong to someone, or something.'

'Is that a fact?'

'As sure as the Earth turns.'

To whom do I belong? Oliver, Kathleen, & Co? I am from them, but I do not belong to them. Do I? And Dundalk? The same. And Ireland? What about Delaney and the IRA and the war? I am a part of that, and yet not a part of it at all. And yet, is that me? And Aisling? Do I belong to anyone or anything?

She watches my perplexity with all the patience in the world held in her green eyes. 'Rest your busy head,' she tells me. 'The pure truths spring from the heart.'

And with that, my truth is released like a great blockage giving way and cleared. 'Cora Flannery,' I tell her, and she raises an old hand and touches the side of my face. She laughs again as she walks away, pushing the bicycle.

Sirens

In the seventh week, I reach Clare and go to Mullaghmore. I crawl over the broken limestone, and examine the fissures and crags. Extraordinary wildflowers are growing there. I look around me.

'I have thought that there are messages here,' I say to Bob.

And what messages would they be?

'One is beauty: that beauty can be found in barren places. The other message is the futility of action if it is measured against time.'

What does that mean, son?

'Well, man has lived in the Burren for thousands of years, and when stone-age farmers settled there, they found it forested and with earth underfoot. These settlers cut down the trees and put cattle out to graze. It was the felling of trees and the grazing of cattle that tore away the land and left the barren rock of today. And if we look at that rock, we see that it is hundreds of millions of years old; we see that it was created under a sea, but not this sea.'

And I point to the coast.

'We can see that the island used to be in the southern hemisphere, in two pieces, and over time it was crushed into one island, and has moved north to where we are today. And we know that our island has not finished its journey. Little by little, it continues to move farther north. We are on the way to the cold north, Bob. And do you know what is there at the cold north, under all that ice? Nothing: just a cold sea. We're on the way to nowhere. And our time on this rock is but a small time, a small time on a rock that changes from two pieces in two continents, to one island, to be under warm seas, to volcanic mountains, to ice, to forest, to a barren mountain — an island rock that is on its way to nowhere. So what tribal claims we make, ultimately, don't make sense.'

Be-god, Bob says. *This is some place all right, when it can say all that.*

There is a hullabaloo when I arrive on Station Road. My arrival has caught Bella by surprise, and she is emotional in her welcome. Mick and Marcella, too, are warm in their greeting, and when we all eat together I am forced to detail the accident, the convalescence, and the walk. It is the middle of the seventh week, and I am tired. I sleep in my old bed for two days, which is a total joy, and on the third afternoon there is a knock on my door. I open it, and Éamon is standing there, with a backpack in one hand and a pair of walking boots in the other.

'Thought you might need company for a few days,' he says, 'just to make sure you don't slacken off.'

I laugh as I hug my friend, and that evening the five of us go to Brogans Hotel and drink beer. The next day we are on the road south from Ennis and I have to encourage Éamon to slow down, so keen is he to attack the walking. We walk for long hours that first day, the journey easy with my friend alongside, and we only rest up when we find a lodging house as we approach the Shannon estuary. The next morning, we cross the river from Killimer on a small ferry — like the one I took at Strangford — and Éamon and I spend the following days walking the coast of Kerry, travelling south and staying in Listowel, Tralee, Dingle, Killorgen, Glenbeigh, and Cahirciveen, before finishing our week in Portmagee. We stay in a farm guesthouse on the edge of the village, and the next morning the landlord takes us on a boat trip to the Skelligs, a crop of rocky islands ten miles out in the ocean. The sea is calm as we leave port, but the ocean swell tosses the boat around as we near the islands. We both hold to the side of the boat.

Our landlord-skipper tells us that the island has a stony, monastic settlement that was founded in the sixth century and that, though remote and difficult to reach, it was raided by the Vikings.

'No matter how well you hide, it's very hard to get left alone in this country,' I say. 'Some bastard always shows up.'

The skipper ignores me, but Éamon flicks his head back and laughs.

'People are peculiar, Éamon,' I say to him, as the boat lands and we begin to climb Skellig Michael, a dark rock that bursts seven hundred feet out of the ocean. 'I mean, what class of a lunatic would live out here in the ocean, out among the puffins and gannets?'

We look on the stone cairn cells, man-hives like beehives that cling to ledges on the rough rock. 'They must have been some nutcases altogether. What was it all about?'

We spend an hour on the rock, breathing the wet, tangy air of the island, and then we board the boat again.

'In Ethiopia,' I say to Éamon as we leave the rock, 'there is a mountain, a high tabletop mountain, called Debre Damo. And on top of this mountain there is a religious settlement, an ancient colony of men, a monastery. The settlement can only be reached by climbing a cliff on a goatskin rope. No woman is allowed go there — no woman has ever been there. Even the goats they keep at the top can only be male. And here's the thing: it was also in the sixth century that it was founded, and it has existed unchanged ever since. I mean, how mad is that? There must have been some universal lunacy going on at that time. And for what? Some great self-delusion?'

'God-sakes, Donnelly, will you give it up? It's just not as simple as that.'

'Yes it is, and that's the tragedy.'

'You are being too harsh, Johnny-boy. They are sacrificing things for a higher goal.'

'That's the killer, Éamon. There is no higher goal.'

We thank our landlord-skipper at the pier in Portmagee. I shake his hand, and Éamon — relieved to get back on solid ground — gives him a hug.

'Good luck, my friend,' Éamon says, as he boards his bus home that afternoon. 'May God guard your every step and bring you home safe.'

'May she do just that,' I tell him, and he laughs and waves.

In Caherdaniel, I walk by a windy shore. The weather is rough and the sea thrashes about; the place has a wild hunger about it, as if the land itself resents settlement and taming. I am thinking again about the rocky island I climbed with Éamon and the man-hive beehive dwellings. Bob is walking alongside, his head down against the wind, his hands in the pockets of his green overalls.

'Do you ever think, Bob, about who we are?'

Who who is, son?

'Man. The human race. We're a pretty fucked-up animal.'

There are many faces of man, Bob says, lifting his head and turning to me. *There are many rooms in my father's house.*

'That's what Aisling would say. She always comes out with the God stuff.'

We are all a gathering, he continues. *In each of us there is a multitude. To be human is to be a confusion of many.*

I walk on to West Cork, and in Glandore I find a sheltered cove below a small pub. The weather has improved again, so I sleep in the open air under a moon whose reflected light is carried to shore on a turquoise tide. In the morning, I am thinking of my brain again, about all those cells and connections, about thoughts and actions, and about who is controlling whom. Bob sits behind me on a concrete slab cast against the rock face. He is looking out across the water, with his two legs dangling from the slab.

'Bob,' I ask him, 'do I use my brain to think things out, or does my brain use me to act things out?'

Later that day, as I rest in a hostel in Clonakilty, I think about Bob, the Bob I knew alive, the Bob who sat across the bench as we ate lunch in the oil store. And although he carried contentment as lightly as others might carry a morning newspaper, I thought then that sometimes there was a shadow about him. I asked him once if he found life lonely. I asked him if he would not have liked his own family.

'I had my own family,' he told me. 'But I know what you mean. We can have two families: the one we come from, and the one we make. There is nothing on Earth that I would rather have done than to have made my own family. But it's just me ...' he looked to me, 'and you.'

'Wasn't it ever possible?' I asked him.

He lifted a teapot and poured the tea into two mugs, adding a little milk to each. He pushed my mug across to me. 'Her name was Ellen. Ellen Finnegan. She was a funny girl, Johnny, a funny girl. She lived life at a hundred miles an hour. She was all go. She lived in Faughart, and every day she rode a yellow bicycle into town. She worked in the post office as a cashier. It's where I met her. It's where I asked her out — the post office. Though we never really went out, just the occasional bike ride to Blackrock. Every day I walked her out as far as Dowdallshill. And if she was coming in on a Saturday, I would go out to meet her, and we would race in as far as the big bridge. I would have gone anywhere just to see those red cheeks and her laughing face, her headscarf loose around her neck, her dark hair flowing. But Dundalk was too small for Ellen Finnegan — she wanted to see the world. She asked me to go, Johnny, to just give up our jobs and jump ship. She was fearless. But I couldn't leave; it just wasn't possible. She went to Birmingham, and for two years we wrote every week, and then the letters stopped. I was afraid to discover why. Then one day she wrote. I kept that letter for over three months before I opened it. It was better to live with the despair and anguish of futile hope than with the pain and desolation of pure loss. I knew what it would say, and I was right. She had met someone else, an American, and they were off to Chicago. I knew it was everything she had ever wanted. I never heard from her again. I can still see her laughing face. I never risked love again — the pain was too much.'

I watched my old friend across the workbench. I said nothing. I knew that in his head he was seeing the girl on the yellow bicycle. I also knew he had sacrificed a life with that girl to stay and care for an ailing mother and a troubled sister. And now they were all gone.

'It is a cruel deal we get in this life, son,' he said to me, as he cradled the mug of tea in his weathered hands. 'Chance can come when we are young and ill-equipped.'

We sat on in a sure silence, secure in each other's presence, as easy with each other's leanings as the meadow grass that sways in a summer's breeze. After a while I got up and touched his head before leaving the oil store.

In the ninth and tenth week, I walk the south and south-east coasts through Cork, Waterford, and Wexford, and in the eleventh I climb inland to spend some days among the stony mountains of Wicklow. As I come down from the mountains, Dublin spreads out to the sea before me and I know I am almost finished and home. I am excited as I am to meet Aisling in the city centre, and I have so much to tell her. I wait for her in a café that is half-filled with women who sit in pairs and serve each other revelations across tables to returns of shock, surprise, concern, and agreement. You wouldn't get better in the Abbey. Three girls enter and pay separately for their orders; they look too young and too poor to push for the communal bill. I am early and so, too, when she arrives, is Aisling. I know something is different when she walks in. I run and take her in my arms, and pull her close and tight.

'You're pregnant, aren't you, Aisling Flannery?'

'Jesus, Johnny. How could you possibly know that?'

'Just a mad guess.'

'So, what do you think?'

'I think it's fantastic. I think it's the best thing ever.'

Aisling breaks and cries. 'It won't be easy. How will we manage?'

'We'll manage fine — better than fine. It will be mad stuff altogether. Don't worry about a single thing.'

Aisling is still crying, but laughing too at the same time in the tricky way that only children and girls can.

'What will everyone say?'

'Everyone will say it's a great thing. And those that don't, don't matter.'

'Are you sure?'

'Sure about what?'

'Sure about the baby?' she asks. 'Sure about me?'

'I sure am. Are you happy?'

'Yes.'

'Are you well?'

'Yes.'

'Then, Aisling Flannery, this is a great day. Shall I sing you a song?'

'No.'

We leave the café to get air and to hold each other, and then we go in again and order coffee and cake.

'We will call her Cora, if we have a girl. Won't we?' she says to me as we travel on the bus to her flat.

'Yes, Aisling,' I say, looking into eyes that are the rustic-gold-speckled brown of the fading fern of autumn. 'We will. And may the gods above grant us that blessing.'

'And if he's a boy?'

'Well,' I say, pulling her close. 'We'll have to think on that one.'

I stay in Dublin for five days, where I cook for Aisling, tell her about my great amble around Ireland, sing songs, and kiss her belly. We make plans, and then I finish the walk to Dundalk.

It is now midsummer, and when the sun shines it bounces off rich greens and yellows. It has taken twelve weeks for me to walk around the island.

'What do you make of Aisling's news?' I ask Bob, on the morning of the final day.

I think it's mighty news altogether, he answers, and pats my shoulder.

It is midday when I approach Dundalk from the south. A pub sits at a junction where roads continue north to the town and east to the edge of the bay. I remove my backpack and enter through an open door. The pub is empty, chairs and stools are upside-down on tables, and barstools are stacked against the far wall. A folded *Irish Times* is on a shelf near the door. I lift the newspaper from the shelf and walk to the bar.

'Hello?' I call out. 'Hello?'

There is no answer. I take a barstool from the far wall to the bar, sit, and spread the newspaper open on the dark counter.

I am reading the sports pages when there is a sound, and I turn to see a girl enter through a side door, pushing a pink mop-bucket before her.

'Oh, hi,' she says. 'We're not really open.'

'That's okay,' I tell her. 'I'm not really thirsty. I just popped in to read your newspaper.'

She looks at me for a while before she speaks. 'You can stay if you want. I'll be making tea when I finish this.'

She cleans the pub around me, reorganising chairs and tables as she goes, pulling the pink bucket behind her with a long mop-handle. I watch her as she works. She has an easy, athletic movement, and under a black top and a short, black skirt there is a fit and toned body. She faces away from me, stroking the long mop across the floor and under tables. There is rhythm in her action, a slight alternate pumping of her arse — left then right, left then right, left then right. It is a beautiful thing.

'Are you watching me?' she asks.

'No,' I tell her, quickly returning to the newspaper. 'Just daydreaming.'

A second girl enters. She has a similar shape to the first; but where the first wears black, the second wears white; and where the first has brown hair tied behind her in a ponytail, the second has blonde; and where the first has dark eyes, the second has bright-blue. As the girls prepare the pub for the day's business, I learn that they are cousins, and they learn of my long walk — everyone loves a story — and when they finish I persuade them to add toast to the tea we share.

When the pot is drained and the toast is finished, I make my farewells and take the road east to the wide and shallow inlet of Dundalk Bay. At the coast, I look out over a level, dark earth. Only at full flood does the bay carry water; at ebb-tide the sea retreats well beyond where the human eye can find it, and the bay appears as a broad expanse of flat sands. A river has cut itself into the seabed, running parallel to the shore before turning and pouring into the eastern horizon. Halfway along the shore is the village of Blackrock, and where the flat plain meets the northern arm of mountain is the town of Dundalk.

It is a fine day, and patches of heat fall through broken cloud. I remove my boots and socks, and tie them to my backpack. I step out onto the sands and push north. I cross the river and walk out into the bay, travelling south to north about a half-mile from the shore. A blue boat sits on the sands, lying on its side like a dog might fall in the shade on a hot day. The hull of the boat faces south, and I stop and rest against it, sitting on the wet sands. To the south, north, and west is land, and to the east is the unseen sea, and beyond that is England. A marine rope hangs over the side of the boat, and I play with it as I sit. The sun finds me, and I look up to the hot light with closed eyes. Behind my eyelids I play with burning, mingling shapes.

The water sparkles as they emerge, rising to stand side by side in the low tide. They both face me, pushing the water back from their faces and into their ponytails. They reach out to me, they beckon with fingers, hands, arms, and eyes. And those faces. The girl with the brown hair turns as the tide rises. I watch the rhythm in her movement, the slight alternate pumping of her arse — left then right, left then right, left then right. It is a beautiful thing. I too rise. It is then I find that in my idle play I have tied the rope around my waist, and now I can't get the knot undone. The girl with the blonde hair steps closer, just beyond my reach. She stands, her legs slightly apart, as the tide rises and a wave catches her where her long legs meet her waist. She gives a short gasp as the wave passes through her — a gasp of surprise, but with a kind of joy. She looks to me as the next wave approaches. Again she gasps as the wave passes, the water soaking the lower half of the short, white skirt. A third wave approaches, and this time a tremble follows the gasp, and she buckles as the tremble passes. She looks on me with her head held at a curious slant. The girl in the black continues to pump in the water. A fourth wave approaches. I desperately try to free the knot, but the rope has welded; I strain against the hold, but I cannot get free from the boat. The wave hits, and the gasp becomes a groan, and when the next wave hits the groan becomes a call. The water rises and sparkles.

I feel a cold wetness. I open my eyes, and water surrounds me.

I get to my feet. I pull at the rope, but the damned thing is tied tight around my waist. How did I do that? The tide is rising, and I panic as I pull at the knot. How did this happen? I pull and grab, but the knot will not give. And the water rises. I hear Bob laughing. I turn and see him sitting in the boat.

Just jump in the boat, son, he says.

I scramble into the boat, and as soon as I do, the knot loosens and the rope falls away. I lift the backpack into the boat and then I lie on the damp wood, looking up to the sky as the boat bobbles in the tide. I wait for the tide to turn, and as I do I look across the water to Blackrock. The village looks different from this view, and when the bay empties and the boat falls, I cross the wet sands to the shore.

I walk along Blackrock's high street in wet jeans. I pass the window of Ramie Knoll's bric-a-brac shop, and stop to look at a framed copy of Robert Emmet's speech from the dock. I scan the familiar text that I know so well:

> … martyred heroes who have shed their blood on the scaffold and in the field, in defence of their country and of virtue … the emancipation of my country from the super-inhuman … I will make the last use of that life in doing justice to that reputation which is to live after me … my country's liberty and independence … when my country takes her place among the nations of the earth, then, and not till then, let my epitaph be written …

I walk on and think on his words: blood on the scaffold, oppression, liberty and independence. It is the story of Ireland. But are we any closer to liberty and independence? And what are those anyway? I think about the war, and I know that a change has come. My old life — whatever that was — is over. I have let it go. There is no regret. There is no joy. Piece by minuscule piece, it has fallen away. Step by step along the walk, it has washed from me; and, like yesterday's rain, it has drained and gone. And, somehow, it doesn't matter at all.

I enter a pub on the promenade, and from a finely dressed barman I order a large coffee with cream. The coffee comes as I take a thick book from a pile that sits on a shelf by the bar. I start into the book, and after a couple of pages I start again, but I cannot make any sense of it. I flick through the book, reading a line here and there, but I can't get to it. I shuffle in my seat. A drum of wind has gathered inside me. I try to get comfortable and read. I try to work the gas free. But I am cramped, and I can't concentrate on the reading. I replace the book on the shelf and, as I stretch, the waste escapes with a loud clatter. The barman looks over and I salute him. What else could I do?

'A fine village you have here,' I tell him.

'Young Donnelly, isn't it?' he says. 'I know your father.'

'Guilty as charged, Capt'n,' I salute him again.

I walk to Dundalk and go to Saint Joseph's. I light a candle. I have lit a candle in every village and town I have walked through.

There is a trail of burning wax behind us, Bob says. *Your walk can be seen from the heavens.*

'So how was your walk really, Johnny?' Anna asks me at the kitchen table when we are alone. 'Did you learn anything with that mad head of yours?'

'I was working on the brain thing again,' I tell her. 'The human brain has been this size for hundreds of thousands of years, but it was only about a hundred thousand years ago that we began to rapidly progress away from what we were. Something must have changed then. And after that change we could interpret things, analyse behaviour, and copy. We must have developed some function to learn, to hold on to, and to teach. To be human is to ask questions. Nothing else that exists does that. That's what makes us different.

And to retain answers and discoveries, the brain must have developed a copycat function so that creativity could be captured and built on. And so we learned fire, and tool use, and how to build shelter. And we developed language, and this led to a collective learning, and so progress was kind of unstoppable, is unstoppable. But something else came with the copycat and with the collective learning — a sort of by-product — and that is empathy, a sense of belonging. And from that came culture and civilisation, and all the rest of the hullabaloo. But belonging, too, came with a by-product, and that was a new thinking: a thinking that there is an us and a them.'

'And you didn't drink too much? Did you, Johnny?'

'No, Anna,' I tell her, and as I rise from the table I reach over and kiss her head. 'I didn't drink at all.'

'So,' Anna says, 'are you going to tell Mam and Dad about this *nature of man* theory of yours?'

'Actually, Anna, could you do that for me? I'm a bit busy with stuff.'

'Johnny,' my sister says to me, as she stands and touches my face. 'You are as mad as the east wind.'

I decide to repeat my college year in Limerick. Until September, I have time to play with. I take Clara to Ennis, and we picnic with Bella and Marcela and Mick at Mullaghmore. I take Éamon to visit Aisling in Dublin. We go on the train — Éamon loves the train. I take Aisling, Clara, and Che to Castlewellan in the Renault 4. We picnic under the twisted oak. I take Mam and Dad for drives to Cooley and Carlingford. I take Che for walks to Soldiers' Point, Ravensdale, and Cúchulainn's Castle. I drink tea and coffee with Anna. I write a letter to Bremen. I don't think about the war.

It is the eighth day of July, and we have a night out in the Cooking Pot. Everybody comes. Congratulations and good wishes are real and warm. Anna and Aisling remain together all evening, and speak in whispers. Eddie and Hannah are there with Mam and Dad, and so, too, are Fionnuala and Gerry Flannery. Big Robbie is camped at the bar with Frank, Peter, and Jack Quigley. Conor has come from London. Éamon has a gift for me. It is a map of Ireland, and on it my walk is traced in gold. I am surprised and don't know what to say, and Éamon Gaughran has his moment. The gathering has travelled to his head like a tumbler of poteen, and all his lights are on. He puts his arm around me and flicks his head.

'He's some lunatic,' he calls out. 'Johnny D is some lunatic altogether.'

A day that started out easy

IT IS THE MORNING AFTER THE NIGHT IN THE COOKING POT. I TAKE A
slow walk to town, pass by the side of the courthouse, and walk
through the Market Square. Every time I pass here, I think of Cora.

I visit the redbrick house near the town centre, and I sit in the
small front room.

'I'm sorry about Delores, Chief. She is a great woman.'

'The very best, John,' Ignatius Delaney says. 'We are fifty years
married next month; it's hard to believe so much time can pass so
easily. But she is fading now from her own person. The memory
started to slip — small stuff at first — but now she seems to be
disappearing day by day, like someone has pulled a plug on her very
self, and the drain cannot be halted, and what's left is just collapsing
away to a nothingness. It's an odd sort of departure, unnatural. It can
be savage on all concerned. But for the day-care centre and her sister's
help, I don't know how I'd manage. Her mother went the same. Of
her own crowd, you know, we never thought she would go first.
Hope can make a blinkered fool of us all.'

'The human brain is a peculiar and delicate thing,' I tell him, but
I don't tell him more. I don't tell him about the hundred billion cells,
about the copycat function, about who is controlling whom, about us
and them. Instead, I tell him about Aisling. I tell him about the baby.

'That's great news, John. No man ever wore a cravat as beautiful
as his own child's arm around his neck.'

I nod to acknowledge the poetry.

'You stay down the country,' Delaney continues. 'Stay well away from this place, do you hear me? You're well away from it. You have done your bit, God knows. It's them against us still, but it won't last much longer — there isn't the will. A ceasefire is coming.'

There is something of the hunt in the Chief's words, something coy, something of the measured cast of the angler's line. I know him too well to be hooked with such bait, and I know he is guarding as much as he is probing.

'You'll retire from the struggle yourself, Chief?'

'I'll still do my bit. It's the old devotee for the long war. An army is in need of all its foot soldiers.'

I remember the time he gave me that small speech about foot soldiers. I look to the old man.

'I wonder about what we do. It doesn't make a bit of difference.'

'We fly the flag, John. We hold the line. If it wasn't for what we do, they would have trampled over what's left of Ireland long ago. They would have destroyed our beautiful country. But there will be no ovation from the masses. Don't be expecting gratitude; don't be hanging about for the applause. People in the Republic have forgotten the value of freedom. They don't care about the cost. They don't want to know — they are embarrassed by the whole thing. We chose a different view, you and I. We chose to look at what they have done: obliterated our language and culture, stolen our lands, scattered our sons and daughters to the four winds, starved the rest of us, made us outlaws on our own ground. They disregard the native man as nothing but annoying flotsam in the tide of their own greed. Sometimes the native man needs to fight. That's what we did. We chose to fight. God alone will judge us.'

'I think you're right, Chief. But that isn't true just of the English — it is true of all humanity. We Irish are well capable of bringing shit down on ourselves.'

[258]

'Yes, but that would be an Irish problem in an Irish land. We have a right to make our own mess.'

'Do you remember all that stuff about original sin, Chief? That man was born a sinner, that being born a sinner is the nature of man? I don't believe that. I believe that man is born with three innate capacities: the love of homeland, the love of woman, and the proclivity to make war. These are our fundamentals. We are born with the tools for infinite joy. We are born with the tools to destroy us. This is the nature of man.'

'We cannot punish ourselves for what we are,' Delaney says.

'True. But who can be blamed? God? We are the product of evolution. We are who we are by natural selection. Aggression is elemental to survival. It is built into us. We are born ready for war.'

'We were born to this war, you and I,' Delaney tells me. 'Rolling over and allowing yourself to be beaten is no answer. Many a coward has hid behind the argument for peace.'

'Yes, Chief, there have been many. Still, though, where has the killing brought us?'

'John, you are looking for a clear path in a forest where there are no paths at all. We must all cut our own way through. We chose our way, and there are many who will condemn us for that. But inaction is no sure key to the door of serenity. That is not how this world works. History is filled with those who tip-toed quietly to their own slaughter. Didn't you learn that in Hamburg? Abasement must be challenged — it must be fought.'

'Yes, Chief,' I tell him, 'that is true.'

'We have a right to defend our Irish nation.'

'Nation? What nation?'

The Chief straightens and his face tightens. I reach across and take the old man's hands in my own.

'Twelve thousand years ago,' I tell him, 'we didn't exist. The ice

[259]

had just left, and all that was here were forests and rivers. Elk and deer and hare and wolf had the land to themselves. And then the first settlers came. And who were they? Who are the Irish? Are we Galician? Asturian? Basque? Gascon? Breton? Cornish? Welsh? Manx? Scottish? Or are we the peripheral deposits of Germanic tribes from the plains of Europe? Who are we? We have not spontaneously materialised on this island. We have to have come from somewhere. And then the Norse and the Danes came, and then the Normans and the English. You'd wonder why they'd all go to so much bother to get their hands on a damp place like this. You'd wonder at the attraction.'

Delaney laughs and relaxes again in his chair.

'You always were of the fecund mind, John. Always a tendency to the discursive analysis.'

'And who are the Normans,' I go on, 'but the Norse and the Danes speaking French? And who are English? They, too, are an invention — a Celtic, Roman, Friesian, Saxon, Norse, French invention. Two inventions fighting each other for identity. Beneath our Irish and our English veneer, we are all someone else. And what are we fighting for? We are fighting for an island that was forged from two continents, an island that was buried below seas, that belongs not to any one place on the Earth, that will be lost again below northern ice, that is on its way to nowhere. Nations don't exist, Chief. We come and we go. The whole thing is mad.'

'We are fighting for our fathers, John. We are doing what they could not.'

'The making of boundary is eternal,' I keep to my argument. 'It is made, broke, and remade. But the making belongs only to land and sea.'

I pause and look away. The beat of the wall-clock fills the silence in the small room. We are different men, the Chief and I. War does that; it builds odd alliances. And, like girls, it can wreck your head. I turn again to the old man.

'War is the worst of man,' I tell him. 'Yet it is the essence of what we are, the consequence of being human. But, yes, it is war, Chief, and it came to us, that much is true. We chose to fight, and who can judge us?'

'You are right, John,' Delaney says quietly, almost whispering. 'Listen to me, John,' he says, leaning across the small table. 'You build a new life down there. Marry that girl and make a family, and do all the right things. But stay away from here. They will never forgive you for those shootings. If they ever knew it was you, they would come after you. You brought fear itself down on them; with that gun, you changed the war. Thank God your identity will die with me. But take no chances — stay well away, and may God bless you. I'll keep the fire lit, others will take on the battle, and one day we will be a nation once more.'

'Maybe you're right, Chief. But the people of Ireland today don't care. For them, a united Ireland is as remote as a parallel universe. They know it is possible. They are not sure if it's beneficial. But, mostly, they just don't give a fuck.'

'Remoteness is a subjective thing, John. It pivots on the personal.'

I lift a framed photo from his desk.

'That's a new photo, Chief?'

'Yes, John, a present. She has me warned to keep it near, to keep her face shining out at me so I won't feel so lonely.'

I now recognise the trace of melancholy in the air, that fragrance that has been on the edge of my knowing since I got here, that sweet mix of carnation and vanilla. I know what it is. It is *L'Heure Bleue*.

'Is she at home these days?'

'No,' he says. 'She is back in California.' And he signals to a letter on his writing bureau.

'And how is she?'

'Oh, you know her, John. She is her own particular person; she likes her own peculiar comforts. She's a mercurial sort — she'd be hard for any man to please. I thought she might be seeing someone here the time she was home, with her comings and goings, her secret dalliances. I think she might have had someone back to the house here. I thought she might stay, but she returned to the States in the end.'

I am probing, but, with other matters on his mind, the Chief is undisturbed by this.

'Why did you call her Loreto?'

'It's after a little hilltop town near Ancona. We visited a church there when we were on honeymoon in Italy. What was it called again? The Basilica Della Santa Casa. When we stood there in the Piazza Della Madonna, the square in front of that beautiful church, Delores said that if we ever had a girl we would call her Loreto.'

I stand.

'You sit where you are, Chief. I'll make us some tea.'

I think about Loreto as I boil the kettle on the gas stove. I know the Chief is not lying; I know he thinks Loreto is in America. But I'm not so sure. I scald the white-porcelain teapot with hot water and empty it into the sink. I spoon loose tea into the warmed pot and fill it with boiling water. I stir the tea, replace the lid, and put the teapot on the table to draw. I lift a ball of green wool that must have been absentmindedly left on the table in what was always a spotless kitchen. I wonder why the Chief keeps the wool, as Delores is now beyond needlework. I guess we all have our sentimentalities; we all have our peculiarities. But we all go in the end. And each in our own way. What matter now the perfect arrangements?

And I wonder. I wonder why the Chief is so coy and guarded. I wonder, but I know. There can only be one reason. I know Delaney will never agree to a ceasefire. I know he believes a ceasefire will be the end of it. And he is right. A ceasefire with no ground won is more deadly than an enemy attack: it legitimises the status quo. Delaney knows this, he understands the consequences, and I know he will fight it. And he will fight it to a bloody end. And if the fight doesn't involve me — and I am the only shooter he trusts — then it can only mean one thing: it has to be a return to the bomb.

I lift the lid of the teapot and stir the tea again. I know bad things are going to happen. I know that concentrating on me hasn't given him the time to replace the volunteer bombers who died when the bomb they were preparing exploded. The recent bombs in England were by Delaney's men, his new men. It was a disaster — two young boys were killed. I step out into the garden and take a twenty-pack of Carroll's No. 1 from the Dunn & Co. I light a cigarette. I am thinking of those two boys. I can still see their faces on the television. I can still see their families. One boy was only three years old; the other was twelve — the same age I was when I first came to this house.

I pull hard on the cigarette. I go over what I know about those bombs. The London bomb was big — it took a tipper truck to deliver it. The Warrington bombs were small, and hidden in town-centre litter bins. The IRA blamed the British for not acting on the warning. But that's not good enough. Putting a bomb in a town-centre litter bin is not war. There are many in the IRA who discredit these distinctions: Irish, Republican, and Army. There are those who bring us no good, and I have warned Delaney before about this. But what's it to do with me? It's not my war any more. I am sure Delaney will now take his battle to the north, and if the bomb is for Ireland, who'll care? What's one more bomb in a northern town? Who cares about any of it anyway? There were bombs before; there will be bombs after. People don't care, not really. I finish the cigarette, and blow smoke high into the town air.

You wouldn't get involved, Johnny, would you? she asked me. *What about those terrible bombs? You wouldn't do a bad thing, would you?*

No, Cora, I told her. *I wouldn't do a bad thing.*

I re-enter the house, and, as I open the back door, a draft enters and the ball of wool falls from the table. I reach to catch it and miss, and it rolls across the grey-tiled floor, leaving a green thread behind.

'You are the best ever,' Delaney says, as I bring the tea. 'How Delores and I wished to have a son like you.'

I tell him about the remainder of my walk, about the long journey home from Donegal, and he laughs and shakes his head at every incident. He wants me to recount every town and village. But something is happening as I talk: one half of my brain has removed itself to another consideration. And that consideration is *L'Heure Bleue.* I just can't get the fragrance from my senses. I think of Loreto Delaney, of the Margaux and the expensive coats, of her own particular wants, of her peculiar comforts, of her mercurial sort, of the secret dalliances, of someone back at the house here, of the letter from California, of the framed photo. Could Loreto Delaney be turned? Or bought? Or seduced and used? But why? How and what could she know? How could anyone know when I would call again on Delaney? That could be a long and useless wait. And how would they know to suspect me of the shootings? Loreto doesn't know what I do. I am being paranoid. I am unbalanced since shooting Declan — that must be it. I try to focus on the conversation with the Chief. But then I think again. What if it isn't me that this is about? What if I have walked into another game? What if …? All the training and the long hours in the fields of South Armagh have cultivated hard instincts, survival instincts. Something here isn't right. I know something is wrong. But what?

Suddenly, the fog of rambling thought is gone. A cold blade of clarity falls, and I turn to what was in my peripheral vision all along — I look to the wall, to the copy of the Proclamation of the Irish Republic that hangs there, to the aged print encased in a simple wooden frame, to the page that has dropped on one side and sits at a slight angle within the frame, to the only thing in this house or about Delaney that is not perfectly neat and aligned. But it is aligned now; inside the simple frame, the document sits perfect and square. And now I know. I know I have surrendered myself to a trap, to a trap that wasn't even for me. I know it's about the bomb. I know the fuckers know about the bomb. That they would use the framed Proclamation must have been their little joke. And that was their mistake.

Delaney is still talking about Tipperary, and only now does he notice my inattention, but I signal him to keep talking.

'How about some music, Chief? What will we listen to?'

I turn the volume to full on Delaney's cassette deck and press 'play'. The slow, dragged intro to Mahler's Symphony No. 1 fills the room. I let it run as I walk to the wall, and when I return I lower the volume.

'Sorry about that, Chief. A bit too loud, even for an old fogie like you.'

The Chief is grey, then pink, but I insist he keeps talking as we look into the rear of the frame that I have taken the hardboard backing from. We both recognise a short-range radio transmitter.

'I didn't make Tipperary this time, Chief. I stuck to the coast. Maybe we'll make a trip down there together. Where will we visit?'

Delaney is shocked, and rattled, but recovers as I force him to talk through a trip to Toomevara.

As he talks, I am thinking that whoever is listening is not far away, and, whatever information they came for, they now know that I am the shooter, and I am sure they will not let me go. Whoever is listening will already have called for back-up; I have to act now. My only option is to find them fast, and attack. I reach across and lift the newspaper from the floor beside his chair.

'Hey, Chief, how about the crossword?'

I lift a pencil from his bureau and write: *New Neighbours?*

'Tricky,' I say, handing him the newspaper.

He writes and returns the newspaper to me. *Yes, No. 5, two men. White Nissan Sunny.*

'Yes, tricky indeed,' he says, rising. 'Have a go from there yourself. I need to use the loo, being an old fogie and all that.'

In the three minutes he is gone, I write the plan on the newspaper. Delaney returns, carrying two Glock handguns. The Chief is a believer in the Glock.

'How did I do?' I ask him.

He reads through my work. 'Not bad,' he says. 'It will do.'

I leave and say goodbye to the Chief at the gate. He hugs me before I go. I watch him return to the house. I walk to the house next door, number seven, and invite his neighbours to a surprise anniversary party that I tell them I am organising for Mister and Missus Delaney. The elderly Missus McKenna doesn't hear me at first but when I explain louder she thinks it a great idea and assures me of their attendance. I get the same response at number six. I approach number five, the first house in the block, without pausing. A white Nissan Sunny is parked by the pavement. From here on, I shall play it as it happens. If they are wise they will not answer, but they don't know that we know who they are, and so might think that not answering will bring some suspicion. At worst, my coming to the door will stall and confuse them, and it will bring doubt. And in war, doubt — and indecision — will kill you.

I press the doorbell. Nothing. No answer. I press the doorbell again and knock on the glass pane in the door. There is a gunshot. A man races into the hallway. He is raising a gun, but he is injured and slow, and I have the Glock ready. I shoot through the glass and he falls. I break through the door and I shoot him again. I hear another shot, and a second man falls into the hallway from the living room.

He, too, is already injured and is on his knees. Delaney has shot them both through the back window. My Glock is still raised, and I shoot twice. I step over both men and take a towel from the rear kitchen. I meet Delaney at the back door, and he tells me to go, that he will take care of things.

'They weren't here for me, Chief. They couldn't have known.'

He nods, but he doesn't reply.

'It was you, Chief. Whatever it is, they were on to it.' I was just talking. I wasn't expecting a response — Delaney has kept me removed from the other stuff.

'They must have some wind of the what, John. They came for the where and the when. It would have been a waste of time. The thing is already in play. And there's no one I would have been talking to; there's no one involved but the two fools.'

'A sacrifice for the common good,' I say, remembering again his speech about foot soldiers, but he is already lost to other thoughts. It is not like the Chief to talk of action, but he is bothered, and has slipped from his usual self. And I know it is not the killing of the two spies that has the Chief bothered — it is the source of the leak.

Both neighbours from numbers four and six are in their backyards and approaching, but they quickly retreat indoors when Delaney gestures to them. People in Dundalk suspect who the Chief is, and nobody will have seen or heard anything. There is no movement from number seven. I guess old Missus McKenna didn't even hear the shooting.

He turns to me. 'We cannot let the war die and leave them in place. What will be left will become the normal and the acceptable, and our long struggle will have been a waste. We must continue the fight with whatever we have.'

'There's no getting clear of it, is there, Chief? It pollutes like slurry tipped into a well.'

[267]

He doesn't answer, and I leave. I climb the garden wall and walk north before turning east along the river.

I walk to Saint Joseph's, enter, and take a pew near the Sacred Heart shrine. I revisit the events of the day, and I think about how a day that started out simple became another killing day; and how quickly the whole thing turned, and how easy. I try to think about what to do. My plan was to exit the war, to finish with the gun, to finish with Ireland. Instead, I killed two men. Another two men. I didn't have a choice, I know. It was kill or be killed, wasn't it? That's what they say, *kill or be killed*. Like they ever knew anything about anything. But isn't that just it — you can step into war whenever you like, but leaving it …? I consider my options, and, as I think about things, about a day that started out easy, I see their faces again, those young boys in Warrington, those faces I saw on the television.

You wouldn't get involved, Johnny, would you? What about those terrible bombs? You wouldn't do a bad thing, would you?

I look up and see Siobhán McCourt.

'No,' I answer. 'I wouldn't do a bad thing.'

But Siobhán is gone, and a small girl stands by the shrine. I have seen her here before, I remember. The girl looks at me with her face held open. I look away, and when I look again to the shrine the small girl is gone, and an older girl is there, a good-looking girl, and this girl, too, I remember seeing once as she cleaned the windows of the chip shop.

Those bombs, she says. *Those bombs kill people, ordinary people, men like Gerry and Éamon, girls like Aisling and Cora, children like Cormac and Clara — kill them as they wait on a parade or do their shopping. Children, mothers, fathers. You wouldn't allow that, Johnny. Would you?*

'No,' I tell her. 'I wouldn't allow that.'

But this girl, too, is gone, and another girl is there. She, too, is a good-looking girl. Her blonde hair is tied in a Grecian braid, her

[268]

pretty face and clear skin show above the pulled collar of an American college jacket, and her arctic-blue eyes lock me and hold me to her. I remember her, too, that time I thought she was being friendly and saying hello, but she was selling sex.

'You appear in strange places,' I tell her.

Well, I work in mysterious ways, don't you know? she answers, and I raise my head and laugh up into the high church roof.

I lower my head again and look on her. 'Are you real?' I ask her. 'Or are you like Bob?'

But this girl, too, is gone, and another girl is there, a girl with long, orange-red hair and pale-blue eyes in a white face.

'Hello, Aoife Jensen,' I greet her. 'Welcome to me.'

Who's Bob? she asks.

'Very funny,' I say. 'So who are you, really?'

I am the mother of all living things; only from me does new life come.

I think about her words for a while.

Do you want to tell me your story?

'No, thanks. And don't you already know it? But it's not too good for me, I guess, that you should show your face now. I'll tell you something. I have known heaven, the days I spent with Cora. And I have known hell, these days without her.'

She looks on me, but she does not reply.

'I told my story to an angel once,' I tell her. 'But that turned out to be Aisling Flannery. Girls, they do things to you.'

And why do you think you were mistaken?

I laugh again. And as I sit there I see those two boys in England and I remember what Delaney said today about fools and foot soldiers and the common good, and I remember who he had been speaking of when he used those phrases before. I try to think. I have promised Aisling that we will build a life together — a new life for the three of us, a life away from war. I have promised that we will be together. But

I promised Cora that I wouldn't allow a bomb. What was that I said about a bomb in a market place? And now I know about a bomb, and I cannot pretend ignorance. What do I do? If I go after that bomb, I am dead. The bomb might explode, and I might be near it. Or the British will take me, now they know I was the shooter. And if I escape all that, if I get to the bomb, if I get away from the Brits, the IRA will come after me for sabotaging the mission. Those are the rules of the game. What a fucking game.

Take care, my young friend, with what rope you take hold of in this life, I remember Bob telling me in the oil store. *Without great care, a rope becomes a whip.*

I decide what to do, and I make to tell the girl. But when I look up, no one is there — only the statue with the gentle face.

It doesn't take long to find Sloane. He is home alone. I kick his door in and shoot him in the leg with the Glock. Once you start, the shooting is easy.

Sloane roars. I give him the towel I still carry, and tell him that I will kill him if he doesn't answer my questions. His protests are short, and he cries when I put the gun to his leg.

'I'm going to ask you some questions,' I tell him. 'And you are going to answer. Then you can call for an ambulance. Otherwise you will bleed to death. Are we clear?'

He nods once.

'Tell me about the bomb.'

He doesn't speak at first, and I move the Glock to his wound.

'We're sending those bastards a message,' he says through a heavy breath. 'We're sending those bastards a big fucking message.'

'When?'

'Tomorrow, dickhead. You know something, Donnelly? You always were a bit fucked up.'

'Where?' I lift the Glock and show it to him, and then I press the gun into his wound.

He doesn't answer, and I press the gun harder into his leg.

'Banbridge, cunt.'

'Who is delivering the message?' I ask, though I already know.

'Boyd. Pitiful Bobby Boyd is going to be a star, a big fucking star.'

It doesn't surprise me that Boyd is being used. If it doesn't work out, Boyd knows nothing. There's a touch of self-protection in the plot. It has Delaney's watermark through it. The weakness in the plan was involving Sloane in it.

I look at Sloane. His resistance is gone; he's tiring, and his blood crawls on the floor. 'What time?'

'Twelve o'clock rock, Johnny fuckhead Donnelly.'

'Sticks and stones, Slime.'

'You are too fucking late. He is on the road already. You can't stop him.'

'Where in Banbridge?'

'Right in the fucking middle,' he answers, suddenly fading.

'What kind of car?' I ask. But Slime Sloane has gone. I call for an ambulance and leave.

I go home, shower, drink coffee, and make a plan. I drive the Renault north and arrive in Banbridge in the early morning. I walk through the town as the streets fill with Saturday shoppers. The main street is adorned with the union colours for the festival of the twelfth. The flag of the enemy is tied to every pole. I make some guesses. I guess Boyd will deliver the bomb as late as possible to minimise suspicion. I guess Delaney will not allow enough time to defuse the bomb — he will have arranged a phone warning only in the last hour. But I know Boyd. If something can go wrong, it will go wrong with Bobby Boyd. If Boyd gets that bomb into town, hell itself will release.

At ten o'clock, I walk up and down a long main street that rises and falls over the crest of a steep hill. Because of the climb, a long central underpass has been cut along the length of the street. The underpass is built in granite and is open to the air but for a central tunnelled section that carries a bridge at a crossroads in the middle of the town. Along both sides of the underpass the original street climbs the hill, and cars park here by the pavement beside the town centre commerce. If Boyd has been instructed to go for the town centre, he will try to park the bomb here.

I keep watch for an orange head. At eleven o'clock, I am standing on the bridge over the underpass. I scan every car that travels on either side. What if he has already delivered and gone? I have no idea what type or colour of car I am looking for. Every parked car looks like it could have a bomb in it. I have no real idea why I'm here. What lunatic thinking took me here? Cars arrive and park. Cars leave. I run to both sides of the street. I don't see Boyd. I run to both ends of the street. I don't see Boyd. I check my watch. How long do I wait? I see two policemen on the east side of the street. They are relaxed and chatting to each other. I guess Delaney hasn't yet made the phone call. I am out of time. I have to tell them to clear the town.

I walk across the bridge towards the policemen. One of them, a middle-aged, round-faced man, notices me approach. Suddenly, he reaches for his radio. Just then I see a blue Ford Sierra pass on the west lane. I see an orange head. I turn and run after the car. Boyd is driving slowly, searching for a parking place, but the available free spaces are all tight, and I guess Boyd is not confident enough to parallel-park with the bomb, and so he continues and the blue car with the orange head drives north to the end of the street and turns west and away on the Downshire Road. Shit and be fucked. I run to follow. I know Boyd will panic. I know Boyd will dump the car in the first easy place he can find. I run to the corner, but the blue Sierra is gone. Shit, Boyd could put that car anywhere. I am close to a full panic. I run two hundred yards along the Downshire Road and see the blue Sierra abandoned in front of a small stone lodge beneath the overhang of a broad sycamore. The lodge is some sort of Saturday school; children and parents are moving in and out. The school is open to the road, and that bastard Boyd has parked in the front yard. I look west to see an orange head hurry away. I run to catch him. Boyd is a slow mover. At another two hundred yards to the west, outside the Railway Inn bar, I close on him. He doesn't see me coming. I hit him hard, from behind, and he falls. I fall on him, driving my knee into the back of his left lung. Boyd is hurt and he has lost his breath.

'Key.'

He doesn't answer.

I rise and drive my foot through Boyd's leg, smashing his knee into the pavement. Boyd cries out. I search him and find the key in his jeans pocket, and I run to the car. I look back. Boyd doesn't move. Ahead of me, people are running. People are running to me. I look and see shoppers running out from the main street. Shit and be double-fucked. I run on past the car, against the flow of people, and into the main street. I see the two policemen, one each side of the street, shouting and waving people out of shops and out of the street. People pass me as they run. They are running towards the bomb. I turn again and run back to the Railway Inn, where Boyd is still on the ground. Two men have come out from the bar and are helping him up. I burst between them and hit Boyd hard again in his back. I take his left arm.

'How long?'

He doesn't answer. One of the men, a big, heavy man, is trying to push me away. The other man is running into the pub and calling for help. I break two of Boyd's fingers. He screams. The heavy man now tries to grab me, and I hit him hard and fight him off.

'How long?' I shout to Boyd, driving my knee into him.

[273]

'Fifteen minutes, cunt.' And because my head's all a bit messed up and excited, I am thinking that's not fair — that's the second time someone has called me that, and here's me trying to do a good thing. It's not really the time for this kind of pondering, but, like I said, my head's getting all messed up.

The heavy man attacks me, and I beat him off again as he tries to grapple me, and I run again to the car. I am tiring and short of air. I turn to see a group of men from the pub running after me. Shit and be treble-fucked. This whole show is going arseways: I have been outplayed by Bobby Boyd. I think of my options. If I shout a warning, what chance is there of people believing me? Anyhow, I don't have the wind to make a decent shout. The men from the pub are closing in — I could get dragged away before I get the story out. I have to do something. I have a mad idea. I decide that I have to get the bomb away. I get into the blue Ford Sierra and start the engine, and I am thinking this is when the car explodes, because that's what happens in all the movies. But the car does not explode.

I drive into the road and try to get away to the west, but the street is full of shoppers who have gathered there, and some cars have stopped and blocked the road. The men from the pub are reaching for the car. The only clear way is behind me. I turn the car and drive towards the main street. I try to calculate the time. How long is it since Boyd parked the car? Two minutes. Five minutes? Ten minutes? Fourteen minutes? I have no idea. At the junction, I look north across the river, but I see that people have congregated on the other side of the bridge and that traffic there, too, has stopped. I have no choice but to turn south into the main street. I know now what to do. The street is empty of people but for one of the policemen halfway up the rise. I drive towards him. I see it is the policeman with the round face, and he is running towards me, waving. I stop and open the window. I know he recognises me from the street.

[274]

Suspicion and doubt and fear are held in his eyes.

'Keep calm and do not speak,' I tell him. 'The bomb is in this car. It was parked back there. There is no time. I am going to put it in the underpass. Get on the radio and keep everyone away.'

As I drive on, I notice a single dark shape swoop low overhead. I continue up the rise of the street. I straighten the car between the granite stone walls of the underpass. I look into the rear-view mirror and I see the policeman. He stands and watches me before lifting his radio to his mouth and running. Oh, sweet hallelujah, this is not good, this is not good at all. Suddenly, I notice someone beside me in the front passenger seat. It is Bob. But Bob is not in his green overalls. He is dressed in a white shroud, and by his side — where the red rag should be — he holds some kind of a lance of blue flame.

'Nice to see you dressed up, old-timer.'

Well, it's important to make the effort now and again.

'You never did before,' I say. 'What's with the magic spear?'

But Bob doesn't answer.

'I messed up, Bob,' I tell him. 'I'm all out of rope.'

'*Níl saoi gan locht,*' he says.

'There's no wise man without fault,' I acknowledge, as Bob pats my arm with his free hand.

I drive the blue Sierra to the central tunnel section. I stop the car under the bridge and pull the handbrake. I open the door and I run from the car, and I'm climbing up stone and am almost over the damned wall when a white heat bursts from the earth.

The death of Cúchulainn

I DON'T KNOW HOW LONG IT IS BEFORE I KNOW THAT I AM NOT DEAD.
I am lying in the road that runs west from the central crossroads.
There is a peculiar silence and the air is strange. I try to stand, and I
am surprised when I can. I check my arms and legs, and they are still
there. The Glock is still tucked in my belt. Something is wrong with
my face and my side, and my hearing, too, but I'm not sure what. My
left leg is torn and I can see flesh and blood.

I move away from the town centre. My left leg is not working and
I am dragging it along, but I am moving, and I take the first side street
and then another and then another. A car has stopped in the road
facing me, and a silver-haired man is in the driver's seat. He doesn't
see me at first; he is watching the dashboard panel. I move to the
front passenger door, open it, and sit in.

'Drive,' I tell him, but he recoils, with his eyes and mouth wide
open. I'm not sure what to do, so I don't do anything but look at him.
He recovers and steadies himself with a shake, and takes the steering
wheel in both hands.

'Drive,' I tell him.

He speaks, but I can't hear him too well. He speaks again, and I
watch him. I think he is saying something about a hospital.

'Drive,' I tell him again, and point to the Glock, and wave in the
direction away from town.

He is calm now, calmer than a man could be expected to be in this
event, and he rolls the car off with another shake of his head.

'Thank you,' I say to him, and he shakes his head again.

I know I have to get out fast before a security blockade closes the town down, so I direct him to drive out of town on the Ballygowan Road and then to take the A1 south. We get free of the town, and after a while he adjusts the car radio and listens intently to the news report he must have had on when I got into the car. He speaks to me. I watch his mouth and read the words.

'Was that you?' he asks. 'Did you plant that bomb?'

'No,' I try to tell him, but I don't have the breath to explain further. I'm not sure if the words are leaving me or if they are only in my head and all he is getting is used air. 'Big mountain,' is all I can say.

Something in the way I look or speak, or try to speak, I think persuades him, and he remains calm as he asks, 'Then why do you need that gun? And why do you need to get away?'

I try to answer, but can't. 'Big mountain, no rope,' I tell him.

My head is hurting and I am feeling sick. I open a window and throw up out onto the road. He is speaking again to me, and I turn to read the words.

'You need a hospital, son,' he says to me. 'If not, you are going to die.'

Son. It is a kind man who would use that address in a circumstance such as this. I look inside my coat. It's a mess. I know some of the blue Sierra is inside me. I feel a wetness, too, on my face. How did this all go so wrong? I am all out of plans. I don't know how all this happened. I don't know what to do. It is difficult to breathe. I try to relax, but it doesn't help. I just can't get enough air.

I check his fuel gauge and again point him south. We approach the border on back roads I know well, and I direct him into Dundalk from the north-west through the outlying roads of the town. It is Saturday. I hope she will be home. We stop at 16 Níth River Terrace. I try to get out, but can't. I try again. I make it, but I cannot straighten, and I struggle to push through the gate. I drag my heavy body to the low wall that separates the front and rear gardens, but I can go no further. I go to the ground and try to rest with my back to the wall. My head hurts bad, bad, bad. I see the kind man's car, but he is gone, and I see a black shape fall on the pillar of the front gate. I'm sure it is a raven. Somehow, amidst all this chaos, it registers that this is not good. I'm sure the thing is watching me. My head hurts so much, and there is a big fire in my chest and nothing is working right and I can't get air, and I know my lungs are finished. I see some movement to my side and try to turn, but my head is heavy and my neck won't work. My head has fallen to my chest and I cannot lift it. From the edge of my vision, I see the silver-haired driver coming from the front of the house, and then suddenly Aisling is with me. Sweet hallelujah! If I could do anything in the world now, just one thing, I would sing this beautiful girl a song. But I can't. I see her as she looks at my face and then at my side, and she is panicked and shouting, but I cannot hear and I can barely get a word out.

'Aisling.'

She is speaking to me, and crying, and shouting towards the house. But I don't hear anything. She is holding my head, pleading with me. I know she is calling for help. But I have watched men die. I know I won't live. I know there isn't time.

'Isn't life a bastard, Aisling? *Just when I thought I was out, they pull me back in.*'

I deliver the line in my throaty Al Pacino New York Italian. I look to her, but she hasn't heard me, and I know the words haven't actually left me. She would not have got my Michael Corleone joke anyway — it's probably not a good time to be funny. I can't get air. I try to smile to her, but I don't think my face is working.

'It got all messed up, Aisling. It got all messed up.'

She is speaking to me, but I don't hear her voice.

[278]

'Aisling.'

I try to raise my hand to touch the side of her face. I can't. I try to lift my hand to her belly, to our baby. I can't.

'You are some lunatic,' I tell her, but there are no words left in my body. I smile to her, but there is no movement left in my body. Nothing is left in my body. I am not working. Nothing is working. And there is no air. I hear music. It is a cello. It is 'El Cant dels Ocells.'

'I hear it, Aisling. I hear it. How mad is that?'

Tír na nÓg

I CLIMB CLOCKWISE ON A PATH OF WORN EARTH. THE PATH IS DARK under beech trees, and elm, ash, hazel, and hawthorn are scattered in outer ditches. Here and there, stone ramparts are built into the hillside. Through the trees, I look down on lush, green land. Great clearings are corralled by woods of oak and chestnut, and copses of pine, birch, rowan, and juniper scatter to mountains of purples, blues, and browns. In one clearing, a wooden trellis holds two or three dozen goats, and in another I see a golden wave of grain. Behind a clump of alders I glimpse the reflected-metal run of water, and from the water and through the alders a blond boy walks. Nearby, I see a family sitting in a meadow. I watch the father pull apples from a basket and wipe each one with a cloth he takes from his robe pocket before turning to smile at me. There is a large clearing in the near distance. A man is working among lines of fruit trees, and a woman is milking a cow in a fenced patch near a farmhouse where geese forage around a tall ash tree. The man sees me, gives a broad wave, and calls out. And though he is a way off, I hear the words clearly, as if the man has spoken from the near ditch. The man says, '*So the last shall be first, and the first last: for many be called, but few chosen.*' I wave and walk on — I never did know what that meant.

There is a sudden movement in the air as something bursts through the hedge and drops before me. I pick the thing up from where it lands. It is a sliothar: the small, hard ball used in hurling. A boy follows the ball through the ditch and onto the path. He is dressed in a tunic of white linen edged with a twist of red and gold, and wrapped around his shoulders is a tightly woven purple cloak. The cloak is pinned across his chest with a golden brooch, and a twisted golden torc sits around his neck. He carries a wooden hurley in one hand.

'Well met,' he says, through a look of expectation, challenge, and humour.

'Do that again,' I tell him, 'and I'll kick your arse.'

'Yeah,' the boy replies, still holding the look. 'You and whose army?'

I throw him the sliothar, and he volleys it into the air and runs off in chase.

He turns his head to me whilst running away. 'Catch me after and we will have a game,' he shouts back, before turning again to chase the ball.

'After what?' I call to him, but he is gone and there is no answer.

I continue on the path and I see a girl sitting on a low wall, her head buried in a book. There is something about the girl that is familiar. She has long, dark hair, and her skin hints of other lands. She looks up from her reading as I near.

'Hello,' she says. 'What will we talk about today?'

I don't know what to answer, so I say nothing.

The girl laughs. 'Come down to me after and we will swap some stories.'

'After what?' I ask.

But the girl just laughs again and returns to her reading.

At the top of the rise there is a clearing, and I step onto a grassy plateau. A single dwelling stands in the centre. It has a thatched roof, and tufts of white smoke push through the reed on the northern facet. The walls atop a ridge of stone are of oak beam, wattle, and earth, and from an east-facing opening I catch the flavour of a stew

[281]

cooking. I walk around the dwelling, and look north and west and south. Farmsteads are sprinkled on a land of green and gold. I turn east and look out to a wide bay. The water of the bay is blue, and below me I see the silver curve of a river as it flows to the sea. To the north, a long, stretched arm of mountain cradles the bay, the lower hills are dark under wood, and beyond the near mountains are distant rocky peaks.

She sits beneath a single oak on the northern ridge of the plateau. She wears a cloak of green silk, and hung around her neck is the flat crescent disc of a golden lunula. She has hair of gold, and the long, golden threads fall in soft waves over one side of her face, resting lightly on her pale skin. She wears red boots, and they are tied in extravagant bows with green strapping. She looks to me. Her eyes are the lightened green of an August meadow.

'Isn't it great, Johnny?'

'Yes, Cora.'

I sit beside her. I raise my hand to touch the side of her face as I kiss her.

'You are unbelievably wonderful,' I say to her.

'You are not too bad yourself, Mister Donnelly,' she says, and smiles.

She rests on me, and I hold her easy in my arms. It is joy itself to hold her. She moves closer, and I can feel her breath on my throat. It is pure pleasure.

'Will we sing a song?' I ask her.

'Okay. What will we sing?'

'Any song you want, you mad and wonderful thing.'

She smiles and holds my arm.

'We'll sing Liam Clancy.'

'The very man, Cora. Which song will we sing?'

'We'll sing the whole lot.'

'The whole lot?'

'Yes, Johnny, the whole lot. Haven't we all the time in the world?'

Acknowledgements

Thank you, Veronica Maye, Laura Susijn, Henry Rosenbloom, and Margot Rosenbloom. Thank you, Rina Gill and Bridie Riordan. Great women all; except for Henry, of course, who is a great man amongst great women. Thanks to everyone at Scribe. Thank you all for sharing the load, for lighting the path, for making it happen, and for your kindness along the way.